SAVED
BY HER
DRAGONS

SAVED BY HER DRAGONS

FATED MATE OF THE DRAGON CLANS, BOOK THREE

by

GINNA MORAN

ISBN 978-1-951314-58-3 (soft cover)
ISBN 978-1-951314-59-0 (hard cover)

This is a work of fiction. All of the characters, organizations, and events portrayed in this novel are either products of the author's imagination or are used fictitiously.

Cover design by Silver Starlight Designs
Cover images copyright Depositphotos

For Inquiries Contact:
Sunny Palms Press
9663 Santa Monica Blvd Suite 1158
Beverly Hills, CA 90210, USA
www.sunnypalmspress.com
www.GinnaMoran.com

Dedication

For those who love dragon-sized batons...just be careful on top. Fractures can happen when you get a little wild.

CHAPTER 1

A Dragon's Heart

MY EARS RING WITH MY screams. The pain of searing magic cutting through my skin and breaking into my chest leaves me incapacitated. It's unlike anything imaginable, and I pray to the fates for the bitch-witch to hurry and finish me off. Death will be the only reprieve from this torture.

I've never felt this helpless in my life, not even when my mates fell from the sky and captured me. Not even when the Darkonians twisted the fates to bind me to them. Not even when Lazlo Infinity tried to collar me. At least in those moments, I could fight. I could think things through and figure shit out. I had help, guidance, and my strong will to get me through.

But now? All I can do is lose myself to the pain of a magical athame cutting into my chest one agonizing inch at a time. The witches purposely drag out the pain, carving something into me as part of their ritual. Twisted dark magic steals away the good inside me, leaving me broken and in agony.

I never knew this was my worst nightmare until now. I always thought it would be something else—losing my mates or returning to the Maximum Magical Penitentiary. It never crossed my mind that the worst thing that could happen to me was that someone brutalizes my body in such a way that I beg for death. This is far worse than the last time a knife met my skin. I'm paralyzed by magic. It's not being able to do anything as they end my life that truly gets to me deep in my soul.

Fates help me.

"Careful, Marjorie. Slow down," McKenzie mutters, stroking her fingers through my hair. Magic sparkles from her fingers, shocking me. "It must come out whole."

I wish I would pass out from the pain already, but it's like McKenzie and the other witch purposely keep me aware, yet they ignore me as if I'm already dead despite the ringing of my voice piercing the air.

And I'm the one called a monster.

"Shut up, sister! I know what I'm doing." The older witch leans over me and grabs my chin, shocking me with magic again. She bares her monstrous fangs as if her intimidation will scare me more than she already does. "Stop screaming, beast! You're only making the pain worse. I want this to be over as much as you do."

I can't react as the edges of my vision crowd with shadows. I just keep screaming.

Another shockwave bursts through me, and I fall to sweet, peaceful nothingness. Am I dead? I don't know. My mind still whirls with millions of thoughts. I envision Kash, Rowan, and Maddox experiencing the same pain as I do—Theo and Ambrose too. And Tiernan? Fuck. He can't be dead. How could the fates be so twisted to allow such a tragedy?

"Delphia, hang on. Please, don't die. Fight it. Fight the magic caging you. Fight with the strength of the stars. With the power of those who yearn for a life with you. Fight!" Tiernan's sharp voice explodes through my mind.

Instead of bringing me relief, it ignites all-consuming agony as I flutter my eyes open to the most horrible sight. Blood covers everything, sizzling with spicy smoke as Marjorie uses her magical athame to crack my sternum. I should never have to see my insides, and my stomach twists so hard that my body jerks despite the freezing magic.

I scream again, sending a stream of dragon fire from my lips. My dragon awakens, blasting through the magic. Neither of the witches can do anything as I light up the world around me. The orange flames crackle and pop. McKenzie claps her hands, shouting a spell I can't hear over my fire, but it's enough to suppress the pain trying to kill me.

I suck in a sweet breath of relief. She healed me. I can't believe it.

Her gesture gives me a blip of hope that gathers my thoughts together. Dying isn't on the table any longer. I can fight. I will fight.

"Damn it, Delphia. You almost made her mess up," McKenzie snaps, scowling at me. She curls her fingers, summoning lavender power in her palms. "Now she has to start all over again."

Oh, no. Oh-fucking-no.

I can't go through the agony all over again. I won't.

Rage bursts through me, and I scream a loud, long wail, summoning the dragon fire of the caged beast inside me. Fire radiates under my skin, and my body glows brighter than the magic zapping through the air.

I don't know if being on the brink of death unleashes the most powerful part of me from the magic trying to hold me hostage, but I'm thankful. The witches can't seem to break through the fire to get to me without being burned.

Thrusting my hands out, I thrust a wave of fire at them. It's enough to get the witches to back up a foot and guard themselves instead of focusing their efforts on me. They can't use offensive magic if they have to constantly protect themselves. I know this. I've seen it.

Their self-preservation gives me the moment of reprieve I desperately need. Exhaustion fights with my stubborn survival needs, and the flames lessen the longer I tap into my beast. It's harder to keep her uncaged, but I'll do this until I can't any longer. Maybe my mates or someone on the staff will realize what's happening.

"Stay the fuck back," I snap, heaving deep breaths. "You can't do this to me!"

McKenzie scowls with my words, her determination exploding in a wave of sparkling magic. Fear strikes me in the heart as she dares to step closer, preparing a counterattack. But I won't give up. I won't let them hold me captive. They'll have to knock me out completely if they want to get the glowing blade anywhere near my body again. Hopefully, someone can hear me before then.

Opening my mouth, I screech, my dragon's voice booming from my mouth with her fire. Scales dance across my skin, but I can't break free and unleash my dragon completely. The chain on my ankle suppresses my beast. I've been deemed too dangerous in my dragon form.

Maybe I am. I want now more than ever to prove to the world that they were right about me. They should fear me.

The suite shudders under my exertion, and McKenzie shouts another spell, creating a glowing shield of magic around her and her coven sister. Pushing to my knees, I glance down at the blood soaking my clothes. I gasp in relief, thankful for being right about McKenzie healing me to an extent. A shallow wound still mars my skin, but the damage of the athame is nowhere near how vile and disgusting as it was. I hate that the only purpose of healing me was so the bitches could start over, and I use the anger to give me more power. Because fuck that. They will not get me again.

"I said, stay back!" I yell, inhaling and exhaling deep breaths. Dragging my chain, I shuffle farther away from them and toward the balcony. "Tiernan! Tiernan, get help! Someone! If you can hear me, help me!"

My voice carries out the wide-open archway and into the night. I glance quickly, hoping to spot a dragon in the sky, but I only see stars. I swing my attention back to the Lioht witches, holding hands and chanting another spell. They just won't give up. How can I fight against their magic? It's impossible. I'm sure their next spell will either hinder me or protect them. They're far too determined and desperate. This is why McKenzie helped my father all along. She didn't want to help him bring me home. She wanted me somewhere that she could have her way without the High Council or my mates trying to intervene.

"Help!" I scream again, kicking my foot, testing the strength of the chain. I've tried to break it already, but that was before I managed to summon my dragon fire. If I can heat it up, maybe I can break the spell restraining me. I could get out of here. I could uncage my dragon and fly.

"Settle down, Delphia. Fighting is pointless. You can't break the chain, nor will someone save you. No one can hear you with the magic shielding the room. Now, if you behave and submit to your fate, we will work quickly. This will be over soon." McKenzie shuffles another step closer, and I glower, thrusting a ball of fire at her.

"Fuck off!" I shout, trying to look for something I can

use to block me long enough to focus on my chain. "You can't have my heart!"

"That isn't up to you. Plus, you couldn't possibly want to live your fate at the Litendrake mercy. Franco Litendrake will surely waste the precious gift you are, arranging something far more torturous than death." McKenzie smirks, gathering a ball of lavender power between her palms. "Show me that you can be a good girl now. Maybe I'll do something for the pain. Come on. Vi ke lota fi—"

Screaming, rage blasts through me, cutting off her spell. I swing my arms, throwing my dragon fire at the glowing metal binding me. My vision turns red with McKenzie's words, and I yank my chain, heating it up until I can't go any farther. I'm just shy of being able to jump over the balcony. I'd rather risk falling to my death than experience another moment of agony by these witches.

Magic buzzes and zaps through the air, and I nearly falter at the sight of the magical cage blocking me from jumping from the balcony. Even if I break the chain, I'll have to get through the shocking wall containing me in my room.

"Last chance, Delphia. Don't make this hard," the other witch, Marjorie, says. She strides closer, pointing the athame at me.

"You're dead if you come closer. This is your last chance!" I say, threatening her by whipping my chain. Closing my eyes, I try to summon more dragon fire, but something stops me. Ice sneaks across my back, suppressing my beast.

"Eht va lote Drakovich heir ti ata!" McKenzie shouts, throwing her hands up.

Blinding light shoots from her hands, sending an orb of magic over me. My fire hits my magical cage, ricocheting around the person-sized bubble. Heat licks my skin, but it doesn't burn. If anything, it settles the raging beast inside me, making it harder to call her.

Or maybe it's because of the looming shadow suddenly falling over me. My beast senses the protection that comes with the man I've agreed to give a chance to be my mate.

The floor quakes as Tiernan lands on the balcony in his huge, black dragon form. His roar booms through the air, and instead of startling me, my heart leaps in relief. I never expected to be so thankful for my wayward unintended mate's arrival, but I'm so glad he showed up tonight before all of this. I don't know what I'd have done otherwise. I can only keep the witches back for so long. With him, I can fight.

"Nogard ef slo que tatita," McKenzie chants in

unison with her coven sister.

Magic entangles with my chain, ripping me away from Tiernan before I can duck under his gigantic form for protection. My back stings as I skid across the floor and into the suite. Fuck me. He can't come in. There is only a small gap between two different magical walls on the balcony that we were able to touch in before. Whatever McKenzie does closes it more, keeping Tiernan out and me in.

"Vi tat lo conduita!" Marjorie shouts, focusing on me while McKenzie keeps Tiernan back by strengthening the shield he attacks.

Tiernan snarls and blows a breath of fire, hitting the shield of magic again. The intensity of his flames shocks the magic, and lightning bolts shoot through the air. The floor quakes again, and the two witches chant louder. Exhaustion doesn't only affect me. Fighting us weakens them.

"Don't stop, Tiernan!" I shout, the sudden realization of their weakness and the strength of Tiernan fighting on my behalf ignites me with hope. I just need to coax out my dragon. I need to get my shit together and join Tiernan.

Magic and fire battle it out against the shield, but Tiernan doesn't back off. His powerful flames never waver. I can almost imagine the heat of them coursing through me and filling me up. I'm so close to igniting fire again. I can feel it.

A loud boom shakes me to the core as fire explodes over my head. McKenzie's cage of magic falters, dissipating. I scramble out of the way, taking cover near a decorative table. Bolts of magic zap around, shattering and destroying everything in their wake. Panic tightens my chest. If one hits me, I don't know what will happen.

"Nova, can you summon your dragon fire again?" Tiernan asks, his words swirling through my mind. His powerful presence loosens my muscles, and I tip my head up to acknowledge him, my voice refusing to work. "I need you to help me. I'll keep them distracted. Watch for their magic to falter. They're growing weak." His confirmation of what I noticed gives me the determination to try to summon fire again. I want to make him proud. I want to prove I'm not a damsel mate.

Without responding to his words, I close my eyes. I imagine unlocking the magic imprisoning my beast in my soul and gather the strength of my Darkonian prince to get my dragon to fight once again. Billowing flames explode from my hands, and I screech, shooting fire at the two witches. McKenzie screams a spell, sending a shield over her, but the other woman can't say the words fast enough. My dragon fire swallows her in a glowing lightshow of orange and yellow flames swirling with her lavender light. Her screams echo through the air, and lavender magic crackles and pops, sending sparkles raining through the vaulted room. Her silhouette vanishes as my dragon fire disintegrates her body, killing her.

"No!" McKenzie yells. She jerks her attention to me, her hair lifting with static. Fury lines her face, and she strides closer, drawing her hands together. "You bitch! I'll destroy you!"

Tiernan uses her second of distraction to ram his hulking dragon body into the magical wall keeping him out of my room. The whole room shudders, the magic fissuring under his power. McKenzie's eyes widen. Calling out another spell, she tries to divide her attention between the two of us, but it's no use. She can't win. I won't let her.

"McKenzie!" The door to my suite flies open with the booming voice. "Delphia is mine! How dare you deceive me!"

McKenzie claps her hands together at the sight of Franco Litendrake rushing into the room as magic no longer hides me. Bright blue light engulfs her, and she disappears with the shocking magic. I drop to my knees, my legs giving out on me. The adrenaline that kept me going fades, and I roll to my back and stare up at Tiernan's hulking form. He squats down butt-ass naked, but I can't even find the energy to look anywhere but his face. He bares his teeth and snorts a breath of smoke. Gliding his hot fingers over my forehead, he gently combs my messy hair from my sweaty forehead. His eyes scream that he wants to pick me up, but Franco's presence stops him. Tiernan wasn't supposed to be here.

"That blasted traitorous witch. She is just like her sister. I should've known she'd try something." Franco clenches his hands into fists, jerking his attention to me and then to the charred remains of McKenzie's coven sister. Smoke billows from his flaring nostrils as fire dances in his eyes. He finally processes my condition and towers over me, looking down. "My fates." Loosening his fingers, he holds his hands above me like he's unsure of what to do. "Delphia, are you injured? Your chest—I can't tell whose blood is all over you."

Reaching down, Franco attempts to graze his fingers over me. Tiernan growls in warning, his guttural dragon voice vibrating through my soul. And thank fucking fuck. I don't want this strange man, even if he's my father, coming anywhere near me. It's his fault I'm here in the first place. He never checked on me once until now.

"She was mutilated by the witches, but they healed

her because they messed up." Tiernan's chest rises and falls with his heavy breathing. "It could've been so much worse. I tried with everything in me to get to her sooner, but they spelled me."

Once again, Franco tries to touch me, but Tiernan growls protectively.

Franco hesitates, dropping his hands by his sides, and finally acknowledges Tiernan, tightening his jaw. The two of them stare at each other in silence. I had expected more from my father's appearance, but Franco's small and un-threatening in his human form compared to the massively stunning beast Tiernan is. But it means nothing. I know that Franco is the king of this territory. He wouldn't have such a title if it didn't come from power. He is the author-itative force of all the dragon clans beneath him who stay in the Litendrake Territory of the Dragon Lands.

Raising his hand, Franco silences Tiernan's threaten-ing growl. "Please, Prince Darkonian. There is no need to threaten me. I won't hurt her. I just want to ensure she's okay."

"She's not if you keep her locked in here and unpro-tected." Tiernan glowers, not backing down.

Franco sighs. "If I had known...I apologize. This has been quite complicated, but I know I can't avoid my heir forever."

I wish he would look at me instead of Tiernan.

Tiernan's muscles ripple and bulge. "You could've just agreed to let us keep her contract instead of putting everyone through this mess, your majesty. I—"

"You don't understand how difficult that decision was to make. Allies are hard to come by, but you've seemed to prove that you might make a good one. As a reward for your actions, I give you permission to visit and protect Delphia despite your initial intrusion. Please accept my offering or leave. I must handle the witches."

"Just a visit?" Licking my lips, I manage to find my voice. "He saved me. He deserves more. McKenzie and her sister were trying to take my heart. Please, I don't feel safe here. I'm sure the princes will give you whatever it is you want for me." The thought reels through my body, the memory of the pain coming back at full force. My voice hitches, and I inhale another breath, trying to suppress my nerves.

Two hot arms engulf me, lifting me from the cold floor. Tiernan's toasted marshmallow scent hugs me in the fragrance of his safety, and I relax.

Franco doesn't react to my pleas, remaining expressionless. His ageless face makes him look not even that much older than me. I should be used to it, considering that our species lives hundreds of years, but it's weird. I had always expected that my dad would be middle-aged.

"Like I said, Delphia. It's complicated. I should've suspected the Liohts would do something rash, and I've failed you for that, but I need time," Franco says, shooting me down and ignoring the fact that all of this bullshit falls on him.

"Rash? Rash?" My voice rises in pitch, my stomach roiling again. "How is trying to cut my heart out rash? It was fucking insane! What the fuck was it even about? My Aunt McKayla? I—I don't understand."

Tiernan hugs me to him, unfazed that he's completely naked and cradling me in front of Franco. "Nova, we're going to fi—"

"You're not going to do anything," Franco says, his voice turning guttural with his sharp words. "I will handle the blasted witches." Turning to me, he adds, "And McKayla is not your aunt. She was your kidnapper. Don't forget that."

I tighten my jaw, desperate to argue. But it's pointless. He obviously has something against the woman who raised me. It was my mom who gave me to McKayla after all, so...

"I also expect you to be prepared to go over everything you know about the Liohts with me in the morning. I need to take care of the security of the palace," Franco adds. He runs his hand through his dark hair. I study his features, trying to see a part of myself within him, but I see and feel absolutely nothing but annoyance for the man who imprisons me in this room as if I'm truly a criminal.

"Your majesty, I'd like to request temporary guardian status for the princess instead of visitation," Tiernan says, speaking up. He straightens his back and puffs out his chest like towering over Franco will intimidate him into agreeing.

"Granted." Franco flicks his gaze to the archway to my balcony. "It's only appropriate since you fought so courageously for Delphia."

Whoa. I'm shocked. I thought his request would've been immediately denied.

"You have until morning, and I expect you to guard her with your life until things are handled." Franco jerks his attention to me. "If I unchain you, do you agree to not try anything stupid? The High Council was very clear with our arrangement. If you leave, you will face unbearable consequences."

I bob my head, a blip of hope and elation igniting inside me. "I promise I won't leave. I just—thank you. You won't regret it."

Franco nods, dipping his chin low. "I understand the circumstances around your arrival home haven't been ideal, but I hope you know that I've done everything I have with your best interest at heart. No Litendrake Heir will ever waste away at the wretched prison. I never wanted your mother there, and I surely don't want you there." His face softens with his words, easing the anxiety tightening my chest. Reaching out, he touches a spot on my shackle. Magic sparkles across the metal, and it releases, showing off my bruised skin.

"Thank you," I repeat, afraid if I open my big mouth to say anything else, I might end up chained again.

With one more silent stern look at Tiernan, Franco strides away and slams the giant door closed.

"My fates, Nova. I need you close right now." Tiernan adjusts me in his arms without waiting for my response.

Like his closeness releases the wild beast inside me, I crash my mouth to his and kiss him with all my desperation. Whatever bad feelings I had for him over how I ended up here vanish, and all I can think about is how safe I feel in his embrace, how good his lips taste, and how free my soul feels in this moment.

"My beautiful mate," he murmurs with a groan against my mouth. "Can I help you clean up? Feed you? Cuddle you? I want so desperately to show you that I don't give a damn if I can't solidify our bonding of souls yet. I want to prove to you that you're mine. I'll do anything for you."

I smile against his lips and nod my head. "Whatever you want. Just...keep talking. Tell me everything that has happened. I need to know about the others."

He hums against my mouth. "They're going crazy. It's taking everything in them not to storm the palace and tear the place down for you."

"I want that so badly," I say, mapping his shoulders with my fingers.

Sliding his tongue into my mouth, he silences me from talking. "Careful, Nova. They might sense your desire, but Franco wasn't kidding. You can't leave the palace."

My brows crinkle together. "What?"

"Ambrose said that you've been branded with dark magic—forbidden magic. If you leave...it's just, let's not think about it. He'll figure it out. I know he will. He has never let us down."

The desire that rose inside me sputters out, and my whole body cools. How can my life go from shit to bearable to fucking awful in such a short time? I miss my mates more than I ever thought possible, and despite Tiernan being here, it's not the same. I want them all.

Groaning, Tiernan hugs me tighter and doesn't put

me down until we reach the bathroom. It's the first time I don't have to maneuver the heavy chair around. Setting me on the grand rock counter with a crevice wide enough to create a sink, Tiernan stands in front of me and drapes his arms over my shoulders.

"I wish I alone could be enough for you, Nova," he murmurs, a flame of sadness dancing across his jade-green irises. He must've heard my thoughts. I wasn't sure if he could like the Drekis. "But I understand. You're not intended for one."

How do I respond to that? I want to deny it and say that he is enough, but then I'd be lying. We haven't even had a chance to really bond. The connection I feel is purely magical because of the mate bond to Theo.

If I lied, he'd know it immediately, because when I think of love and pleasure and happiness, it always revolves around several men. It revolves around the Drekis. He's right that my heart claims many, and without the others, I feel as if I'm incomplete. Like I'll never be whole again.

"I just pray to the fates that you'll be intended for me," he murmurs, combing his fingers through my hair.

I force my mouth to smile despite my heart not really being into it. "I'd like to try, Tiernan. But not until I'm free of this mess. I just—I just need you to be here for me, okay?"

"I will never be far. Promise." His green eyes light the fire in his soul. "You're my mate, whether or not the fates are in our favor. You deserve better than what the witches have granted."

If only I could feel that he's right.

If only the fates could truly be on my side.

CHAPTER 2

Warning

"DELPHIA." THE SOFT WHISPER OF a feminine voice tugs me away from the sound of Tiernan's heart beating.

I wasn't sure if he'd ever fall asleep if I didn't, despite looking exhausted from fighting against magic. He only relaxed after I closed my eyes and pretended to try. A part of me thought it was sweet for him to make sure I was okay, but I felt bad about it. Just because I couldn't relax enough to drift off doesn't mean he shouldn't get to.

"Delphia." I hold my breath and concentrate on the world around me. I'm so shaken that I wouldn't put it past me for hearing things that aren't there. Especially because I'd recognize the familiar melodic voice anywhere.

It's not in my head. I know it. It might have been years since I've seen Aunt McKayla, but I'd never forget the soft yet sharp tone of her voice. Her murmur of my name reminds me of the simple things in life I took for granted—like believing I was human with criminal parents and how she was always around. I wasn't sure I'd ever hear Aunt McKayla's voice again, and hearing it now? Whoa. This is crazy, right? Why would she contact me now? And here? She made sure with a spell that I would know that she'd no longer be in my life when the Drekis and I searched for her. A part of me hopes she changed her mind and is reaching out. Another part of me knows it's wishful thinking.

Ugh. I'm afraid to find out, but I'm desperate to know.

I gather my bravery and get the nerve to shift from Tiernan's embrace. Easing upright, I study his sleepy features as his bottom lip puffs out with each of his breaths. He doesn't stir or move, and I lean over and kiss his forehead softly. Unlike Maddox, Kash, and Rowan, who are extremely light sleepers, Tiernan either trusts the protection of the palace or truly believes there won't be any more threats tonight. Regardless, I won't wake him.

"Eht rorrim ile gra ti ra," Aunt McKayla whispers, her voice sounding as if it comes from nowhere and everywhere. It swirls through my mind and in my ears. It's like she uses a spell to call to my soul. "Delphia, open your mind to me. I must be quick." McKayla's words sharpen with urgency, reminding me of the hundreds of times she spoke to me in such a tone. When I was growing up, it was like this when she thought I was acting like my mother. Now? I can't stop the worry rising inside me. This isn't a casual summons with magic to check in on me. It's more.

I peer around the dark room, using only the soft magical candlelight within the glass sconces outside my bathroom to light my way. My bare feet thump quietly against the cool rock floor, and I hug my arms around me tighter, wishing I had grabbed one of the blankets from the bed. I only wear a nightie, where Tiernan remains naked in all his delicious glory. His unashamed confidence reminds me of Maddox, though he's not as rough around the edges.

The thought of Maddox cracks my heart. I can almost hear him grumbling about the fact that I haven't had sex in...what feels like a long fucking time. He'd be both annoyed that Tiernan didn't try hard enough to seduce me or because he wasn't here to do it himself. I never knew how much I'd love Maddox for his attitude, but it makes the strange entanglement of my soul to both the Drekis and Darkonians that much easier.

Another whisper of my name laces around me, drawing my attention to the tingling sensation crawling over my skin. I stare in shock at the bathroom mirror. I knew I had been strolling this way, but I was so lost in my thoughts that I missed exactly how I got here.

"Eht rorrim ile gra ti ra," Aunt McKayla whispers, her voice growing in volume.

I notice a red spark of magic streak across the mirror like a lightning bolt, and my reflection blurs. My heart rams against my ribcage the longer I stare at my wavy reflection until it morphs and transforms into an eerily familiar face. I clutch onto the countertop, the sight of Aunt McKayla in the mirror staring at me worse than I thought because of her similarity to McKenzie.

Fear engulfs me.

The memory of the searing pain cutting open my chest forces me to step back. How can just an image in the mirror—one who I know but with an evil twin—ruin such a reunion for me? Tears threaten to spill from my eyes, and I clutch the countertop to stabilize me.

It's Aunt McKayla. She would never hurt me. If only chanting these words helped.

A dozen thoughts race through my head as I finally convince myself that the woman in the mirror won't turn into McKenzie, step through, and steal my heart. "Aunt McKayla?" I ask with a hoarseness in my voice. I need to hear her confirm that it's actually her and not McKenzie to get my heart to settle.

"I'm so happy to find you in Magaelorum," she says, her eyes flicking around like she drinks in my reflection through this strange looking glass. "I assume you found your mates, yes?"

"Found them? More like they found me. And what the fuck to everything. Why didn't you tell me? Where are you? I got your message at our old house when I went looking for you." Everything gushes from my mouth as if I need to spit the words out before I forget them. "You have no idea what I've been through."

Her features tighten at the heat of my anger. "Delphia, please. I'd love to answer your questions, but I don't have time. My connection to Magaelorum grows weak, and I need you to listen."

Is she serious? Rage rushes through me like a tidal wave of destruction, and I smack my hands on the countertop. "No, you listen to me. I'm in trouble. I'm being imprisoned at the Litendrake Palace. You told me my father was dead. He's not. He's—"

"What? No." Her eyes widen with a spark of her magic. "No. Delphia, listen to me. You need—"

Green magic sets the dim bathroom aglow as Ambrose materializes beside me with four hulking figures. I gasp, my heart speeding up. I want to throw myself at my mates, but I can't take my eyes away from the mirror.

"Delphia, you must run. Run now. Take your mates and go into hiding. You have to. It's not safe. There is something I must make right, and it'll bring many enemies from the shadows. Please, you have to go." Aunt McKayla rubs her hands together, sending sparks of red power zapping across the mirror.

I lean on the counter, slapping my hands to the mirror as if I can break through to where she is. "I can't, I'm—"

"Delphia, run!" The mirror explodes, and if Ambrose didn't summon a protective shield, I'd have been cut by the thousands of sharp pieces raining across the grand bathroom.

Two hot hands squeeze my waist and lift me off my feet. I stare in shock, meeting Maddox's dark eyes. He flares his nostrils, drinking in my features. My body refuses to react as McKayla's demands rage inside me. I should kiss him and show him how much I missed him, but no matter how hard I try to get myself together, all I can think about is listening to McKayla and running.

"We must take Delphia away. Now." Maddox's voice booms with his words. "She feels as if she will die otherwise, and I cannot bear the thought of her fear being all-consuming."

"My brother is right." Rowan steps closer, crunching glass under his boots. Leaning over Maddox's shoulder, he reaches out and caresses his fingers to my cheek. "We've waited long enough. Now is the time."

"Be reasonable, Drekis," Ambrose says, snapping his fingers. Green magic crackles around us, eating away at the glass on the floor until the mirror returns as it was. "We can't run with her. The power imprisoning her here will rip her apart if she leaves."

I blink a few times at his words but don't look at him. I keep my gaze trained on my reflection in the mirror as if I can summon Aunt McKayla back. How could she make such demands without listening to me? Would she if she knew any better? She cared enough to contact me, but what now? Was it a courtesy because she raised me, or was it because she cares? Fuck my life.

"Then fix it." Theo growls, drawing my attention to

him as Kash quietly joins Maddox's other side to pet my hair. "Do what you must. I don't care about the consequences. Our mate is too important."

My eyebrows shoot up on my forehead, his words prodding at my soul. I can't stop my wild emotions from getting the best of me. "You haven't earned the right to call me that. You stood by and did nothing as they brought me here." Are my words unfair? Yes. I just can't help the bitter feelings. My good senses know there wasn't much they could do, but my heart wants to still hold it against him. Maybe it's because he's more of an asshole than Maddox. Maybe it's because if I never ended up here, I would've never gone through the agony of the witch attack. I wish things could return to what they had been before when we fought about our bond and none of the other messy shit and worrying about my life and heart.

Theo narrows his eyes at me, one look into his face reminding me of our moment of heated passion—of how I basically hate fucked him and loved the hell out of it. My body hums with the memory, and I squeeze my thighs together. My traitorous vagina doesn't give a fuck if we don't get along. But damn it, I do. He will hold it over my head if I don't stand my ground and make him prove to me that he can be a mate.

"Do I need to remind you that I have earned the

right?" Theo glides his tongue over his bottom lip, revealing the glittering barbell in his tongue. "Because you say one thing, but your mind says another. Stop resisting our bond. You're mine, and I'm prepared to prove it and claim you over and over again."

My body reacts at his comment, and I break my gaze from his first, wanting nothing more than to shut off my lust. It's growing harder to think, especially with all of my mates surrounding me. Each of them showers me with attention, their gazes and touches only arousing the beast inside me instead of settling me down. Like they can't resist testing me, they quietly close in around me until there is no possible way to leave their circle, not that I want to. The only place I want to escape is this palace.

"Show me." Whoa. Did I really just say that? My lust gets the best of me, giving my mouth permission to egg him on without thinking things through. Who knew I could be this horny all the time? My mates are right about me having needs. I thought they were joking and just wanted to satisfy me because they could. Now? The feelings of desire grow intense. All-consuming.

Theo flares his nostrils and whips his attention to Ambrose. With a growl, he says, "Ambrose, take care of it now. Do whatever you have to and break the magic caging her here. Our mate needs us to be here for her, you included." Theo tightens his jaw and motions toward the doorway. "Go wake up Tiernan's lazy ass. How he even can—"

Fire sets the world aglow, and Theo growls, spinning and shooting dragon fire back in Tiernan's direction. Usually, a fight like this would knock some sense into me, but my body still refuses to chill out. I can't think. I can barely catch my breath. All I want to do is jump on someone and have my way until I can leave this hellhole disguised as a palace.

"Get them out before they start something Delphia might not be ready to finish. She hasn't allowed a claim from all of them, and it will not be this way. She deserves intimacy on an individual level first." Maddox shifts me, hiding me behind his back.

I stretch up and peek over his shoulder. "Don't try to control my relationships. You agreed—"

"Out! Now," Maddox demands, baring his teeth. Fire lights his eyes, and Kash and Rowan do as he asks and shove Theo along with Ambrose from the bathroom. They all flock to the door, looking ready to start a war to get back in, but Maddox gathers an orb of dragon fire in his palm. "The three of you better fucking figure out what is going on in regards to McKayla. Nova needs you to deal with it while she needs us to care for her. You agreed not to overwhelm her and swore to learn what she wants and expects from you alone first. So hurry the fuck up and deal with shit. If you can manage at least a blip of a plan in getting her out, you can have your turn. But it must be earned."

Is he for real? Absolutely. My infuriatingly dominating mate doesn't joke around when it comes to my needs. If we weren't in this situation, I'd argue with him, but he's right. What I need is for the Darkonians to figure this stuff out while someone takes care of my damn needy body. I can't think about anything else.

"What he means is that if I allow it," I mutter, smacking Maddox on the chest. "And right now, I just—I need you all to do this for me."

Tiernan's features soften, our conversation about what I need from him swirling through my mind again. Locking his fingers to both Ambrose and Theo's shoulders, he drags them away and shuts the door to the bathroom. The Drekis stare at the bathroom door for only a short moment. Turning to me, they each devour the sight of me in my nightie, their desire prominent as their cocks threaten the state of their pants, so hard that I can imagine their boners poking free.

My emotions get the best of me, and tears prickle my eyes. I haven't felt such relief in a long time, and I throw my arms around Maddox, hugging him tightly. Kash and Rowan join our hug, and I take a moment to kiss each of them, giving them the affection they crave.

"I missed you all so damn much," I whisper, my voice sounding with a small whimper.

"Not as much as we missed you, kitten," Kash says, nuzzling his face to the crook of my neck. "It's taking everything in me to even wait for a second longer to show you exactly how much."

I grab him by his waist. "It has been so terrible. I didn't think I'd survive. I need all the distractions. All your love."

"You've been starved for us, haven't you?" Rowan brings my hand to his lips and kisses each of my fingers.

"Not just for us. For all affection. What I don't understand is why you didn't let Tiernan fulfill your desires if you were in need. He's been with you all night. Are you not interested in him like you say?" Maddox pulls the strap of my nightie off my shoulder and kisses my skin with his hot lips. "I don't smell him on you at all."

I release an exasperated laugh, combing my fingers through his long hair. "We were bonding on a soul level, Maddox. And so you know, I could've showered and rinsed away the evidence." Actually, I did shower with him.

Maddox scoffs and nips the top of my breast, using his teeth to tug my nightie down even more. "No, cookie. I don't think you understand. His seed would linger, trying to dissuade us from having our share."

Rowan whacks him on the side of the head. "Shut it, Maddy. You're going to make her worry about her scent when you know all it does is drives us wild. It makes me want her more." Burying his face into my neck, Rowan inhales a deep, dramatic breath like it's my scent he needs to survive.

"Is that so?" I tease, bending my neck for him to kiss my throat.

Tearing my strap, Maddox rips the bodice of my nightie. "I'll prove it." He grabs my hand and brings it to his hard-on. "Feel what your scent does to me."

Oh, fuck. I don't even want to think about my scent. I just want to push them to hurry and do what they want with me. Sucking in a long breath, I do the only thing I can think of to initiate things and wiggle from Maddox's arms. He play-growls, trying to keep me locked in his hold, but I throw myself back and balance on my palms. He releases me only to have Rowan try to grab me away. I lock my ankles around Rowan's neck, using his sturdy form to swing myself toward Maddox again.

Hooking my fingers to his belt, I lower myself to my

knees. I unfasten his pants and pull them down, not waiting or allowing them to make the first move. Maddox moans as I lace my fingers around his thick girth in determination and suck his tip into my mouth. His fingers tangle in my hair, and he slowly guides me to suck him deeper. I don't have to hear his thoughts, but it's taking all of his control not to get rough, but that's what I want. His spicy cinnamon flavor of his pre-cum sets the wild beast inside me off, and I grab his hips, bobbing my head, imagining what it would be like if he turned primal in his need, not wanting a blow job but to fuck my face and watch me deep throat him.

He tries to pull back, yanking my hair, but I cling to him, pinching his ass. I know it drives him crazy to stand here and let me have my way. I want to push him until he can't take it anymore. I want him to dominate me.

Growling, he narrows his eyes, listening to my thoughts. Our gazes remain locked on each other, and fire lights his irises. "You're in so much trouble, Delphia," Maddox murmurs, tightening his fingers through my hair even more. "I fucking love your mouth, but damn it. Your needs come first. You're not supposed to be pleasuring me until you've had your fill."

I roll my eyes and hum my disagreement, loving the hell out of teasing him. I ease back but stroke his cock with my fingers slick with spit. "What are you going to do about it?" Again, I take him into my mouth and moan in my throat, using my voice to vibrate over him.

He grumbles, his muscles rippling. "Brothers, punish her. Show her what happens when she's not letting us perform our duties as her mates."

Laughing, I shake my hips teasingly, feeling Kash and Rowan's stares on my back. They would stand and watch until one of us invites them, and all I can think about is how tough my body is and how my species has evolved to handle a mate-bond with a whole clan.

"I don't know if they have it in them," I tease, licking my way to Maddox's balls.

"Keep it up, doe-eyes. Your ass is mine." Rowan growls deep in his throat, the noise sexy as hell as he shoots his dragon fire at my ass, smoldering the nightie and leaving my body exposed. Swatting me with his palm, he sends blooming tingles stinging over my ass cheek.

Kash joins me on the floor and drags his sharp nail over the bodice, ripping the front open. If they had it their way, I'd never wear clothes at all. Maybe they plan to burn everything I have once we get out of here. I'm not even sure I'd mind at this point. I never want to be apart.

"We'll never leave you again by our own freewill," he murmurs, caressing his fingers to my hard nipple until he bends down and sucks my nipple into his mouth.

Rowan kneels behind me, unbothered that I still stroke and play with Maddox. He slips his finger over my clit, feeling exactly what the three of them do to me. I moan and suck Maddox again, humming with pleasure, and Maddox groans at the sensation.

"Let's move her to the shower. There's a seat. I want her on my lap," Rowan says, sliding his arms around my waist.

I hum my agreement, slowly easing Maddox from my mouth. "Whatever you want. All of you. I need you more than I ever knew possible."

The world blurs as Rowan lifts me up and carries me under his arm like a damn caveman or something. I laugh and wiggle, not making it completely easy for him, especially pulling this move and manhandling me like Maddox usually would. He must sense my playful mood and how my desires morph into filthy fantasizing with the reminder of how they fucked me at once. I want it again. I want them to test my body and get the pleasure they crave because they're always focused on me.

Maddox undresses completely and enters the shower first, turning the hot water on. Steam fills the huge rock room, dampening our skin. His glistening bare chest is so sexy to touch and explore. I kiss each of his pecs and rub my fingers over his abs. Spinning, I tease the hell out of him by stretching my leg up and using his cock to rub myself as we wait for his brothers.

"Fucking hurry. I'm about to have my way first," Maddox mutters, grabbing my wet hair to pull me to him for a kiss.

I curl my fingers at Rowan. "You can together. I want it. Rowan wants my ass."

Rowan growls with a smile, rushing to kick out of his clothes. I spin around and touch my toes, letting him spank me again before brushing his lips to the stinging spot. I expect him to do it again, but he hooks his arms around me and turns me for a deep kiss. Strolling the short distance to the bench, he flips me around and drags his hand down the length of my stomach, putting pressure with his fingers between my legs as he guides me with him. My whole body goes crazy at the sensation of his naked chest sliding against my back, and he sits down with me, letting his cock rest between my legs without entering me.

I automatically rub his tip and roll my hips to grind against him. I can't see his reaction, but I can feel his muscles bulge. I smile and watch Kash undress outside the shower, loving how turned on he is. He strokes his hardon, never taking his gaze from mine. Maddox touches my chin, guiding my face to his, and he kisses me deeply and desperately, not letting me watch as his brothers surround me and reposition my body open for them.

"Get her nice and worked up, Kash," Rowan says, kissing my shoulder. "Make it feel good. Make her shower you."

Oh, fuck.

I moan so embarrassingly loud, feeling Rowan re-adjust me on his lap, tucking his cock along the seam of my ass to give Kash the perfect view of me. Maddox steals the noise from my mouth, sliding his tongue over mine, stopping me from seeing anything and only allowing me to feel the sensations. I squirm in anticipation, desperate to know what they're doing.

"You want to watch, don't you, cookie," Maddox murmurs, smiling against my mouth. "It drives you crazy that you can't see."

"Mmhmm," I practically whine. I try to pull away from his mouth, but he holds my hair, stopping me.

"Too bad. I want you to just feel. Feel the passion and pleasure. Feel our love and desire." Maddox nips my bottom lip. "Let the sights be for us this time. Watching you get off—so sexy."

Kash's thoughts entangle with mine, and he stretches my legs wider to accommodate his broad shoulders. I tremble in anticipation at the sensation of his hot tongue licking down my thigh and to the apex of my legs. I arch my back as he sucks my clit into his mouth, the intense pleasure stealing away my thoughts. They're going to withhold my orgasm. I know it. I can sense it, and it sends my body buzzing.

Goosebumps prickle over my skin, and I pant and squirm, losing myself to the ecstasy Kash creates with his fingers and tongue until I feel as if I'm going to explode. I cry out in desperation, arching my back. Stopping, Kash uses my excitement to slicken his finger to test my ass, slowly fingering me and getting me ready for what's to come. I bite my lip and close my eyes, letting go of my reserve and embrace whatever they have to offer me. I lose myself to the sensations each of them creates separately yet together, working as a team to take care of me.

Rowan sucks my shoulder, leaving his mark. I pant and gasp, biting Maddox's lip and going to war with him through our kiss. My toes curl, and I wiggle my hips, try-ing to pleasure myself because Kash keeps me on the edge far too long, teasing and stopping, using both of his hands to his advantage as Rowan restrains mine.

"Make her scream, Kash. She's ready." Maddox final-ly eases from my mouth and stands up with his words. I grab his cock and stroke him, watching Kash fingering both my holes and rubbing my clit, preparing my body for Rowan.

I gasp and arch, my body finally exploding over the edge of ecstasy. My muscles tighten with my orgasm, and Rowan quickly lifts me up, letting my body squirt across his cock. I should be weirded out by it, but I know what I'm capable of as a female dragon, and being with multiple mates at once is my very nature. I'm made for this and will embrace it as much as the Drekis do.

"Ready, Nova?" Rowan asks, his breath tickling my ear. He flexes his cock against my back. "I'm dying to be inside you. I want you to feel my pleasure and to drown in yours."

Kash lifts me up by my hips as Rowan aligns his body with my ass. I pant at the pressure of being lowered onto his cock, getting used to the sensation of my body stretching to welcome him in. Maddox's eyes burn with firelight, and he rubs my clit, ensuring I feel the pleasure I crave. My body adjusts to Rowan, the pressure subsiding, and I rest my head back, just wanting them to take over. I want to be their perfect mate and give them whatever they crave. I want to be used and enjoyed, tested and treated like their ultimate fantasy.

Kash strokes his boner in front of me, watching my ass slide up and down his brother's cock in a way that steals my thoughts. I automatically reach out and silently ask him to join in, and Kash positions himself between both our legs, resting on one knee while propping his other foot on the bench seat.

"She's so tight," Rowan murmurs to his brothers, moaning with his heavy breathing.

"She's going to get tighter. Just wait. It's going to be unlike anything imaginable." Kash bows to kiss me. "You ready, kitten?"

I gasp and bob my head, tilting my head down to watch Kash join his brother. Stretching my legs out, he puts me in the splits and moans his enjoyment, following Rowan's rhythm, the two of them sliding easily with my slickness. Maddox strokes himself, and I reach for him and pull him closer. He climbs on the bench and lets me guide him into my mouth, bending his knees to work with his brothers. Talk about feeling completely stuffed in the best way possible.

Maddox holds my head in place and rocks his hips, making me deep throat him. I hum and moan against him, losing myself to every sensation they create. Explosions ignite between my legs, and I orgasm again, feeling myself squirt all over Kash. He growls in bliss, his pride as palpable as his pleasure.

It triggers Rowan, his grunt huffing into my hair. I

clench him tighter, digging my nails into him. He stiffens beneath me, his muscles rippling as he cums, but he doesn't stay in me for long. Sliding his cock out, he whispers his love for me in my ear. Maddox pulls his cock from my mouth and takes Rowan up on his silent offer to trade places, and I tip my head back, my mind whirling, my body so excited to take care of my mates.

"Make her cum again, Kash," Maddox demands. "Two more. Ten. I want to hear her scream and feel her shake. I want her to feel so good that she can't think of anything else."

"Maddox," I gasp, sinking my fingers into his hips.

Rowan cuts off my attempt to speak with his sensual kiss, stopping me from saying that one more orgasm is enough. My body shakes, the pleasure mind-numbing. Maddox groans with his thrusts, acting a bit rougher with me than Rowan had, but pleasure explodes through me all the same. Kash bows into me with his orgasm, but he doesn't pull out. He remains in his place and rubs my clit as fast as Maddox claims me until I scream a wave of fire toward the ceiling, my wild nature unleashed by my mates.

"Fuck yeah. We got her all wild like she loves," Maddox mutters, using his hands to guide me up and down a few more times. He finishes with a grunt, and I practically melt into him, unable to do anything but breathe.

Kash and Rowan take seats on each side of Maddox, and they adjust me to sprawl across them, still craving to kiss and touch me, showering me with their affection. Water cleanses our bodies, and I savor how they trace me with their fingers, showing me the attention I can't get enough of.

Our bodies hum, feeling as if our souls twine and merge, and I listen in silence as their dragon natures think about things I have yet to truly consider. Our passion awakens and strengthens our mind-link, and their emotions feel so raw and vulnerable, but they feel safe and unashamed as they allow me to know them on the level we share with our soul bond.

They desire more than my body in this moment and relish how amazing it is to just be with me. I knew this. Maddox alone was never secretive with his desire to bear children with me, but it's like the need turns more desperate, so much so that both Kash and Rowan think the same.

I had no idea what even a small amount of time apart could do to us, but it's like we've grown closer together. And now that they think such things, I can't help myself. Because I need something to hold on to. To look forward to. I need to know that no matter what or how shit goes down, the Drekis are mine. We will create a future together. No one can keep us apart.

"Nova," Kash whispers, massaging his fingers into my thigh. "You're going to make it impossible to leave this shower if you continue to be so open with your new desires."

"It is impossible to leave. I need to give her what she wants immediately. Mating season is close. Can't you feel it?" Maddox starts to lift me up to begin fucking me again, but I grab him and block his entrance with my hand.

"Maddox, we can't," I say, my voice lacing with sadness. "Not yet."

Rowan sighs. "She's right, brother. Things with—"

A strange alarm blares through the air, making the lights flicker. Maddox growls under his breath and stands, clutching onto me as he snatches a towel and wraps me in it. Handing me to Kash, he gathers his dragon fire in his palms and strides toward the bathroom door. Rowan joins his side, and the two of them prepare to charge into the bedroom with their power blazing and ready to destroy.

"Vi telo at vita yo tiater," a familiar voice chants. McKayla's spell hums through the door, and I tense. What the fuck is going on?

"Magaelorum, I've come with a message," McKayla says, her voice even.

Maddox shoves the door open and races with Rowan into the room. Kash strides behind them more cautiously until he sees that only the Darkonians wait near my bed. Ambrose laces his fingers behind the back of his neck, and he glances at me and back to the magical projection lighting over the wall.

"My name is McKayla Lioht, shunned High Priestess of the Lioht Coven, and my former coven faked my death. Their reign must come to an end. Too many innocent people have paid for their crimes." Red magic flickers across her gaze.

My eyes widen in shock.

McKayla smirks, but it's not in happiness. Something darker lies in her mind. "Dear sister, it seems you wanted a war, so you get your wish. Blessed be your fate."

CHAPTER 3

Trouble

"FRANCO IS COMING," AMBROSE SAYS, narrowing his eyes at the door. He stands rigid, his back straight. I don't have to hear his thoughts to know he fears getting discovered. It could end with a fight that could jeopardize all the work he put in to get through the magic that kept them out. "We have to hide."

Digging my nails into my palms, I focus on settling

my nerves. He said hide and not leave like I thought he might. If he took my mates and vanished...I can't stand the thought. I never want to be apart again. I don't care if it makes me seem clingy. I will cling to them like a sloth with a death grip and never let them go.

"We could take flight," Theo says, his forehead wrinkling in annoyance. He snaps his attention to me, the regret of his suggestion prevalent with his furrowed reaction.

I wave my hand toward the bathroom. "No fucking way. Go in there and use magic or something. I don't want any of you leaving." I know it's risky to ask my mates to stay, but just the thought of them leaving and struggling to return because of the magical shield scares me. I never want to be apart again. "I need you here and not risking getting locked out."

"Just keep him by the door, princess. We should be safe enough." Ambrose zaps magic at the Drekis and Theo's feet, forcing the four of them to head into the grand bathroom. "He shouldn't be able to catch anyone's scent from a distance."

Now that he mentions it, I realize I can smell my mates too. Shit. I say a silent prayer to the universe that we don't get caught.

"Let him fucking get close enough to smell us. I'd like to—" Maddox grunts as Kash punches him in the gut, getting him to move his ass.

"We can't fight now. It could dissuade him from ever agreeing to hand Nova over." Shoving his hand into Maddox's back, he gets my grumpy mate to keep moving.

"Tiernan, keep Franco distracted. Don't let him think you've been doing anything else just enjoying Nova," Ambrose adds, his words sending heat to my cheeks.

Scooping me up, Tiernan runs with me to the bed and tosses me on it. He yanks my towel away and shoves it under one of the pillows, surprising the hell out of me. I can't even open my mouth to ask what he's doing because he crashes his mouth to mine. And fuck. The heat of his skin lights up my body, and I react to his passion with my own. If the door to my suite didn't boom open, I'm certain I'd have guided Tiernan's cock into me. His hard-on rests on my pelvis, flexing with the same need I feel inside me. What the hell is wrong with me? Stupid horny vagina.

Franco clears his throat, his annoying announcement grating on my nerves. He didn't even knock and could've seen me naked. "You've had quite enough time to satisfy your mating desires, prince." Wow. I can't believe he expects us to just stop and acknowledge him instead of leaving and coming back later.

I almost yell at him and throw a fire ball because it's so weird.

Tiernan must sense my anger, because he restrains my hands in his.

If this isn't awkward, I don't know what would be. Dragons are so casual when it comes to nudity and sex compared to humans in the Mortal World. And mating desires? Is that what this carnal need to have my brains fucked out is? Because hell. I still can't grasp the thought of having animalistic tendencies even though I have turned into a dragon. I know it's what I am.

Tiernan blows a breath in my ear. He's as caught up as I am and doesn't want to give in to Franco's rash demands to just stop even though we're only pretending. "Yes, your majesty. Please give me a couple minutes to finish up."

Heat burns my cheeks. This is fucking awful.

"You have five and must ensure Delphia is dressed appropriately. I have some important company arriving as we speak." Franco steps closer, his shoes tapping on the rock floor. "If you'd like to call your brother to join us, I'd like to extend an invitation to him. As crown prince, his presence will be appreciated by the other clans."

What the hell? I thought he'd be barricading the castle because of McKayla's message or throwing a fit and threatening me, blaming me for something out of my control. I wouldn't put it past the man holding a never-ending grudge against my mother, which is how I ended up with him in the first place.

I want to ask Franco about it and what he plans to do, but I'm afraid. I'm terrified to even leave this bed. I hate being a prisoner, but I hate the idea of having to parade around and act as if none of this bothers me. There is no way he didn't hear McKayla call out McKenzie to all of Magaelorum.

"Delphia," Franco says, finally focusing on me. I can sense his gaze on my bed. I refuse to peek out from under Tiernan though. If I do, I might explode with my rage. He has the audacity to touch my foot, sticking out from the blanket. "Wear a gown. I expect you to be on your best behavior and not give anyone a reason to see you as the criminal Magaelorum deemed you to be. These alliances are important for the sake of all of the Dragon Lands and for our kingdom. If you can't act as the princess you were born as, you will be treated as the prisoner you've become and not be allowed the socialization you need to learn the things kept from you. Do you understand?"

I glower into Tiernan's shoulder, my skin blazing with my anger. I catch the faint scent of smoke as I burn the sheets with my hands. "Yes, Franco. I understand. I won't cause any trouble." I mean, unless someone provokes me. I don't say as much. He's letting me out of this damn room. I can look around and memorize everything to make it easier when we can go.

"Call me Father. It must be known that you are my heir and the Litendrake princess despite your Drakovich lineage." Franco's voice sharpens as if it pisses him off to even make the suggestion. He really hates my mother, and I wish I could know with absolute certainty how things went down between them. They had to have some sort of connection, right?

Not if they were betrothed like Franco tried to do to me.

I grind my teeth, scratching my nails into Tiernan. "Yes, Father. I understand the importance of the familial title." It's what got me out of Max, after all. If only it felt like he deserved it. He's been nothing but a mystery and absent...I guess the same as it's always been. At least how it was before, thinking he was dead, I could shrug it off since there was nothing I could do about it. I hate thinking that I prefer to think he's dead. It shouldn't be like this, but it is what it is. Sharing blood obviously doesn't make him a father to me. All it does is give me another reason to fight my way out of here and never look back. Fucking disappointment of a man.

"Good, now hurry. I don't want to keep my allies waiting. We need all of the power we can get to protect this territory. I will not bow to whatever the fates have in store. We are better than that." Franco's shoes squeak as he turns, and I close my eyes and count his footsteps as he strides away to exit my suite.

Neither of us moves, listening to him lingering without shutting the door right away. My heart beats thud in my head. It's like he purposely waits to drag on our anxiousness, trying to kill a mood that died with his arrival.

Finally, with the loud boom of the door, Franco leaves in a flurry. Still, we remain frozen, our chests pressed together and Tiernan's naked body between my legs. A dozen thoughts swirl through my head as I process Franco's words.

"He's up to something. Why would he invite other clans over?" I ask, tightening my arms around him. "Why do I have to dress up?"

"I think he wants to show you off and use you to get attention. Clans use females for alliances, and I damn well know that the Litendrakes' run thin. Fucking shit. He's strategizing his options because of McKayla's announcement. He did say he needed to keep power," Tiernan says, his rumbling voice vibrating over my shoulder. I don't know exactly what he means by any of that, but I know it can't be good.

"What do we do?" I cup his face, staring into his eyes.

His body arouses again, no longer tamed by Franco's interruption.

"First, I need to move before I lose control and claim you." Tiernan rolls off me and covers his eyes with his hands, inhaling a few deep breaths.

My body hums with need and desire. If I didn't hear the others drawing closer, coming from the bathroom, I'd roll back onto him and claim him first.

"Fuck, she's insatiable," Theo mutters, jumping onto the bed beside me. He snatches me before I can roll out of his way and pulls me on top of him. "My sexy firecracker, give me a moment of your time. I want to kiss you."

I press my hands to his chest. "I have five minutes to get ready, so no."

Theo snaps his fingers at Ambrose. "Help a familiar out."

Green magic sparkles through the air, and I blink and stare down at my cleavage peeking out of the slim-fitted black satin gown. My long hair billows around us, dry and pinned out of my face. Fire smolders within the jade depths of Theo's eyes, and I find myself getting sucked into his wave of appreciation as he drinks me in. I should resist and play hard to get. We haven't exactly been on the best of terms with his entitlement, either. But the forced bond between us consumes me, and I brush my lips to his, giving in to my dragon.

"I want to make things right between us, Nova," he whispers into my mind, keeping the conversation between us. It's the first time I haven't had to yell at him for not using my chosen name. "I know you hate the bond we share, but I don't want it to be like this. I want you to know how much I want a future with you as my mate and by the sides of the men your soul has chosen before me."

I ease away, rubbing my lips together. "See, was that so hard?" I tease. I can't help it. Something in my nature wants to give him a hard time. "Though I'm still unsure. That hate-sex..."

Theo play-growls. "Hate? No. That was completely and utterly primal and exactly what I'll give you every time."

Whoa, fuck.

Maddox groans in his throat, drawing my attention to him. He elbows Kash, chuckling. "What did I say? She loves it rough and wild."

I roll my eyes and wag my finger at Maddox, getting him to raise an eyebrow. I turn to Kash and wiggle my fingers, asking him to come closer. "Don't listen to that asshole. I enjoy making love to you as you want. You fill a need unlike anyone else...sweet yet steamy and something I crave over and over again."

"You're all right. Wild and insatiable. Just look at her now." Rowan winks at me, getting everyone to smolder me with their gazes.

I rub my legs together and hide my face. They love what they do to me.

Cocky fucking bastards. All of them.

Holding my hand up, I get them to settle down before they try something and say, "I can feel all of your damn beasts getting riled up, and you guys need to chill. As much as I want to stay here...fuck."

I groan and flatten myself to Theo. His hard body ripples under mine, his desire as prominent as the rest of my mates. If they had a choice in the matter, I'm certain we'd never leave the room. I am even more certain that if we ever make it out of here and to wherever our new home may be, we'd never leave the bed. It's fucking insane. I feel like I should want to do other things—like explore the Dragon Lands, fly through the skies, anything—but my damn body can't stop thinking about any of them and how I crave to bond with them in a way that puts us all on the same level. I'm addicted to them in mind, body, and soul and feel incredible being with them as our nature intends.

Ambrose scrubs his hands over his face, composing himself before he gets too wrapped up in his familiars' emotions. "Things will clear and you won't feel so out of control after mating season, princess. Their scents trigger your desire, so unless you force space between you—"

"Space is out of the question." Theo growls and fakes Ambrose out like he's going to blast him with fire.

I sit up, straddling Theo, and link my hands with his, stopping him from messing around. Swiveling my torso, I glance at Ambrose. "We need to leave. Now. I can barely keep my mind clear long enough to process things. The warning from my aunt doesn't help...I don't like any of this. Something is up. Wasn't it strange that Franco didn't even mention it? He had to have seen it, right?" With my thoughts of my aunt and Franco barging in here, I can finally gather my good senses to stop thinking about all the things my mates want to do to me.

Ambrose presses his lips together, the green sparkle of magic glittering across his silvery irises. "He knows. I'm sure of it. Like my familiar mused, it's probably why he's brought in other clans. I just—I'm sorry, princess. I'm incapable of freeing you at the moment. I need more time to study the spells and learn what I need. The magic used here...and on you...is incredibly dangerous. It takes a coven to accomplish such a spell or something darker for an individual like me. Sacrificial magic. But I will not leave your side. No one will see me with my shield."

"We need to see what Franco has planned too," Tiernan says, stroking his fingers across the satin fabric of my hiked up gown. I try not to react under his soft touch, but damn it, does he make it hard not to. "If he's called in the clans, he might have some sort of bargain for them. I worry about what it means. Something like this could affect all of the Dragon Lands—mountains, skies, everything."

Rowan growls under his breath at the thought. "The only important thing right now is Nova, and if you three can't see that, then—"

"She's why we're here. She's what motivates us to ensure the safety of our home. You can't just turn your backs on all of this." Theo cuts Rowan off with his reasoning. "The Mortal World might be acceptable to you, but our mate needs a home here. She's been deprived of everything her whole life, and I know we must do this and think about what's good for her now. We have to think about our offspring and clans. Nova is everything in our worlds, so we need to ensure she gets everything."

Nerves bunch in my stomach. I know the two clans see things differently. I worry that these differences in their ideas of how to create a future with me might make things more difficult than they should be. The Drekis know we can survive without having a kingdom and unlimited resources. What's important is us first. The Darkonians agree, but they see the importance in the world outside of us too.

"Please, you guys. That's enough. We can compromise and still have the future you envision for us." I scramble to my feet, shutting them all up before they try to voice their reasons why each of them thinks they're right. "We'll be discussing all of this as a group when we can, but now isn't the time. I love that all of you just want what's best, but I need to have an opinion too. You're my mates. My futures. I demand to be included."

All six of them remain expressionless, their bodies clearly struggling not to speak up to dominate me or whatever. Even Ambrose looks to have something to say, and I can imagine just what every single one of them has in mind. I'm what brings them all together, and I'm thankful they can at least agree on that. I'm all of theirs. I might've said I'm only giving the Darkonians and their guard a chance, but that's not exactly true. My dragon claims them. They're not going anywhere.

If the loud clap of thunder—no, of flying dragons—didn't boom through the room, I might've backed down and let them hash things out because their intensity zings to my very core. Thinking about anything other than Franco and witches, even if it's an argument on what happens next is what I crave.

But unfortunately, our future isn't the priority. Surviving this moment is.

I rush toward the balcony only to have Kash hook his arm around my waist and stop me from going out. I peek from his arms at the giant, mesmerizing beasts soaring in the direction of the palace to land below. And damn. I pray to the fates that they all put some clothes on or something. Watching the men transform and gather naked, even from here, steals my attention. I'm not sure how my eyes will survive having to stare at a room of big beastly men in all their nakedness. That's one way to know what they think of me, and the last thing I need is to know that they are thinking dirty thoughts as their cocks rise to point in my direction. It's weird as fuck.

"What the fuck? Those aren't all Litendrake allies," Theo murmurs, coming up to our other side. "It looks like the leading clans from everywhere."

"Shit." Tiernan clenches his fingers into fists. "I have a bad feeling."

I do too. I don't say as much. I can't. A massive golden dragon lands on my balcony, surprising the hell out of us, and Ambrose shoots magic through the air. Everyone vanishes from my sight as he shields them from view. The beast swings its neck, peering around. He searches the area as if he's making sure no one sees his arrival.

Billowing smoke escapes his nostrils, and our eyes meet from a few feet away. I scramble away as the dragon pokes his big head into my suite, practically chasing me with his eyes alone. My whole body cools at his intrusion. Who the fuck does he think he is?

Opening my mouth, I summon my voice to scream. The hulking dragon cuts me off by nudging his gigantic head into my stomach, knocking me off my feet. I land back on the floor and jerk my legs up, kicking the dragon in the chin.

"You fucker! Get out of my room!" I yell, kicking him again.

The dragon growls at me, leaning closer. He doesn't react as I smack and kick him, trying to keep space between us as he tries to sniff me. I expect one of my mates to react, but they don't. Ambrose keeps them hidden. This is one of those times I wish I had better control over my dragon. I'd knock him out of here and make him regret sneaking into my room uninvited.

The door to my suite creaks open, and Franco claps his hands and rubs his palms together. Instead of scowling and starting a fight with this bastard dragon, all Franco does is stare at the dragon in amusement. My chest heaves, and I remain frozen in my place. Taking advantage of my shock of seeing Franco not reacting how I expect, the dragon presses his nose right to my pelvis and inhales. I swear and punch him as hard as I can.

"You creep! Father, do something," I snap, shoving my hands to the dragon's snout. Asking Franco for help feels utterly wrong, even more so than calling him Father.

Franco crosses his arms. "Be respectful, Delphia. He's an admirer."

I gasp in irritation. "Admirers fucking introduce themselves and ask permission to enter someone's room."

Transforming, the dragon morphs from his beast form and into a man, completely naked, hairy as fuck, and smelling of something wild—musky. I hate that I pick up his scent from here, and it scares me. He bellows a laugh and smooths his wild hair with his hand.

"Feisty, isn't she?" the man asks, ignoring me to bow to Franco.

"What did you expect? I should disembowel you for entering my daughter's suite uninvited, Santino," Franco says, his voice teasing instead of threatening. "You were to ask permission."

"She didn't say no when I saw her. She was playing hard to get, running before I could speak," the beast man, Santino, says, whipping his attention to me. I can't believe him. "I should burn this place down because you haven't already offered to arrange her union to the Battle Clan. She's exquisite."

I want so badly to snap at them to stop acting like I'm not here, but Franco snatches my hands and drags me to my feet, restraining me to his chest. I freeze, my soul screaming to get away from Franco. It yells at me to override my good senses and to fight, because something is so incredibly wrong.

"And lose my ability to incite the clans to join us to stand together? You can bow along the rest of them, you bastard." Franco growls deep in his throat, gathering my hair to hold it out of my face. Is he silently letting Santino look at me? He is. This asshole. "I'll not waste my restitution this way."

"Smart man," Santino says, striding closer. He tilts his head and gazes at me without touching me, but my skin crawls anyway. He licks his lips, traveling his gaze to my breasts as he undresses me with his mind, turning himself on in the process. If he gets any closer, he'll get a knee to his hard cock. "Your father doesn't control the Mountain Lands for no reason. I hope you appreciate his efforts in arranging your upcoming union, Delphia. I look forward to pledging my loyalty to bring you home."

Oh, fuck. What?

I frown, my body cooling. "Excuse me?"

Stepping closer, Santino gets in my face. "Wouldn't you like that? My brothers can't wait to meet you."

Breaking free of Franco, I slap the beast man in the face. This can't be happening.

Santino laughs and snatches my wrist, pulling me to him. Getting in my face, he releases a hot breath. "I love a good fight, princess. Keep it up, and I'll show you how much you'll crave to be mine."

CHAPTER 4

Broken Contract

A SNARL SOUNDS THROUGH THE air, and the suite quakes as Theo and Tiernan land on the balcony in their massive dragon forms. Ambrose must've used his magic to get them outside. The threat of their roaring beasts is enough to get Santino to back up a few feet, though Franco doesn't release me.

Tiernan transforms first and strides closer. Surprising

me, he punches Santino in the face, knocking him off his feet. "I leave for two minutes to call for my brother, and you come in here and try to lay a claim on the princess I will win the union with? You better return to your clan, Santino. She is ours."

Franco tightens his hold on me like he expects the Darkonians to snatch me away. I wish they would. I'd risk my limbs to punch Franco in the cock to get him to release me. I don't care if it starts shit. He just casually mentioned that he's going to give me to another clan, and not necessarily my mates.

Santino raises an eyebrow, unfazed by Tiernan's threat. Smirking, he glances from me and back to Tiernan. "My apologies, prince. I thought your contract was forfeited. The dishonor in breaking an exquisite arrangement spread quickly. I'm surprised you even decided to show your face around here."

"I've welcomed him into the palace for assisting in private matters, but it doesn't change the fact that you are correct. The Darkonians do not have my daughter's contract," Franco snaps, finally releasing me. "Which is why the Darkonians will be in line like the rest of you assholes. Now leave Delphia's quarters and join the others. All of you. You've had enough of her private attention. Another visit must be earned."

Grabbing my wrist, Franco drags me toward the door leading to the rest of the palace. I peer behind me, watching Tiernan shove Santino toward the balcony where Theo waits in his dragon form. I'm surprised they exit that way instead of following behind me. Ambrose materializes into view near the bed, and I can't stop my eyes from watering in dread. This can't be happening. I refuse to accept any other clan. The Drekis and Darkonians are my mates.

Whatever Franco is up to with my union won't end in anything other than a war between the two of us. He's planning to use me to gain stronger alliances, and I won't stand by like a complacent female getting told what is supposed to be good for her rather than letting her stand on her own and choose what's best for herself.

This whole shitshow is definitely about McKayla and her declaration, and I wish with everything in me that I could escape. What if Theo and Tiernan don't get me like they want and plan? What if Franco gives me to the vilest clan as punishment? I know he holds something against me for being my mother's daughter. I shouldn't have gotten my hopes up after he caught McKenzie trying to steal my heart. He was only mad because he had other plans in mind for me. Which of them is worse? I wish I knew. Right now, Franco and McKenzie are up there with Lazlo Infinity and Quillon on my list of most hated people.

"Remember what I said, Delphia," Franco says, forcing me to run to keep up with his quick pace. "The Darkonians still have it in their heads that you're their intended mate, and you need to deal with the fact that it no longer is the case. I will put you with the clan I see most fit to ensure our power. The High Council wants to steal our lands and place the blame of the blasted Liohts upon us, but I will not let them keep us down."

I remain silent, peering around the arched tunnel leading us deeper into the mountainside. I can't find the nerve to speak. He's using me. Fucking using me. All because his dumbass made some sort of deal with the Liohts to hurt another coven, and it's coming back to bite him.

"Delphia, are you listening?" Franco snaps.

I hum my agreement. "Yes, Father."

Damn it. I hate sounding so obedient, but the fire in his gaze frightens me. He doesn't care whether or not I'm happy. He doesn't care about me at all except for what I can bring him.

In this moment, I can't believe I ever felt saddened by his absence from my life. Knowing that he's been alive all this time and carrying such hatred toward me just because of who gave birth to me pisses me off.

Heat builds in my chest as my dragon reacts to my darkening emotions. My veins light aglow like lava, and I try my best to squelch my urge to explode into my beast form. It would be a tight squeeze in this tunnel but not impossible. I'm sure that dragons can fit everywhere in this massive palace built for them.

"Now lower your gaze to the ground and only show attention to the clan leaders I give you permission to acknowledge. I will not allow those who I know will betray me to think they have a chance with you under their terms." Franco releases a breath of smoke and slows down outside a towering archway. He narrows his gaze on me, but I refuse to look at him, following his instructions like the good little girl he wants me to be. "Also, pull up your tits. Give the clans more to appreciate."

Oh, fuck no. The only reason I adjust the bodice on my gown is because Franco looks as if he'll do it for me. I hug my arms around myself, stopping him from trying to drag me around by my wrist again. Voices hum through the air, growing louder as I shuffle behind him, keeping my gaze lowered. All I want to do is look around. I need to see everyone here and know what I'm dealing with. Fuck. Fuck. Fuck.

Silence settles over the grand ballroom, the stone walls glittering with crystals of different colors I'm not sure I've ever seen in the Mortal World. It almost looks as if the sky has been placed within the rock, bringing the heavens to Earth in this mountain palace. The room warms, the heat of over two hundred dragon men smoldering through the air. Their gazes penetrate into me, and I stare at my bare feet peeking out from my gown because Ambrose never summoned me shoes. If I didn't see the fabric hugging my silhouette, I'd think I were naked and on display.

"Welcome!" Franco says, his voice booming through the room, echoing within its vastness. "It's an honor to have the strongest, fiercest dragon clans in all of Magaelorum present. Allow me to offer you an endless feast to celebrate your arrival to my kingdom."

I can't stop myself from peeking up as dozens of men carry out huge plates of meat to set amid the long, clothed tables. It's elegant yet feral, the gathering strange to my mortal upbringing. This is how I imagine things to have been like in the long-ago mortal past.

The silence breaks, and I try my best to sneak a couple glances at the legs of the men in the room. Thankfully, it seems that they all wear some sort of coverings but not exactly the formalwear I've been dressed in. Franco places his hand on my lower back and guides me to the head of a broad table with a high-backed chair decorated with gemstones. He motions for me to sit at his right, and I watch one of the servants pull out the chair for me.

"I got you, firecracker," Theo murmurs, surprising me by grabbing the chair next to me. Another man growls, one who clearly wanted the honor of sitting by my side, and Tiernan shoots a burst of fire at him, the force knocking him away.

Damn. These dragons really do flex their power and strength with each other.

"Santino, please join us. I'm sure Delphia would enjoy your company." Franco plops into his chair and touches my chin, forcing it up. "Isn't that so, daughter?"

I slowly nod, afraid he might hurt me.

"Invite your brothers." Franco grabs a leg of some sort of meat and waves it into the air. "Boynton, join me as well. I'd like to introduce your clan to my breathtaking heir."

"Who is the spitting image of her mother." A man slouches in the seat across from me, beating the Battle Clan. Tiernan sits beside Theo, and I force myself to keep my stare on the pile of dripping meat. There is no fucking way I'm going to even touch it. I draw a line of my compliance on what I put in my mouth—food, cocks, what the fuck ever. "Just beautiful."

"If only Delilah wasn't such a disappointment," the man, Boynton, adds. He stretches his arm across the table, sticking it in my line of sight. "What about you, Delphia?

We've heard the rumors of your imprisonment."

Still, I don't look up.

Franco kicks me under the table, making me jump. "Complete rumors. As is what I'm sure you've all heard from the blasted traitor witch, trying to sully my name."

It takes everything in me not to roll my eyes. He's so full of shit.

"I'd love to know the truth, your majesty. I remember the trial as clearly as if it were yesterday. I hadn't seen the High Council dish out as harsh a punishment since you accused the Tenebris Coven of murder." This comes from a man toward the end of the table.

I snap my gaze to his, regretting it immediately. The whole table, all men, stare at me like I'm the only thing any of them wants to look at. Luckily, Franco doesn't notice. He growls deep in agitation and gets to his feet.

"The Liohts tricked me. Used magic. Something. Because what I saw that day—the Tenebris Coven slaughtered McKayla Lioht." He smacks his hands into the table, heaving a breath in anger. "McKenzie even came into my palace after helping me bring Delphia home only to try to take my daughter's heart. I was set up. The traitor witches want to draw attention away from their wrongdoings and place the blame on the dragons. They want our land. They want our power. This is why I've called you—ally or not—to gather. We must unite and be ready for the war the witches started."

My jaw slackens at his words. He's so damn convincing that I can't tell if what he says is true or not. What if all along he was just a puppet being played by the Liohts? I know that the High Council rules all of Magaelorum despite it being divided into territories.

"We need more than your word for it, Franco," another man says, not calling him by the title the others have used. "My clan has a guard contract with a High Council member. We need more than a fucking feast to even consider taking sides."

Santino nods his head in agreement. "I must agree."

Franco snarls and blows a breath of fire down the middle of the table, smoldering his food offering. "I have two things you might consider. Land and Delphia. I will grant one of your clans a contract with her if you all confirm your alliances."

"No," I whisper under my breath.

"A union with the princess?" a man murmurs in consideration.

Franco snatches me from my spot, hoisting me up and forcing me to stand on the table. "She's the most breathtaking woman in all of the Dragon Lands. She will bear strong children with the Litendrake lineage."

My stomach clenches at the thought. No one apart from my mates should ever think of making babies with me.

I open my mouth to argue, but electricity crackles through the air. A strange alarm blares.

Franco jerks his attention toward the archway. "Do you see that? They're here! We must band together. Show me your worth, and you will be rewarded."

The room bursts with growls and fire, the whole place shaking.

I've never seen such a sight.

All of the clans take Franco up on his command, including the Darkonians.

They all leave.

CHAPTER 5

Union

"COME ON, DELPHIA. LET'S WATCH." Franco doesn't give me the chance to respond and snatches me off the table, slinging me over his shoulder.

I always thought Maddox was a bit Neanderthal in his behavior, but Franco is far worse, treating me like a piece of property or some shit. I wonder if the other drag-on clans are just as bad or if it's only because Franco holds a grudge for my mother's wrongdoings.

"I want to see which clans are worthy of such a bond to you," Franco adds, heading into a tunnel that spits us out on the ledge of a steep cliff that drops into fog too thick to see the bottom.

The world booms and quakes, and I gape in awe as hundreds of dragons, more than the men invited into the palace, soar through the air, peppering the twilight sky with their massive forms. Clouds of fire and smoke fill the air, and I can't stop myself from clutching onto Franco's sleeve as I spot bursts of magical power light the storm of dragons aglow with bolts of red electricity.

"The High Council will think twice of trying to intrude on our kingdom without the proper warning," Franco mutters, bouncing on the balls of his feet. "This might've been a good thing for us after all."

Us? No. Him? Fuck him. Damn it.

Anger coils around my being, and I imagine my dragon bursting free so that I can take flight and disappear. If only the thought also didn't steal my breath, sending me stepping away from the ledge.

"I know you enjoy the company of the Darkonians and had they kept their agreement, I would have never thought twice about our alliance, but that was arranged so long ago and by your grandfather. If he were still alive today, I think he'd consider the Battle Clan. A bigger clan is a stronger clan, and they will serve us right." Franco stares at the side of my face, waiting for my reaction.

"I've already bonded in soul to them," I say, not mentioning that it was only Theo. "Please don't reconsider."

Franco narrows his eyes. "Maybe that's why I should."

The edges of my vision shadow, and I peer around, wondering if I surprise Franco and manage to kick him off the cliff if he'd be able to transform into a dragon before hitting wherever the ground is. Probably.

The last thing I need is for him to get even angrier at my existence, but his words twist my stomach. I refuse to let him just betroth me to a clan. It was bad enough to discover that the Litendrakes had done so with the Darkonians. Had circumstances been different, I'm not sure how that would have turned out. I think it was the fates that brought the Drekis and Darkonians together with me in the center, and I don't want to lose them. I've already lost enough as it is.

"Look at the sight. They're fleeing," Franco says, pointing toward the red electricity dancing through the sky. "I knew our strength would keep them away."

"I don't understand." My rebel mouth says the words before I even realize I just spoke what's on my mind. Fuck it. I might as well try to figure him out more while I have his attention. "Why have you given the witches control over you in the first place?"

Franco scoffs like it's the most ridiculous question. "My dear Delphia. Do you not know of our circumstances? Have you learned nothing about who you are?"

"I have, but I still don't understand why the clans turned their back on the fates instead of just working out the differences between clans. Seems stupid to force bonds. It does nothing to build alliances and only maintains them."

"Stupid? Hardly. Do not voice your opinion about things you know nothing about." Franco huffs a breath of smoke through his nostrils. "And if you can't grasp the concept now, you might never. I will not waste my breath teaching you. Your soon-to-be mates can handle that task and mold you to their wills."

This asshole.

Fury rises in my heart, and I summon my dragon fire in my palm. I don't get a chance to act, though. A familiar roar echoes through the sky above me, and I catch sight of my beautiful Dreki mates circling in their dragon forms.

I inhale a sharp breath. Now that their arrival sinks in, fear ignites in my heart. Franco tips his head toward the sky, following my gaze. He tightens his jaw and drags me back, leaving the balcony clear as the hoard of dragons nosedives toward us. I yank my hand away from him, spinning and pressing my back to the rock wall. The first dragon lands with a quaking thud, and I brace myself. Franco has no choice but to abandon me or risk getting trampled on.

Another enormous dragon lands behind the first, swinging his long neck in my direction. The yellow-orange beast with gold eyes lowers his head, getting into my personal space. Breathing deeply, he sucks in my scent, sending my hair flowing around me.

I smack him on the snout. "Get back, asshole. You have no fucking right to scent me."

The dragon blows a hot breath back out, and Maddox's huge glittering green form knocks the bastard away from me and roars, shooting a stream of fire to keep him back. My eyes widen in fear. I don't want Maddox to start shit here, and definitely not over some random ass trying to get a whiff of my scent. Franco could do something crazy like demand the dragons who want a chance to claim me tear him apart.

"I should nip that sweet ass of yours for thinking I can't handle myself, cookie," Maddox thinks to me. He narrows his dragon eyes and flicks his tongue across my face. "But leaving my scent all over you should do for now."

I swipe my arm across my wet face. "Seriously?"

"Next time, I'll bring out my baton for punishment. I think I need to remind you that I handled Magaelorum's worst criminals. We own the damn skies despite what all these assholes think."

"I'll bring out the cuffs," Rowan teases, his voice swirling through my mind as he lands behind Maddox.

"Come on, kitten. I'll protect you from my brothers. Cuddle you and keep all the other assholes away." Kash shoves Maddox away with his big head and snaps his teeth to the hem of my dress, pulling me away from the wall.

I finally get my body to move and duck beneath his massive body, using his dragon form to shield myself from the others trying to get a second of my attention. I peer around from Kash's shadow, my whole being on alert. Franco didn't wait to drag me away like I expected, and I catch sight of him at the head of the table once more.

I stroll only a dozen more feet beneath Kash until his shadow disappears. My heart picks up pace at him transforming and leaving me exposed.

"I love how she craves me to be in my most powerful form," Kash murmurs, his voice sounding from behind me.

I twist to rush to him, but one look in his eyes stops

me in my tracks.

"And I fucking want to burn this whole place down for denying her closeness," he adds, flaring his nostrils at Maddox.

I compose myself, thinning my pouty mouth. From one look around, I spot all eyes on me, including Franco's, and his reminder about not showing attention to anyone he doesn't approve of rushes through my head.

"Princess, may I escort you back to your seat before someone else asks?" Tiernan's voice floods me with relief as he falls in step by my side.

I automatically take his outstretched hand and tuck myself under his arm, not even caring about the low growls of jealousy humming through the air. "You left me." I don't know why I say it, but it's like my whole being demands answers.

"I had to follow orders and prove my worth, Nova. As much as I hated bowing to Franco's whim, there is no way we're letting him try to give you to another clan. He'll learn soon enough that you're ours whether he agrees or not." Tiernan keeps his comment between us, speaking to me telepathically. "Accept my vow that I'll never abandon you."

"Abandoned? No. Delphia just missed us," Theo says, striding up on my other side. "Isn't that right, firecracker?"

I sigh and ignore him, reminding myself that everyone scrutinizes us.

"We won't be far, Delphia," Maddox says, his voice caressing my ear with his whisper. It's like he knew I had to hear them out loud just to be certain. "We still need to prove our rank. The Drekis Clan has been under contract to the High Council for far too long that these bastards seem to have forgotten."

A loud roar echoes through the ballroom, and Tiernan practically carries me forward as Franco calls attention to all the clans present. What started off as an okay gathering turns into a damn cockfest. Now that my brain realizes my mates are fine, my body notices they're naked. And not only them. Every damn man in the room except for Franco and the staff remain in all their rippling, muscular, nude forms.

Don't look. Don't look. Don't fucking look.

I chant my new mantra to myself, wishing with everything in me that I was used to seeing dragon dicks. I mean, I see my mates naked more than I see them clothed, but I still can't stop myself from getting entranced. With so many naked fuckers, I want to look around—but then again, I don't. Stupid curiosity.

"Dun eht edih be." Ambrose's soft voice trickles

through the air with his spell. A sparkle of green magic dances across my vision.

Whoa. Fuzzy spots bloom around the room, blocking out every damn ass and cock from my vision. I could kiss the sneaky warlock for helping me out. I had no idea he could cast such spells, and I'm so thankful for the selective vision. Because funny enough, I can still see Tiernan and Theo. With one look behind me, Maddox, Kash, and Rowan remain clear in view.

"You can thank me later," Ambrose murmurs, still hidden from sight.

Franco claps his hands together, getting the rumbling beast men to settle and return to their seats at the long tables. He locks his gaze on mine, remaining expressionless as I allow Tiernan to pull out my chair for me.

"My fellow clans, what did I tell you? Together we are stronger. More powerful. The witches of the High Council don't stand a chance if they believe they can test us." Franco rests his palms on the table. "Do you believe me now? Do you see what we can accomplish?"

"And what about the contracts? You have a lot of ideas, but you know we rely on many covens to help us. Our unions are important. We can't leave the future of our species to the fates." A man with intricate tattoos stands near the end of the table and crosses his arms over his chest. "They could destroy everything we currently have in place."

His concerns ignite chatter among the clans, and I can't stop from peering around, wanting to take in as much of the discussion as I can. I'm rather relieved they all don't just fall at Franco's feet and do as he says. He might be the ruler of the Mountain Lands, but it's not all that there is.

"You're thinking like a weak, worthless pet. That's what the High Council wants," Franco snaps, sending smoke billowing through the air. "There are enough females within our clans that forming our own unions won't be a problem."

"What about those fated?" Kash's question rings through the air, drawing the crowd's attention.

I clutch Tiernan's hand under the table.

"Fated? Where the fuck have you been, boy?" an older man asks, scoffing at his question. "It's been a millennium since the Fates graced our species. The witches ensured it."

"How can you be certain?" Kash straightens his back, not letting the older dragon intimidate him.

"Ask fucking anyone in this room," another man says, waving his arms around.

"Or maybe you should ask Franco. Isn't that the reason Delilah went to prison? She killed the crown prince because she found her true mates." From a table off to the side, a massive man gets to his feet. "That's what my father said. He was in Max when she was. It's why you managed to get Delphia as restitution."

What?

"Enough!" Franco shouts, glowering at the room. "This isn't about my family's wretched history and failed bonds. This is about the High Council and their plans."

"You liar!" The words escape my mouth before I have a chance to even comprehend what I'm saying. "You were never innocent in any of this. I spoke to the witch coven you accused. I know you were working with McKenzie."

Franco bursts into his massive dragon form and snarls. His huge wings stretch across the room. Screeching, he blows a breath of fire through the air and whips his head at me so quickly that Tiernan loses his hold. Franco lifts me in his mouth, the pressure of his bite enough to turn my body placid in fear.

Tossing me away from the table, Franco puts space between my mates and me. Pain erupts through my whole body. Franco will hurt me. I know it. The only reason I'm alive is because he can use me to his advantage. Unlike with the witches, I'm better off alive and not dead.

I scramble away, crab walking and struggling to move in the tight gown. The room quakes as Franco charges at me in his beast form, spitting fire at me. The world ignites in flames, burning my clothes and exposing me completely to all the clans who already fantasize about having their way.

"How dare you try to humiliate me and make the clans question my authority, Delphia!" Franco's voice rips through my mind, his anger as hot as the fire surrounding me. It doesn't hurt, but his power steals the breath from my lungs. "I will break you into the obedient female your mother should've always been...or better yet, I'll let one of them."

Franco screeches again in his dragon form and locks his teeth to my hair, yanking me from the floor. He dangles me from his teeth, showing me to the crowd of men throwing punches and fighting amongst themselves. Men from the Battle Clan fight with Tiernan and Theo, keeping them away. Maddox and Rowan tackle a couple other guys. Kash glowers at Franco, his eyes lighting with his dragon fire. Fuck. He's going to do something crazy. I know it. I want it. But I'm scared.

I cover myself the best I can, searching for one of my mates. "Put me down! I don't want to fight!"

"Too bad, Delphia. I'm done." Franco swings me back and forth as Kash dodges around people, trying to get to me. "Listen up!"

The room falls silent with his booming telepathic command.

"Nova!" Kash hollers, breathing fire. A man jumps on his back, forcing him down.

"I'm ready to give my heir to the strongest clan here. If you catch her, you may claim her. I just want her gone." Whipping his head, Franco throws me across the grand ballroom.

I summon my dragon beast and roar.

I've never seen so many men want me.

They might tear me apart.

CHAPTER 6

Submit

FIRE EXPLODES THROUGH THE ROOM with my anger, and I gnash my teeth, trying to bite anyone who dares to come near. Surprisingly, none of the men change into dragons, and they focus on fighting each other once again, trying to get the competition to back off.

"Nova!" Kash yells again, his desperation to get to me running hotly through me.

A man punches him, setting him off. Exploding into his monstrous dragon form, Kash grabs a table in his teeth and knocks at least twenty guys off their feet, clearing a path for his brothers. I blow another breath of fire, trying to keep anyone brave enough to approach me away.

Where the fuck are Theo and Tiernan? Ambrose? I can't see them from my spot, and I worry that the Battle Clan might've hurt them.

Franco's dragon roar steals my attention, and I watch in shock as he goes after Kash, knocking him across the ballroom. Men scramble out of the way, and a couple men attack Kash in their human forms, helping Franco.

I lose focus on what's in front of me that I don't catch sight of the man closing in on me until he locks his arms around my neck and hoists himself up. The second he straddles my shoulders, he transforms into a dragon, and his weight crushes my body to the floor. I thrash and try to break from his claws, but he sinks his teeth into the side of my throat, squeezing down, stealing my breath.

My dragon abandons me, and I can't stop from transforming into my human self. The world drops out from under me. I freefall a dozen feet, unable to catch myself. Landing on my stomach, I try to push up, but a hot body sandwiches me to the cold rock floor. I nearly lose my mind, feeling the man's fingers grab the back of my neck.

He restrains me, trying to lie on top of me. Fuck. He's going to rape me. He's taken Franco's demand literally and will try to force me to submit to him this way.

"Vi ta co lata!" Ambrose's spell sparks through the air, raining green magic over us. "Release her!"

The man's death grip on me doesn't loosen, the shock of power not even fazing him.

"Ambrose!" I scream, thrashing and bucking. My stomach twists at the sensation of the man trying to shift my leg to give him space. "Ambrose!"

I try to summon my dragon again, fire, anything, but it's like my body refuses to react.

"Beast! Vi lat go tienat eht at!" Ambrose shouts, sending brilliant light through the room.

My vision turns white with his hot power, and the weight of the man sinks harder into me, but not because he fights. Ambrose flicks his hand, knocking the man away from me and gathers me into his arms. The world quiets, and he snaps his fingers, dressing me in jeans and a shirt. I cling onto him, my whole body shaking. I've been manhandled and hurt before, but having Franco—my own father—sentence me to this fucked up fate breaks me. It scorches me to my very soul.

"Princess, I'm so sorry. I'm so sorry," Ambrose says, petting my hair and adjusting me in his arms until I wrap myself around him. "I was protecting my familiars and couldn't react fast enough. I'm so sorry."

Tears burn my eyes, and I blink them away. "He's a fucking lunatic. You have to do something, Ambrose."

"Ambrose!" Theo's voice rings through the air. "Ambrose, get her out of here. Take her somewhere safe."

A screeching roar stings my ears, deafening me. I watch as Franco knocks Kash away and dodges around Maddox. He launches into the air and flaps his wings, blowing fire as he soars the short distance toward us.

"Release my daughter!" Franco shouts through his telepathic link. "Release her now. I've made my decision. She will now belong to the Battle Clan! Everyone else must now wait for her to have an heir!"

Shit. What?

"If you take her, I'll call upon McKenzie. You will regret it, warlock!" Franco lands on the rock ground a dozen feet away and transforms back into his human self.

Ambrose summons an orb of green power in his hand and throws it at Franco. "She's ours!"

Everything happens so fast that I can barely grasp the world changing. The noise from the fight fades, and my heart sinks into my stomach. Fear prickles over my skin. I blink a few times, clearing my vision of the blinding light. I find myself with Ambrose in a dark room, cool and damp like we're deep and low within the mountain palace.

Clapping his hands, he sets the room aglow with magic, giving me a view of the dank room that feels more like a crevice within the glittering rock. A small hole, barely big enough to accommodate my body, leads into pitch blackness. I hug Ambrose tighter.

"We're safe," Ambrose murmurs, summoning a blanket. He wraps it around me and sets me on my feet. Scratching the back of his neck, he sighs and shakes his head as if he hears something I can't. And maybe he does.

"This is a shitshow," Ambrose murmurs, nearly too quietly for me to hear. "Yeah, I know. I'm sure we'll have to face the Liohts. You two need to fucking figure out exactly what Franco wants and just give it to him. Arrange some alliances with other clans. Tell the Drekis to use their influence to scare others into compliance."

I inhale and exhale, calming my racing heart. Ambrose sounds like he's communicating with Theo and Tiernan through their familiar bond to him. I shift on my bare feet, the coolness of the room sinking into my bones.

"Ambrose," I say, finally finding my voice. "I don't understand any of this. What have I done?" I don't know why I ask him, but I can't help it. I need to figure out what I've done to deserve such monstrosity from a man that is supposed to be my father.

"Hurry and let me know," Ambrose mutters under his breath. He turns his attention to me and puffs a long breath of air through his nostrils. Silently, he opens his arms and coaxes me back into them, hugging me. "Nova, I'm sorry. There is so much going on, and I just want to keep everyone safe. I'm afraid I'll let you down."

"He needs to die, Ambrose," I say. Fury ignites in my heart, sending the warmth of dragon fire through my veins, pushing the cold away. "You need to take me back and let me kill him. He won't stop otherwise. I believe him that he'd call McKenzie."

"Just give your mates a few minutes, okay? They will show him reason. Something is hot under his ass right now, and he's a scared coward." Ambrose strokes his fingers up and down my arms, smoothing out my goosebumps through the blankets.

"He could hurt them," I argue.

"Your absence will settle everyone down. I assure it." Ambrose leans in and kisses me, stopping me from arguing again.

My body reacts to his closeness, his strong arms filling me with the sense of safety I've missed in the last hour of madness. Even being in the same room as my mates doesn't compare to being in their arms. And Ambrose? He might not have a soul-bond with me, but I find myself drawn to him just the same.

"You know Maddox and Theo would be furious if they knew you thought they couldn't handle the situation," Ambrose murmurs, easing away from my mouth when he's certain I'm calm enough to think about anything apart from the destruction of my life.

"Then they can come here themselves and punish me together." I bite my bottom lip between my teeth, trying to send my words to them telepathically, but neither of them responds.

"I'll pass on the message, princess." Ambrose combs my wild hair away from my face and tucks it behind my ear. "And I'm sorry I had to cut you off from everyone. It's the only way I can guarantee you'll remain hidden."

I frown. "Ambrose, I don't like this. What if they need you?"

"The only thing they need is for you to be safe and away. It's getting far too close to mating season. It fucks with their dragon natures—and not just your mates. Every damn bastard in there thinks that you're fair game, and Franco didn't help any by letting them all unleash their wild beasts." He swallows, his Adam's apple bobbing in his throat.

"You make us all sound...so feral." I crinkle my nose, hating to think about how the beast side of us runs wild with a mating need out of our control—at least, if we let it. "Isn't there something you can do? Use some magic?"

"My familiars wouldn't be happy if I...turned you off." He chuckles, a small smile lighting his face. "Neither would the Drekis. It's in their dragon nature as your mates and their need to protect you that makes them strong enough to take on the dragon clans, you know."

"Really?" I tilt my head, staring into his silver gaze. "What about you? I know you have a connection to Theo and Tiernan. Does it fuck with you?"

He tightens his mouth. "Not wanting to turn you off isn't entirely on them either. It feels wrong to even consider it."

"Is that so?" I smile and stretch up on my tiptoes. "It feels worse knowing that you're too afraid to distract me and give in to this wild nature. How else am I supposed to settle down?"

I intend for my words to come out teasingly, but a whine lines my voice. Ambrose's silver eyes flash with his green power, and he whispers a spell under his breath and sends a burst of magic over the wall. A strange portal manifests, almost like a window to another world, but the looking glass gives us a view of the ballroom.

I stiffen at the sight of the damage and destruction caused by the clans turning against each other for a chance to claim me.

"This wasn't what I had in mind," I say, my voice coming out a whisper. Hoarse. "But thank you. I appreciate getting to see things for myself."

Ambrose turns me, engulfing me in his arms from behind. He rests his chin on my shoulder and watches as Franco throws his hands up, arguing with one of the men from the Battle Clan.

"See, your mates are all fine. They know what they're doing. Franco has to prove his intentions." Ambrose points to where the Darkonians and the Drekis stand side-by-side in what is the sexiest wall of muscle and badasses I've ever seen.

"Why do I feel like you're afraid to distract me how the others would?" I can't help teasing Ambrose, even keeping my gaze trained on the looking glass. Now that I see that he wasn't lying about my absence settling all of the clans down, I need to figure out how to settle my own ass down.

"Princess, control yourself," Ambrose says, sliding his hand across my stomach. "I want to. I do. But it wouldn't feel right to give in to my desires...before Tiernan. I've heard him worry about it a dozen times. He would never admit it, but the lack of your magical bond still makes him nervous."

"Oh." How do I even react to that?

"Please don't think too much into it. It's not him. I just—they're my best friends. I want you badly. But I also want it to be perfect." He's rambling and we both know it.

I spin in his arms, needing to meet his gaze. "You're nervous. Be honest. It has nothing to do with Tiernan or wanting things perfect."

He groans and shakes his head, resting it on my shoulder. "The things you do to me, Nova. I just—"

"It's okay. You don't have to explain." I brush my lips to his again, savoring the taste of his lips and the tingle of magic he releases from his very being.

Ambrose sighs against my mouth and eases away, offering me another gorgeous smile. "I think things have settled enough. Look."

Spinning me around, he positions me in front of him, pressing his taut body into my back. His hard-on grazes my lower back, though I don't think he intentionally pokes me with it. Not like the others would do. And damn it do I want to stand on my tiptoes, arch my back, and tease him.

"I knew my familiars could handle it with the Drekis backing them up. Our clan will be unstoppable once we have a chance to unite and bond." Ambrose nuzzles his nose to the side of my neck.

I hadn't even noticed what was happening on the other side of the looking glass. Stupid body. I should learn my lesson by now, but my damn defense mechanism in dealing with basically anything these days is to drown myself in the affection my guys give me.

"What do you think they're shaking on?" I ask, forcing myself to concentrate. I can't hear anything through his magic, or maybe it's because my heart beats so loudly that it's all I can focus on. Regardless, it freaks me out a bit that Theo and Tiernan shake hands with Franco. Even weirder is that they also shake hands with the Battle Clan and then motion for Maddox, Kash, and Rowan to join them.

"Franco agreed to re-negotiate a union between you and the Darkonians." Ambrose continues to explore my stomach with his fingers, grazing them up and under the hem of my shirt.

"What?" I don't understand. He was so adamant about torturing me and ruining any sort of chance I had at happiness. What changed? Something doesn't feel right.

"Give me a second, princess. Tiernan asked that I not be the messenger and to retrieve him." Ambrose breaks the magic on the looking glass and steps away from me.

I spin and try to grab onto him. "Ambrose, wait—"

Bright light flashes through the room, and my fingers

only grab empty air.

Ambrose disappears, abandoning me.

If only it didn't feel like it could be forever.

If only I could follow after him.

CHAPTER 7

Dragon Vow

I CROUCH ON MY HANDS and knees and stare into the hole in the rock wall, trying to summon my bravery to crawl into it. My mind keeps flashing to every horror movie I've ever watched, and I can't stop thinking about some monster or deathtrap or whatever waiting for me within the narrow tunnel.

"Ambrose, damn it. Hurry up," I say, squinting my eyes. I tap into my dragon fire, the warmth bursting across my hand easily, no longer completely contained and caged like my dragon was before under the influence of magic.

I flick my fingers, tossing the orb of dragon fire into the tunnel, trying to get a glimpse of where the fuck it goes. The tunnel lights up a little, showing off the glittering stones embedded into the rock but nothing else. My dragon fire can only light up about ten feet. Beyond that, more pitch darkness.

"Just crawl in already. You're a fucking dragon. You can eat any damn monster that tries to devour you. You can burn the world down. Don't be afraid of the damn dark, Nova." My pep talk doesn't do much to assure me, but I crawl forward anyway, trying not to let the tight space scare me.

"Go any farther, and I won't be able to reach your cute ass." Tiernan hums in amusement, swatting my ass with his hand.

I startle and bump my head on the top of the tunnel. Groaning, I blink away the stars peppering my vision and act like a damsel in need of rescuing. I flop on my stomach and whimper, loving how Tiernan sucks in a breath, his nerves as palpable as his happiness to see me.

"Fuck, Nova. Let me help you," he says, his voice rising with concern. "Ambrose, summon some blankets or something. She hurt herself." How will blankets save me?

Well, at least he tries.

Locking his fingers to my ankles, Tiernan drags my defeated ass from the narrow tunnel and flips me over. I pop out my bottom lip, fucking with him. I don't know if it's because his emotions are still wild from the whole dragon clan gathering bullshit or what, but he misses the fact that I'm only teasing him and quickly scoops me onto his lap.

"What were you even doing?" he asks, caressing his fingers to my jaw. He tips his head back and glances at Ambrose. "Did you make a detour or something? She was trying to get out. She could've gotten stuck."

"No, I went straight to you and back." Ambrose squats beside Tiernan and lifts an eyebrow, studying my face.

I stick my tongue out at him. "It felt like an eternity, warlock."

He chuckles and ruffles his fingers through my messy hair. "Come on, princess. Tiernan can't understand that you're fucking with him. He's too caught up on everything. You might want to tell him you're okay."

I feign weakness and slump in Tiernan's arms. "But I'm not okay, Ambrose."

Tiernan lifts me higher, studying my face. "Summon Maddox."

"No, it'll take too long. I'm hurting. Everywhere. There's only one cure." I bat my eyelashes, loving his smoldering intensity.

Glancing at Ambrose, Tiernan furrows his brows in confusion. I nearly break from my fake pouting to kiss him. Ambrose chuckles, stepping back, keeping out of arm's reach. If I wasn't on Tiernan's lap, he'd lunge at Ambrose for not taking things seriously.

I snatch Tiernan by his chin, forcing him to look at me. "I need you to tell me everything is okay and the others are safe first."

Cocking his head, Tiernan's features soften. He finally realizes I'm not in distress or hurt. "We are fine, Nova. We've come to an agreement with the Litendrake Clan. The Drekis used their ties to the High Council to sway the other clans. They purposely took Franco's side and got the others to agree to stand together. Theo also bartered with Franco to protect his palace. We were able to prove our value. The Battle Clan also got a formal alliance with us, which means that it's possible to arrange future unions with our children if we want."

Ugh. What? "I'm not forcing a union on our children," I say. Anger rushes through me at even the thought. How could they even consider such a thing?

Tiernan plants his mouth to mine, stopping me from

blowing up. He kisses me softly, sensually, silently begging me with his thoughts to calm down. "We would never. Not after this. But the Battle Clan needed to know that it could be on the table. I promise you, Nova. We're going to change how things are. Our clan dynamics won't be like anyone else's. It'll be in our vows to you. You're our mate and the most important woman in the world. We want you to rule by our sides. Now that Franco finally got what he wanted, we'll be able to. He agreed to allow us to formalize our union in good faith. Ambrose will get everything together to make it happen. The Drekis and Darkonians will unite under the Drakovich Clan name."

My heart skips, his words igniting something fierce and all-consuming inside me. Did he really say what I think he said? The Drekis and Darkonians are uniting for me? They're taking on the name of my dragon clan? Whoa.

"That is, if you agree to bond with me in soul, Nova." Tiernan captures me with his gaze, a soft smile turning him even more handsome. "It would also mean you will bond with Ambrose. Tying your soul to his will also allow him to tap into your dragon. It won't be the same as you bowing to him, but far more powerful."

I slowly nod, shifting my gaze to Ambrose. "And you're okay with this?" Just as I don't want a bond forced on me, I also don't want to force one on him.

Green power sparkles in Ambrose's silver gaze. "More than anything. I'd love to share a future with you indefinitely. You will be my soulmate."

"Everyone is in agreement," Tiernan adds, stroking my cheek. "All you have to do is say yes."

My heart and body feel as if a weight lifts off of me, and my dragon soars through my being, the excitement of solidifying our mate bond singing in my essence. I throw my arms around Tiernan and kiss him deeply, passionately, and then I reach for Ambrose and do the same.

"I'll be back in a bit, okay?" Ambrose murmurs. "I must prepare."

Without waiting for a response, Ambrose chants a spell and disappears.

The sneaky bastard. I don't have to read his mind to know the real reason he's left me alone with Tiernan. Our conversation from earlier floods to the front of my mind. He wanted to ensure that Tiernan got to sleep with me first. Most women would be a bit what the fuck about it. Me? I'm a dragon, horny as hell, and I'll go with the flow.

"Nova?" Tiernan asks, drawing me from my thoughts. "So, it's a yes, right? You never confirmed."

I tip my head back and laugh. "What? Was my kiss not enough of an answer?"

A shy smile crosses his face for what seems like the first time ever. Tiernan lifts and drops his shoulders, and I wonder if a verbal agreement is what's needed.

"My answer is yes." I bite my bottom lip with my comment. "I want to unite the Dreki and Darkonian Clans...because you guys are mine. I've already decided and have accepted it." Maybe it was a bit fast, all things considered, with the forced bond from Theo, but I don't care. I don't have to have the same mortal expectations I grew up believing. I don't even want to think about those standards ever again. All I want to do is embrace my life as a dragon and fight beside my mates for a future of our choosing.

Tiernan grins, his wave of pure happiness lighting up my very being. I know he was worried that he'd never get to bond our souls—hell, I wasn't sure if I'd want to—but it feels like how things are supposed to be. No magic. No arrangements. Just trust, honesty, and the same desire to be with one another.

"You've made me the happiest man, my beautiful Nova," he murmurs, kissing me again, pulling me so close that I can feel the extent of his happiness as his cock hardens against the clothes Ambrose summoned for me with his magic.

It's now that it registers in my mind that Tiernan is

still naked. It's funny how sometimes it feels so natural that I don't notice right away. Or I do and I just accept it as part of our lives. But now? Holy fuck. I want him. My dragon whimpers inside me, needing to feel him and be close. To embrace him as I've embraced my other mates.

Reaching down, I lace my fingers around his girth and moan with his sharp intake of breath. Grabbing the back of my shirt, Tiernan tugs it off. His tongue glides across each of my nipples, and I stroke him, bouncing with my movements, wanting to grind on him. Desperation consumes me, and I unbutton my pants before Tiernan gets a chance to do the honors. He growls and snatches my wrists, flipping me onto my back.

My body buzzes with a jolt of electricity as he raises my hands over my head and pins me in place with one hand. Using his other, he drags my pants down and bows in, kissing me deeply at the same time his finger draws up my thigh. He rubs my clit with enough pressure to make me arch my back and moan, and I squirm beneath him, trying to playfully break his hold on me.

"Don't fight me, Nova," he mutters, his grumbly voice vibrating over my lips. "You're mine, and there is no fucking way I'm letting you pleasure me first. I want to taste every inch of you. Touch you in ways that will make you scream my name. I want to ensure you think about me for days. But you have to let me have my way. Can you do that?"

I gasp a breath and arch forward, brushing my lips to his. "I can." Because fuck, it's what I want too. "I just—"

He nips my lip and sinks his finger inside me. "No excuses or pleas to pleasure me. You're cumming first. You're mine, and that's how it will always be. Your needs before mine. Okay?"

I slowly nod my head. "Then hurry." I can't resist pushing back, testing him and teasing him. He has a wild side I know he dies to unleash, and I want to see exactly what's in store for me.

"Hurry? No. I'm going to savor you." Tiernan repositions my legs, adjusting his body between them to lower himself on the blanket Ambrose left behind. He lifts one of my legs and kisses my knee. Gliding his tongue across my heated skin, Tiernan tastes me from my thigh all the way up until he stops between my legs. Using his fingers, he shifts my body, exposing my clit more to him, and he trains his eyes on mine, watching my reaction as he flicks his tongue, keeping the perfect rhythm and pressure. I moan, wiggling, dying to touch him. Combing my fingers through his hair, I play with the strands and pull him closer to my body, quietly getting him to suck and lick me harder as I come to my peak.

My muscles spasm, my body stiffening. I yank his hair, struggling to stay still as he keeps going, drawing out my orgasm until I trap his head between my thighs. My eyes water with my ecstasy, and I can't stop myself from leaning up and resting my legs on his shoulders. He smiles at me with fire lighting his eyes.

"You taste amazing. The best thing I've ever had." He rubs his lips together and teases me with his finger, only to pop it into his mouth. "Incredible. I want more."

Fuck, do I want that too.

I wonder what it'll be like. If he'd fuck me hard and rough or if he'll treat me with the same tender love Kash does. Tiernan doesn't give me time to think about it, because he pulls me to him and kisses me, lifting me up enough to align our bodies. Our moans echo through the room, his tip vibrating with the magic of his piercing. Holding me by my ass, he keeps me balanced on his palms and rocks into me. I clutch onto his shoulders, getting used to the crazy-amazing sensations humming through my body.

It's enough to make me cum again, and he's barely even started.

"You're so tight," he murmurs, getting me to open my legs wider. He adjusts his hands and uses my wetness to slide his finger into my ass, increasing the pressure even more. "You feel so good. Fates, I knew you'd be perfect, but this is far beyond anything I could imagine."

I smile, loving how much he enjoys voicing his pleasure. He moans just as loudly, the noise so sexy. I love hearing him, feeling him, letting him just do what he wants. Picking up his pace, he thrusts into me, managing to keep me balanced despite my body trembling with bliss. I rest my head on his shoulder and watch our bodies together and how deep he slides into me.

Changing positions, he carefully sets me onto my back without pulling out and uses his hands to get me to do the splits. He eases me up a bit, still holding me and curling my torso. He groans and swings his body to mine, thrusting deeper, harder, getting me to scream in pleasure. Strumming his finger over my clit, he plays with me, and my whole body heats up until my dragon fire bursts over my hands and sparks against the blanket, setting it ablaze.

But he doesn't stop.

He growls in pleasure, his own fire sparking wildly as his scales blossom over his skin, his dragon form begging to break free. If the room was big enough, he might. And I might. And now my dragon wants to experience the same pleasure as I do with our mate.

"Fates, you have no idea how much I want that," he gasps, dropping my legs to fuck me harder, rougher, switching from loving to full-on beast. He sucks my neck, leaving his mark, and I tense with another orgasm, feeling as if my dragon and soul both fly free.

"I never thought I would," I say, my breath panting. "It's the strangest thing."

"It's not," he murmurs. "It's perfect. You're perfect."

With his words, he grunts, his muscles flexing and rippling with his orgasm. The heat of his body on mine prods at my nature as a dragon. He lies on top of me, his heart thrumming against mine. I kiss him as he rolls over, pulling me on top of him, his body already hard and waiting to go again. I nearly let him.

If green magic didn't sparkle through the air, I'm pretty sure we'd fuck for hours or more. I can't get enough, yearning to memorize Tiernan's body over and over again as my mate. As the man I just agreed to share my future with and allow to take my clan name.

"I'm sorry for intruding, but I thought you'd like to be relocated somewhere different," Ambrose says, devouring me on top of Tiernan with his gaze. "The rest of your clan is waiting. It seems that Franco wants the union to happen sooner than later. He fears things falling apart."

I blink a few times. "What?"

Tiernan hums his agreement. "I'd like it. I don't want to wait a moment longer. Hearing her claim. Feeling it. I want to feel her on every level. Her mind and body are beautiful, and I'm sure her soul is...Nova, let me make you the happiest woman."

I lick my lips and bob my head. "How about we make each other happy? All of us. I don't need to wait. I'm ready for this union."

Who would've thought? Not me.

But for the first time in a long time, things feel right.

I have hope for our future.

CHAPTER 8

Confrontation

"MY MATES!" I SQUEAL AND rush the short distance to where Maddox and Rowan sit across from Kash and Theo.

The four of them huddle around a pile of documents, reading over what looks like a contract in another language. I don't recognize any of the words, but it's possibly Witchlands tongue. My guys have been working with the High Council long enough to probably know it, but I've never heard them speak it.

"Because we can't, kitten." Kash rises to his feet faster than the others, and I run and leap into the air. Catching me, he spins me around and kisses me, dipping me low until I flip and land between Maddox and Rowan. "It's impossible for anyone other than those gifted with witch magic."

"We can read it, though," Maddox mutters, pulling me onto his lap. "And you smell like you've been celebrating without us. I hope you had a good time with Tiernan."

I crinkle my nose and nod. "Don't make things weird. He proposed the union to me, and it was so romantic."

"Hopefully he fucked you hard." This bastard. Maddox is always so nonchalant about my sexual relations with the others—if anything, he's demanding. It reminds me of the first few days after he declared I was his mate and how he would insist that his brothers take their turns.

How am I going to survive a union to six men with Maddox always being so insistent with my needs?

"Happily," Rowan says, responding to my thought.

I throw myself from Maddox and into Rowan's arms. "You guys are too much."

"Too much? Never. You're insatiable, cookie. I can

smell your desire now. You're thinking about allowing us to claim you in your dragon form. You crave it." Maddox smirks with his words. "I'd be honored to cure your curiosity."

Heat burns across my cheeks, and I kick him playfully with my foot. "I wouldn't even know how to. I'm not familiar enough with my dragon."

"That needs to be rectified, you sexy firecracker." Theo moves from his seat and stacks the papers so that he can sit on the short table in the sitting area of what I think is his suite within the palace. It's not the room Franco had kept me in. "It bothers me that you've spent your life with your most powerful form suppressed by magic. I want to teach you the things that might not feel natural to you yet because of it."

Theo's comment surprises me, and I tip my head to look at him. He offers me a smile and reaches out, grasping my chin with his fingers. I give in and stretch toward him, meeting him for a kiss.

"That's sweet, Theo," I say, offering him a smile.

He tightens his jaw. "As our soon-to-be queen, it's important that you're prepared. Our people will expect you to bear children this upcoming season, and we can't have you be the only dragon who can't properly fly. It's tradition to give birth where—"

I cover his lips with my hand. "Okay, not sweet. You're moving too fast. I'm not popping out a baby yet."

"You say that now, cookie, but you know you want my offspring. I can sense your desire. It'll become strong—"

Kash swings out both his arms and hits Maddox and Theo in their guts. "Knock it off. Both of you. I will not allow you to put words in her mouth. When she's ready, she's ready. She's different, and you all need to accept that her mind and soul still might not be completely aligned. Not to mention that we need to create a home, settle whatever bullshit we have to with the High Council and the Litendrakes." Kash blows out a breath of smoke, his dragon-nature peeking through. "The situation we're in isn't ideal yet."

Theo flicks his gaze around. "We have plenty of time—"

"Brother, enough. You might have claimed her body and soul before me, but I know Nova has mixed feelings about you. You piss her off more than you don't." Tiernan steps from the spot where Ambrose transported him in from the hidden room within the rock of this mountain.

I sigh and get up, drawing everyone's attention to me instead of each other. They all have their opinions on what they think I want and need, and it's sometimes hard for them to understand that I can't read myself like they can. Kash was right about my mind, soul, and body not being aligned, but honestly, none of them are wrong.

I twist my hair in my hands and turn to Ambrose. "Why don't you take me back to the hole in the rock until these guys figure out that my wants and needs might be different for each of them?"

Ambrose chuckles and nods, zapping an orb of electricity at both Theo and Tiernan, stopping them from trying to argue. "Whatever you want, princess. I'm at your service."

I giggle and dodge away from the five dragons and to Ambrose, holding his arms open for me. "I love the sound of that. Let's—"

A playful growl sounds from Kash, and he tries to catch me and drag me back to the couch. He misses me by inches, and I leap, kicking my legs out into the splits, and land within Ambrose's reach. He chants a spell, sending up a shield of green light, cutting the two of us off from the others.

"You're going to be in so much trouble," I say, laughing, loving how my dragon mates look ready to really test the strength of Ambrose's magic.

I grab the hem of my shirt and flash the five of them my boobs. Their expressions morph into ones of lust, and

I shift closer to Ambrose, wondering if I took things too far. Because fuck. If Ambrose lets the shield down, they look like they're going to team up and punish me how I like.

"You bet your ass, we are," Maddox says, shooting a ball of fire at the shield. "We're going to give you everything you want and prove exactly how strong a female dragon is. Six mates might be challenging."

"It's a good thing I'm flexible." I shouldn't poke the beast, but he's trying to get to my nature. We both know it. And damn it. Just the thought of fucking six men? It's a good thing my needy vagina is all in and her asshole friend is just as cool.

Rowan snaps his head back and howls a laugh, and with one look, I realize they all heard my thought. It's getting harder for them to keep it to themselves by pretending that they can't hear me.

"Fucking fates," Kash says, rubbing his chin with his hand. "I hope you're creative with your magic, warlock. Do we need to fucking suit up with all the dick bling too?"

"Whatever you want. Our mate does love it," Tiernan says, smiling at me.

I fan my burning face. My dragon fire feels as if it'll explode from me at any second. If a knock didn't sound on the door, I'm sure I'd be naked at any second, spread open, and double stuffed—maybe triple stuffed. Two holes, a mouth, two hands...is it possible to fit more?

"My dearest daughter," Franco says, his voice booming through the room as he thrusts the door open without knocking.

The warmth that was smoldering through me cools immediately, feeling as if his presence alone cages my dragon—maybe scares her. All I want to do is squeeze in the middle of Maddox and Rowan and let the others stand in front of me. Being the meat in a sexy man sandwich has its perks when it comes to being protected.

"Had I known you had such strong connections to these two clans, I might not have made such a spectacle." Franco remains expressionless. "You see, after the message from the blasted traitor came in, I lost my good senses."

Is this supposed to be an apology? If it is, it doesn't work. There is no excuse for what he did and what could've happened to me.

I close my hands into fists, trying to keep it together. I can't even look at him. Just hearing his voice unleashes a wave of rage inside me.

"I hope you believe me when I say that I had no idea that McKayla was alive. The Liohts tricked me. They have done nothing but destroy the power I worked hard to get.

They tried to keep you from me and denied you your birthright as the princess of the Litendrake Kingdom." Franco steps closer, his bare feet tapping on the rock floor. He's naked. I can't believe he had the nerve to come in here butt-ass naked and offer me a shitty apology.

"I don't know what I believe," I say, my voice coming out shaky. I shouldn't admit it. I should just agree and hope that he leaves. Being surrounded by the Drekis and Darkonians gives me the bravery and strength to face even my worst enemies. And right now, along with Lazlo Infinity, McKenzie, and the High Council, Franco tops the list.

He growls, setting my guys off. I remain stiff and glaring at my hands. His reaction is enough to stab me in the soul. If he was telling the truth, he wouldn't get angry and act like he's about to get defensive. He'd try harder to prove the truth. But this is the truth. I know it deep inside me. He damn well knew that the Liohts were setting another coven up. He had to have known that McKayla was alive, especially because I was with her. He used the whole situation to his advantage. I bet he got perks out of cooperating with the Liohts.

"You believe me. That's what you do, daughter. You cannot possibly trust the witches over your own blood." He growls again, striding close enough to make Theo and Tiernan stand tall, blocking him.

"That witch took care of me all my life!" I snap, summoning dragon fire in my palms. "Everyone claims McKayla is a traitor, but she didn't try to cut out my heart like McKenzie. She didn't throw me to the damn dragon clans like a fucking piece of ass for them to have their way with. She saved me!"

Jerking my head up, I glower at Franco, meeting his flaming eyes. If the Drekis and Darkonians didn't silently warn him to stay back, I know he'd hit me. He'd take out whatever anger he has for my mom and McKayla and lash out at me for it.

"Now, get out," I snap, my words whipping through the air. "You got whatever the fuck you wanted, and my mates will help you keep power. But after today—after my union—I never want to see you again. You mean nothing to me. Your clan only means pain and heartache. I will not let you destroy my life because of a damn grudge you hold for my mom."

"Delphia!" Franco hollers.

Throwing my hands out, I send a ball of dragon fire at Franco, knocking him back. He roars and tries to retaliate, but Ambrose deflects the magic. Furious tears burn my eyes, and I twist and throw my arms around Maddox, wanting nothing more than to have my mates carry me away. If the union wasn't important to them—solidifying their claims with magic—I'd beg them not to put me through this with Franco. He's going to ruin what is supposed to be an amazing moment in my life. I know it.

"I advise you to leave, your majesty," Theo says, his voice deepening. "As the leader of the Litendrakes, you must ensure everything is ready for the union. It is you who gets power, not us, so do not disappoint my mate. We have standards and expectations to live by despite what you think in this moment."

If Franco had his way, I'm sure we'd all be dead.

Spinning on his feet, he storms out of the room in a flurry of flames and smoke, transforming into his dragon outside the door. Roaring, he shouts his annoyance through his dragon and gives us one more look before launching into the air to take off.

"Fuck. I fucked up." I lean forward and cover my face with my hands. "I'm sorry. I couldn't help myself. I'm just beyond pissed. He has no right to think of me as his daughter and shouldn't have the power he already has."

I swear dragon hugs are the cure-all for my unbidden devastating emotions. And being sandwiched between all of my mates? My trembles stop immediately and my anger fizzles out as they fill me with their strength and love.

"This will be over soon. I promise you, Delphia," Theo says. For the first time, hearing him use my birth name doesn't piss me off. "With our union, the High Council will have no choice but to allow us to take you home. You will never have to step foot in this palace again."

I blow out a breath. "I'm just—" I groan, trying to figure out how to voice everything I feel inside.

"Listen to Theo, kitten. I know he can be an entitled asshole, but he's right. We're going to sign the union contract, declare our vows, and get the fuck out of here to celebrate." Kash snuggles his nose into the crook of my neck.

"And then we will remain in each other's arms until you carry my children. After that, we'll show you what life should've always been like. You will know the beauty of our lands and sky. You will be free." Maddox kisses my forehead.

I don't even argue about his plan.

Right now, it sounds like the best thing ever.

CHAPTER 9

Fated

THIS UNION BUSINESS IS STRANGELY like a mortal wedding. I never thought I'd ever put on a white dress that wasn't part of my costume arrangement when I was a Sky Dancer for Galaxy Gold's. And staring at my reflection in the wall mirror? I wish I got to wear something else. I don't know what it is about seeing myself in something comparable to a bridal gown, but my stomach twists with nerves. I shouldn't be nervous. This is the best decision I've ever made. I want a future in the arms of the Drekis and the Darkonians, but it feels like even as I prepare to walk down a magical altar, that something foreboding awaits. This union march feels more like a stroll to my own execution, and it has nothing to do with my mates.

Something bothers me about Franco's hot and cold attitude. Would he have even agreed if he thought he could overpower my mates? Probably not. I just want to run. To fly. To learn what it's like to soar as my dragon and never look behind me as my mates lead me into our future together.

Bright light sparkles through the room, startling me. My vision dims as it adjusts. Spinning around, I automatically summon my dragon fire. Standing behind a magical shield remains McKenzie. I had hoped to never see her again. She's out of her damn mind to show her face to me. Rage ignites inside me, and I blast my dragon fire at her shield. She shouts a spell, keeping it firmly in place.

"You're dead!" I screech, rushing forward. Power sizzles off my skin as my dragon awakens. She wants revenge as much as I do. The room shifts as I transform, towering over McKenzie in my most powerful form. Before, I used to feel weak and a bit afraid and out of control as a dragon. But now? This witch is going to be my snack. I never thought I'd eat someone alive, but here I am, learning something new about myself.

"He tu vi cata!" McKenzie shouts, growing her shield to cascade up and over her in a protective bubble instead of falling away. "Delphia, please. Hear me out."

I roar, my dragon's voice booming through the air. If my mates didn't know something was up, they would know now. I expect them to come rushing in here at any second.

"I have an offer to make you. One that will be better for the both of us." She clenches her jaw and holds her hands up. "Just hear me out. Give me two minutes. If you decide against it, I'll leave you alone."

I blow a breath of fire, sending sparks cracking and popping from her magical shield. It takes everything in me to tame my dragon, and I groan as I transform into my mortal self. I glower at the pieces of white fabric scattered across the room. I ruined my dress. Damn it.

I throw a burst of dragon fire at her again, ensuring she keeps away from me. "You have two minutes. I have to change and get ready again."

Keeping my attention on her, I head into the wardrobe and stare at the collection of gowns. Ambrose had summoned the particular white dress for me, and now gazing around, I realize that I'm going to start off our union by breaking the first tradition. I should care, but honestly, I like the idea of not mimicking a mortal in such a life-changing moment.

"Franco plans to deny your union in front of the clans," McKenzie blurts, her sharp voice sending my heart into my stomach. "He asked me here, but I know he's planning to throw me to the High Council the moment he gets the chance. I'm not going down for his clan's mistakes. McKayla would've never done this to us if they'd just accepted that your mother was never going to bow."

My brows knit together with her words. I snatch a silvery gown from the hanger and slip into it, the flowing fabric like the whisper of wind on my skin. I peek at myself in the mirror. I love it. I think my mates will too.

"So I want to make you a deal, Delphia," McKenzie continues, her voice nasally with her annoyance.

I don't respond to her right away. I hear her, but it's like my mind doesn't want to process anything she says.

"We have a contract with Franco already," I say, strolling from the wardrobe. I glance at the huge door, hoping that Kash shows up soon to retrieve me. As the youngest of my mates, he is in charge of escorting me and handing me to Maddox, who is the oldest. It's a bit weird to think about, but it is what it is. My whole life is one insane thing after another.

"You don't. It won't be signed until the ceremony. Just hear me out, okay? I want to offer you a truce. While your heart is precious and something my coven could use to combat the fucking High Council, I'm willing to take another." McKenzie rubs her hands together, sending lavender electricity across her magical shield. "Do this, and I'll guarantee yours and your mates safety. I will also prove to the High Council that you never committed the crimes they accused you of."

I tighten my jaw, her words piquing my curiosity. "Do you really think I'd believe you?"

She sighs. "I don't care if you do or not. This is the deal. One dragon heart and you can leave all of this bullshit behind."

"I don't know. I need to talk to my mates." I twist my fingers together, locking my gaze to hers. "What you've done...you deserve this fate. You deserve to be hunted by the High Council. You should know how it feels to be weak and helpless."

The more I think about it, the more I get angry.

"You're making a mistake. This is your last chance. Franco will ruin you. You must strike first. We can both benefit from his death—" McKenzie whips her attention to the door, snapping her mouth shut. Chanting a soft spell, she summons a glittering dagger, which clinks on the rock floor at my feet. "Take it and go. Do this, and you'll be heavily rewarded."

I frown, watching McKenzie vanish at the same time Kash thrusts the door open, fire blazing in his palms and anger sharpening his face. He flares his nostrils and jerks his attention to me before searching the rest of the room.

I swallow and release a shaking breath. He rushes to me, not allowing me to close a foot of space on my own, and lifts me into his arms. Clinging to him, I hug him with my whole body, feeling the strength of his arms around me. He spins with me, inspecting the room. A dozen thoughts cross through his mind as he opens up to me. He smells the witch. He wants to fly from the balcony to search for her, but he also doesn't want to leave me and knows I can't go.

"Kash, you need to take me to the rest of my mates," I say, trying to push away the dread roiling through me. "McKenzie was here. She—"

A deep, guttural growl escapes his mouth, and he ignites fire in his palms, heating my back. "I knew it. Are you okay? Did she hurt you? Fuck. I need to call Ambrose. If she was here—"

I crash my mouth to his, silencing the words spilling from him. "Wait, please. Listen to me for a second. She wanted to make a deal with me. She said Franco wasn't going to follow through with agreeing to my union."

"Are you fucking kidding me? What kind of deal?" Kash's chest heaves, pressing into my boobs with each of his gulps of breath. "I've never met a witch who doesn't create shitty deals. She must be scared."

"She's pissed, if anything. She...she needs something for a spell to get her out of the mess with the High Council. If I can get what she needs, she will ensure that I'm free from all charges and accusations against me. She'll clear my name." Now that she's not standing before me, keeping me on guard, McKenzie's words finally sink in. Could she actually follow through? Could I? Fuck me. This is why I need to gather my mates. I can't decide on this alone.

"What aren't you telling me? You haven't said what she wants." Kash eases his head back, meeting my eyes with his beautiful hazel gaze. "It's bad, isn't it kitten?"

"Worse." I rub my lips together for a second. If I can't speak the words out loud, how will I be able to follow through? It's ridiculous for me to even consider. "She still needs a dragon's heart. She wants Franco's."

His features pucker with his crinkling nose. I knew it was bad, and Kash's reaction confirms it. "Nova, that's insane. Impossible. You can't just cut your father's heart out and give it to McKenzie, hoping she stays good on her word."

I slowly bob my head. "I know. I knew it was crazy to even think. I was just scared. If Franco doesn't follow through with his words, then what?"

"We'll consider the alternative. But it won't be you doing it, kitten. You've been through enough." Brushing his lips to mine, he kisses me softly. "It's my job as your mate to take care of you. If it comes down to it, I'll handle it."

"Kash," I say, grimacing with my words.

"Don't even try to argue with me. This is one of the few times I won't let you have your way. I know you, Nova. You will always do what needs to be done, but I want you to know that I will always do the same." Kash hugs me tighter, his whole body humming at my closeness, awakening a wave of warmth.

"I love you, Kash," I say, the sudden need to tell him what's on my mind turning all-consuming. "I love you and will do whatever it takes to give us the life we deserve. I swear to it. We'll get Franco and McKenzie handled one way or another. Then after that, we're going after Quillon. That's my vow to you. I will not have his control of you hanging over our heads."

"It's easy to forget without him here," he murmurs. "And with you in that dress. You look stunning. I'm glad you didn't go for white."

I grin at him. "I kinda ruined that one."

"I wish I was here to see that. I could feel you transform. I thought...I don't know what I thought. I think McKenzie shielded the place. I just knew I had to come." Kash sets me on my feet and spins me around, drinking me in. "And seeing you like this? I never want to leave. I yearn to make love to you this very moment to celebrate."

I grin, shaking my head back and forth. "If I agree, I know we'll never make it to the ceremony, so I'll promise you a moment alone later. I want one with each of you...and one together."

He chuckles. "Maddox was right, kitten. Once we're out of here, we'll never leave the bed...and it's exactly how I want it. So let's hurry. We're going to need to make a detour to talk to Ambrose. The others are already welcoming our clans. All of the Dragon Lands are excited about this union."

My eyes widen. "Did you say your clans?"

"I did. They're anxious to finally meet the woman who did the impossible." Kash touches my warm cheek. "They want to welcome home the lost Drakovich princess and bless us with their approval. Well, as long as we can handle Franco."

We can. I know we can.

I just hope I don't have to steal another dragon's heart.

Music trickles through the air as Kash guides me down a grand hallway and to an open-air terrace overlooking the mountains, forest, and setting sun in the distance. The breathtaking view prods at my dragon nature, and I can't stop the blip of jealousy coursing through me at the sight of several dragon silhouettes soaring over a lake not too far away.

"I hate that he already ruined this for you," Kash murmurs, tapping his fingers to my back. "Try to focus on our clan, okay? Ambrose will handle it. We will put him in his place."

I puff out a breath and slowly nod.

"If he refuses, you know the plan." Kash leans forward to stare me in the eyes. "We're going to take you regardless. Do you understand? You're ours, Nova. We're no longer playing these magical games, nor are we backing down. We're stronger than we've ever been because of you."

His words touch me so deeply that I stop in my tracks and kiss him. I never thought I could feel so powerful in my life. This moment, knowing the truth of his words, makes all of the fear, pain, suffering, and sacrifice worth it.

I would face going to Max all over again as long as it meant that it led me to my mates. I thought I'd carry regrets over my circumstances and choices, but I don't. The only thing I carry now is hope.

"We better get you out there," Kash murmurs, brushing his lips to mine once more. "If we don't, our clan will have a stolen mate on their hands...at least temporarily."

I grin and nuzzle my nose to his, hopping up into his arms. I don't want him to walk me down the aisle. I want him to carry and kiss me the whole way until he can hand me off and allow me to do the same for my other mates.

Kash adjusts me in his arms, hearing what I want crossing my mind, and he strides forward, cradling me like a blushing bride over the threshold and onto the flower-lined aisle with dozens of men and a few women, all dressed in formalwear. Those not of personal relation to our clans stand alongside the balcony, and dragons fly near, watching from above. This is far from anything I could've ever dreamed up—but it's amazing. Incredible. My skin buzzes and the heat of my dragon lights me up in a way I never knew possible.

"Please welcome Princess Delphia of the Drakovich Clan." Ambrose's voice booms through the air, spelled to be heard over the mumbling crowd whispering about me.

The guests on both sides of the aisle rise to their feet

and turn in our direction. I cling tighter to Kash, my nerves getting the best of me. If he wasn't carrying me, I might've fallen on my face. I can't stop the trembles coursing through me.

"Welcome, princess," a man in the back row says, extending his hand to me.

Kash murmurs for me to take it, and the hulking dragon man kisses the top of my hand, leaving behind a spot of warmth.

It's like one person from every row was granted permission to greet me, and our stroll down the aisle takes far longer than anything I've ever seen at a mortal wedding. Maybe because I know no one, really. I keep my performance smile plastered on my face, and go with the flow the best I can.

"My beautiful daughter. I'm so pleased to finally meet you. You will make a fine mother and mate to my sons. I'm pleased to know the fates worked out in our clan's favor." A woman in the front row holds out both of her arms and grasps my face, kissing both of my cheeks. Her raven-black hair twists into an elegant braid with purple flowers pinned to it, and from her jade green eyes, I know she's Theo and Tiernan's mom.

I don't know what to call her, so all I do is smile wider and say, "Thank you. It is an honor to meet the queen of the Darkonian Lands. I can't wait to finally see our home and get to know you."

"I would love that." She kisses my forehead. I don't know what I was expecting—maybe a monster of an in-law or someone completely atrocious and evil because of the circumstances with me wanting the Drekis and Darkonians, but I'm so fucking relieved. I just hope this isn't an act.

"Now, now, mother. There will be plenty of time to get acquainted with Delphia...perhaps after mating season." Theo places his hands on the woman's shoulders and kisses her cheek.

Oh, fuck. He did not just say that for everyone to hear. I could kick Theo in the ass for bringing it up, sending my cheeks flaming red.

"She will need guidance, your majesty. It would be an honor to have you help us through the new phases of our life." Maddox comes up besides Kash and touches my warm cheek. "But first, I'd like to take my mate and complete our union."

I crinkle my nose. "You just want to hurry and try to get started making babies," I mutter, keeping my voice low.

Maddox chuckles and winks at me. "Whatever your heart desires. I just want you."

Theo escorts his mom back to her seat, and Maddox takes me from Kash, setting me on my feet. My knees quake with my nerves, but Maddox tightens his hold on me, ensuring I don't fall or faint or burst into my dragon form to fly away. He kisses me in front of the crowd and turns me to Theo, who kisses me next. Each of my dragon mates takes a turn, greeting me and showing me the affection I crave until Ambrose stands in front of me, holding a candle etched with unrecognizable symbols.

I don't know much about his magic, but I do know that there are different types of things he does depending on what he needs. He casts spells for his shields and teleportation. Then there is stuff like potions and creating magical objects like the cock bling. As for the candle? I think it has something to do with binding our souls formally. He rushed the last time to force my bond to Theo, and this is far from that.

"These candles will bind the clans together and unite the dragon fire of the Drekis and Darkonians with the Drakovich Clan," Ambrose says like he heard my thought. "It is with great pleasure to bring together three of the most powerful clans in this union of souls and power."

The crowd draws silent as he hands Maddox and Theo a candle, the two of them heads of their clans out of their brothers.

"I call upon Franco Litendrake, the ruler and father of this beautiful princess, to please come forth and help Delphia light her candle." Ambrose motions toward the front row.

I still at the sight of Franco. I was so caught up with everything that I hadn't even noticed him. Fear blooms in my heart, tightening my chest, and I dig my nails into the candle. His eyes capture mine, and he scowls. Stomping his way to me, he gathers his dragon fire between his palms. My mates tense around me, and green magic sparkles from Ambrose.

This is it. This is what we've been waiting for. If McKenzie was telling the truth, Franco won't cooperate.

I brace for the worst as Franco reaches me and straightens his back. Growing the fire in his palms, he growls deep in his chest.

My body reacts to his silent threat, and I swing my arm out and slap him.

He roars.

CHAPTER 10

Cut His Heart Out

"GRAB HER!" MADDOX SHOUTS, TACKLING Franco before he can hit me.

Rowan snakes his arms around my waist, yanking me back. I gasp and glare, watching the fight unfold as Kash, Theo, and Tiernan join Maddox to keep Franco down.

"Ezeerf tsaeb won!" Ambrose shouts, shooting his electric magic at Franco.

He freezes mid-transformation, his scales blooming

over his thick arms. Smoke billows from his mouth and nose, and he growls hard and loud, the noise vibrating through my very being.

Everything happens so quickly that my mind can barely process what's happening. Dozens of guards rush my mates and drag them off of Franco. They split the Drekis from the Darkonians, and several more run in my direction. Rowan thrusts his dragon fire, knocking the first guy back into the others.

"I'm rejecting your union!" Franco hollers, sending fire streaming from his hands and across the crowd. "I call upon the Battle Clan and the rest of my allies to escort all members of the Darkonian and Dreki Clans from the palace. My daughter will not be going through with a union to anyone. She will be enslaved like she deserves."

What the actual fuck has gotten into him? He's out of his damn mind.

"I'd rather go back to Max!" I shout. "You can't do this to me!"

Franco snarls, keeping everyone back by creating a wall of fire around him as he strides closer. "I can and I will, you dreadful heir. Your mother killed my brother and rejected me as her mate. You are my restitution, and I have decided not to bind with clans I know that will turn against me the moment they have a chance."

I blink a few times at his words.

"If I didn't despise the Drakovich bloodline so much, I'd claim you myself. And maybe I still will, Delphia." Franco's chest puffs out with his comment, the very thought grossing me out.

"Are you nuts? That's disgusting," I snap, clutching onto Rowan.

"Perhaps if you were my real daughter and not only given to me for your mother's crimes." Fire sparks in his eyes, and he growls again. "You will never bind to anyone. It'll be the punishment your mother always deserved."

He's not my father. What the fuck? How the fuck? How could the High Council even agree to this? They gave me to him because my mother rejected him? That is so wrong. I can't believe them.

"Franco! Stay back!" Ambrose shouts, drawing Franco's attention away. "You might think Nova belongs to you, but she doesn't. She never will. We were only humoring you, but this game is over. You will stand down and sign the contract. If you don't, I will personally summon the High Council and break your magical shields. I will leave your palace open for a takeover."

Franco explodes into his dragon form, whipping his body around. Ambrose shouts a spell, sending an electric chain whipping through the air. It reminds me of the one that Lazlo Infinity used on me, trying to force me to submit to him. The crowd falls silent.

"Allies of the Litendrakes. You will cut ties immediately or face a debt to our warlock," Theo says, raising his hands into the air. "You don't want to go down with this man. He will be your ruin as he was the ruin for his clan."

A few men get to their knees and bow.

Whoa, shit. It's working.

"You will have our guaranteed protection from the High Council," Maddox adds, clenching his fingers into fists.

Franco snarls again, but he stops fighting the chain. His towering form morphs until he stands as a man before us.

It takes everything in me not to fly forward at him and cut his heart out. It's all I can think about.

"If you want Delphia's contract, I want something more in return," Franco says, crossing his arms over his chest.

He ignores the dragon clans and strolls past Ambrose, yanking the magical chain around his neck. I inhale a deep breath, my whole body cooling as he keeps his attention on me. I hate this. I hate everything about this. Franco is psycho and unhinged. He's unpredictable.

"Delphia, I will do as you want and agree to give you

away, transferring you to the Darkonians and Drekis under the High Council law with one condition." He stops a few feet away, heeding Rowan's growling warning.

"And what's that?" I don't know why I bother asking. I should automatically say no.

A sparkle of lavender magic draws my attention from Franco's sadistic eyes, and I catch sight of McKenzie materializing in the far corner of the terrace.

Shit.

"I want your firstborn daughter," Franco says. "I want to raise her as my true heir. Agree, and you will be free from all of this."

I snap, my whole body rejecting even the thought. "Are you fucking serious?"

"I am." He thins his mouth into a line.

"Fuck no!" I scream, breathing a breath of fire.

A glittering dagger clinks on the stone terrace, and I whip my gaze to it. McKenzie twitches her fingers at me, reminding me of what I can do to make things right again. My body reacts without my mind's consent, and I throw myself from Rowan and lock my fingers around the glittering hilt.

Launching from the ground, I crash into Franco and aim the dagger. This is it. I'll cut out his heart. I'll be the monster this world claims me to be. I'll prove them right.

I'll live up to the crimes I've been falsely accused of.

"McKenzie, you have a deal," I shout.

Franco growls and tries to throw me off him, but I stab him in the shoulder. He screams in pain, thrashing, his whole body recoiling at my threat.

"Nova, no!" Blinding green power crashes into me, knocking me away. Ambrose locks his fingers to my shoulders. "You can't!"

"Do it, Delphia. It's the only way," McKenzie says, shocking Ambrose with her power, sending him back.

The crowd disperses, running to stay out of the way as Ambrose and McKenzie fight, throwing magic and sending chairs flying. I can't concentrate with the anger rolling through me in powerful waves.

"Ambrose, stop." I scramble to my feet, glancing between my warlock and Franco. "You can't stop me. You know it must be done. This could fix everything."

"You can't be sure that she'll keep her word, princess. The High Council wants your head. She's on the run." Ambrose summons a protective wall. "It must be someone else."

"It has to be her," McKenzie says, her hair flying around with her magic.

I knew it. My dragon knew it. I know that cutting out Franco's heart was a worst-case scenario and that Kash wanted me to let him do it, but fuck. This guy needs to pay. It should be me. I can't let Kash make another sacrifice for me. I won't let any of my mates.

"What will it be, Delphia?" McKenzie asks. "I need a dragon's heart."

I slowly turn to the rest of my mates, looking to them even though I don't want to know their answers. I want revenge. I want to feel Franco's heart beating in my palm. This is all his fault. He blames my mother because she rejected him so many years ago? Screw that entitled, twisted fucker of an asshole. The world would be better if he was just dead.

"I'm sorry," I say, my voice coming out low. "I'm sorry that I'm going to be the killer you feared was your mate."

Because Maddox, Kash, and Rowan couldn't fathom being fated to be with a murderous criminal.

"I have to do this." Tears burn my eyes, and I clutch the dagger tighter in my hand.

"No!" Ambrose flies at me, locking his arms around my waist.

I screech and try to fight him off, but he grips me too tightly. "Ambrose!"

McKenzie shakes her head with a sigh. "This is a huge mistake, warlock."

"Witch, I want to take your deal." Franco's words sound through the air, zinging to my soul. "We can still work together. We can change things. I will help you if you help me."

"I don't think that'll be possible, Franco." McKenzie tightens her mouth and taps her way closer, rubbing her palms together. "There is one problem. The warlock."

"I'll handle him. Just trap the dragons." Franco's words ignite fear inside me.

Ambrose raises his hands, calling upon magic to protect my mates, but Franco blasts dragon fire at him. Flashes of bright light ignite and several forms materialize as more witches appear.

"Get her out of here, Ambrose!" Theo commands.

Locking his arms around me, Ambrose chants a spell. "I'll be back for you! I swear!"

Pain burns through me, stealing my breath. Ambrose's legs give out on him and he falls to the ground, his whole body jerking.

"Guards, restrain them," Franco commands. "If you don't obey, you will fall by their sides."

Flipping onto my back, I try to get him. Franco stomps his foot into my stomach, winding me. I can't do anything as McKenzie summons magic and freezes me in place. She tips her head to the side and caresses her finger to my jaw.

"It didn't have to be this way," she says, pouting. "You should've taken the deal when you had the chance, Delphia."

"He'll betray you," I snap, trying to break from the magical binds. "He'll throw you to the High Council the moment he gets the chance. Don't do this."

"I'll be gone by then." McKenzie steps away from me. Turning to Franco, she says, "I won't be needing all of their hearts yet, so I will be keeping them as my pets. Only one sacrifice is needed. Who should it be?"

My heart bangs around my ribcage. "McKenzie, no! Please!"

She ignores me and strolls by each of my guys, taking a moment to look at each of them. "Hmm. You all have such strong hearts."

"Take mine," Maddox says, his words growling. "You can have mine."

I scream, trying to break free once more. "No!"

"It's done, cookie. I will do anything to protect you and my brothers." He glowers at McKenzie. "I offer you my heart, but you must let them go."

McKenzie smiles. "Such bravery, but no. You'll all be mine."

CHAPTER 11

Sacrifice

"BRING THE REST OF YOUR clan," Franco says, his gruff voice erupting over the pounding of my head. "We need a drop of dragon fire from each of you."

"What of the others?" Santino Battle asks. "You will ensure a female heir, but you won't give my clan her union. What are you planning?"

I blink my eyes, unable to do anything but watch and listen as Franco stands beside the other clan leader. This is fucked up. So fucked up. My mind, body, and soul ache, and there is nothing I can do about it. I know my mates regret stopping me. I know Ambrose beats himself up. But their hearts were in the right place. If only it didn't come to this.

"They will make their own arrangements. You will have her for the first mating season and be my second in command." Franco flicks his attention to me and winks.

If I could throw up, I would.

"And if I want another?" Santino follows Franco's gaze and drinks me in, not even hiding the fact that he grows hard at just the thought. "I'd prefer her to enjoy our time and would like to give her a chance to mate with my clan willingly."

Do his words make me feel better? Fuck no. I've already chosen my mates. I'll never give in to him like this. I don't care if it makes me a hypocrite because of everything I went through with the Darkonians, but Franco is a monster. The Darkonians had no idea that my soul belonged to another clan. They grew up with the idea that they'd bond with me. I was always theirs to them. With this asshole, he knows he'd be stealing me from my mates.

"I think we could arrange something, but I do not want you growing attached. It will be in the contract, punishable by death. Do I make myself clear?" Franco bares his teeth, his muscles rippling with his movements.

"Perfectly. Thank you for ensuring the arrangement. My clan will be very pleased, especially if what you say will happen. It's been a long while since a female was born to the Battle name instead of brought in by a union." Santino pats Franco on the back and saunters toward me. He kneels on one knee and rests his hot hand on mine. "I apologize for the circumstances, but I know we will have an exceptional time together."

I try to break from the spell, but no matter what I do, I can't get my body to work.

"I am ready for you, Franco," McKenzie says, her sharp voice cutting through the air. "Please bring the dragons to my altar. I'd like to ensure they know their place as my pets. I will need all of the protection and force I can get to see everything through."

Tears burn my eyes, dripping onto my cheeks. Santino tilts his head and reaches up, smearing them across my skin. "I wish I could take you now, but it seems your controller would prefer you to watch."

My soul screams, my mind begging my body to break out of this magic. My dragon roars in my very being, rattling me on a level that feels as if she'll destroy me if she can't get out.

Static buzzes through the air, stabbing into me, and I

inwardly scream as the guards bring all six of my mates to the center of the grand ballroom, where McKenzie created a circle with some sort of strange powder and a bunch of different rocks. This looks nothing like what she did in her failed attempt to cut my heart out, but maybe it was because she was in a rush. Now, she can torture me for however long she wants.

I'll kill her. I'll fucking kill her and rip her head off for this.

"I've decided to reject Maddox's self-sacrifice and choose someone else to provide their heart." McKenzie strolls around the circle and stops behind Maddox. She ruffles her fingers through his hair, making him growl, but like me, he can't move or speak either.

Shrugging into a robe, McKenzie takes her time circling my mates like a hunter ready to devour her prey. Kash's muscles bulge as he fights against the magic, and his veins pucker on his neck. McKenzie stops in front of him and touches the point of her athame under his chin, forcing his head up.

"Be grateful that you're being spared, little dragon. It seems your heart and soul are tied to another who will be useful." McKenzie pops out her bottom lip. "Such a shame. I suppose this is what I get for not helping you in the beginning."

She drops the athame from Kash and strolls to Tiernan next. He remains expressionless, bound by her magic, but he doesn't look at her. His gaze remains on Ambrose as he kneels just outside the circle, wrapped in magical chains.

"As for the young prince," McKenzie says, patting him on the cheek with her blade. "You have a nice, strong, powerful heart, but it seems that you lack the kind of bond I'd prefer you had with Delphia. She must regret her decision not to help me, and I'm just not sure you're enough."

Oh, fuck. Oh, shit.

My heart races, the beats out of control and erratic. McKenzie abandons Tiernan and strolls to Theo next.

"The same goes for you, prince. It seems she rather dislikes you." Locking her fingers to his hair, she tips his head back. "Or am I mistaken? Regardless, your power better serves me alive."

I dart my gaze to Rowan's, and we stare at each other in silence. It feels as if I'll die at any moment. I don't even have to hear McKenzie's thoughts to know she plans to go after my sweet, caring mate.

"Nova, I love you," Rowan whispers, his thoughts breaking through the buzzing in my mind. It's the first time since being bound by magic that I could hear him in my head. "I've loved you since the moment I knew your name and knew you would be my mate. I'll love you long after my life here. Our souls are bound by the fates. I will meet you again in the stars. Be brave, doe eyes. I need it."

Hot tears brand my cheeks, blurring my vision. I never thought much about what happens after death. I never thought I would have to think much about it. I've died before. Lazlo killed me and managed to contain my soul when he broke me out of Max. I don't remember anything from those moments, and I'm terrified it's because they don't exist. I never grew up believing in the fates. The fates have continuously let me down my whole life. And now? They'll destroy me. I don't want to survive this. I don't want to see my mate killed and the others broken and stolen from me. I don't want to be bred like an animal with the clans to force my own daughters into a sick fate. This must end here.

It must end now.

I will burn the world down. McKenzie can't do this. My dragon won't be caged.

Fury builds in my middle, climbing up my torso and twisting around my heart. I imagine my dragon freeing herself and using her power to destroy the magic binding me. A blip of green magic sparks from Ambrose's hands, his back to me. I concentrate on the light, wondering what it would take to use his power as if it's my own. His bond with Theo and Tiernan means we share a bond all the same.

If I can just—

"Vu calla vi tota bienta set!" McKenzie shouts, gathering lavender electricity into her palms to light her athame aglow.

"I love you, Nova," Rowan repeats. "Please, be brave. Trust my brothers. They will save you."

But I'm not the one who needs to be saved. He is.

"Ambrose, help him," I think, sending my thoughts to the universe, hoping he can hear me. "You have to do something. You're strong."

Silence greets me, but his green magic grows brighter in his hands. I know he can hear me. I just know it. He reacts to my despair as much as the others. Their muscles move and twitch, their dragons fighting to be released.

"The middle Dreki. Oh, how the fates have failed you." McKenzie moves behind Rowan and flicks her fingers, shoving him into her circle with her magic. "It's such a shame, considering how much Rhett enjoyed his good beast."

No. No. No.

Every breath hurts me, seeing my mate mistreated and controlled by magic. Heat continues to build in my middle, my whole body warming. I keep my watery eyes trained on Rowan. McKenzie flips him onto his back and slashes his shirt with the dagger, exposing his muscular chest.

"Princess, get ready. I'm going to need you to fight. Your mates are going to need you. I will cast a spell that will channel everything I have and everything your mates have into you. You won't have much time, but I no longer see another way." Ambrose's words swirl through my mind. "Co let ti vi atta go lu." His voice hums in my mind, his spell raining green magic over me.

Theo's head lulls forward. He loses consciousness as I gain movement in my fingers. Whoa, shit. The fire inside me shifts and moves, glowing through my veins. McKenzie is so caught up in her own spellcasting that she doesn't notice Tiernan's head lull next.

"Co let ti vi atta go lu. I call upon the fates to bind my body, mind, and soul to my familiars and their mate. Co let ti vi atta go lu. Blessed be the fates to give Delphia the strength of three plus three. Co let ti vi atta go lu. Unite us as one entity and set her free."

Maddox, Kash, and Ambrose slump within their magic bindings, and Rowan's head flops to the side.

Like someone rips the cage open on me, my dragon explodes free in a hurricane of smoke and fire, my rage stealing all of my mortal senses. I give in to my beast, savoring the all-consuming power that courses from my mates and directly into my heart, the glowing green strings of magic binding the seven of us together.

Opening my mouth, I roar, shooting fire at McKenzie. She shouts a spell, summoning a shield around her. My dragon screams rip through the air. I flap my wings, jumping forward. Slashing my claws at her barrier, I shock myself trying to break it. She holds up one palm and positions her knife in her other hand. Slowly carving down the center of Rowan's chest, she continues with her spell. Electricity zings through me as magic zaps from all around me. I not only have to fight McKenzie alone, but I also have to fight the remaining members of her coven.

Whipping my head, I blow another breath of fire, managing to get through one of her sister's shields. The witch screams as the force of my dragon fire, enhanced by my mates and Ambrose's magic, incinerates her. Ash dances across the stone floor in her wake, and I turn back to McKenzie.

McKenzie shouts a spell, her words incoherent. "Accept this sacrifice, oh good fates. Take this heart and—"

Agony stabs me in the chest, Rowan's pain sizzling through me as if it's my own. I screech and blow another breath of fire, attacking her protective shield. I don't stop.

I won't. I summon all of my dragon's strength and power, doing whatever I can to weaken her shield as my mates remain unconscious.

I shove the pain away, snapping and clawing at the shield, breathing so much fire from my mouth that all I see are flames everywhere. This is how I imagine Hell to look, but instead of burning me, all it does is continue to fill me with everything I need to keep fighting.

A deep, guttural roar hums through the air as Franco lands with a thud in his dragon form. He tries to blow fire at me, but all it does is blend with my own, something about Ambrose's spell giving me the ability to absorb everything thrown at me.

"Franco, stop her!" McKenzie's yells turn into a scream of bloody-murder, and the room lights up in lavender light. She's trying to escape.

I can't let her.

Jerking my head forward, I breathe another breath of fire and snatch the witch up with my teeth. I whip my long neck and toss her into the air. She chants a spell, trying to save herself from the long drop, leaving her unprotected from my beast.

I roar, the ear-piercing call of my dragon ringing through the air. The room rumbles around me, and the sound of thunder—of dragons soaring outside the palace—booms through the air. With one more burning breath, I shoot a stream of dragon fire glowing green with Ambrose's magic at McKenzie. Her whole body lights up, and her silhouette shatters and smolders, turning into ash. She's dead. She's really dead, and I killed her.

"Delphia!" Franco's booming voice cracks through my skull as if it's powerful enough to split my head open. "You will bow and submit to me! This isn't over!"

He's right. It isn't.

He's next.

Spinning my body, I swing my tail, lashing Franco across the face as he tries to bite me. I screech and blow a breath of fire, trying to keep him back long enough for me to transform. If I return to my mortal form, I can run through one of the archways too small for him to fit. It'll give me a chance to find something, anything, I can use against him.

As a dragon, I don't have the skills I need to fight him.

I have to use my brain until my mates come to. The magic Ambrose used knocked them out completely.

"Delphia, this is your last chance!" Franco shouts through my mind. "Submit to me! If you don't, I will slaughter all of you. I will end your life as I had done with your mother's!"

What. The. Fuck!

Fury consumes me, turning my vision red, and I flap my wings, propelling myself forward. Opening my mouth, I unleash a wave of green-glittering dragon fire at Franco. It scorches across his stretched belly as he prepares to jump on me. I skid, dodging out of his way. If he pins me, I'm not sure I can fight the strength of his beast.

Franco chases after me, managing to sink his teeth into my tail. He whips me around, knocking my feet out from under me, sending me sprawling. I skid across the rock floor, clawing my nails into it to try to stabilize myself. Franco catapults in my direction. He opens his mouth wide, preparing to blast me with flames. My whole body convulses, and I grind my teeth as my dragon frees my humanity. The world grows as I shrink, and I make a flying leap, jumping over Franco's tail. I race toward the circle where my mates are, hoping to get at least one of them to stir.

"Ambrose!" I yell, projecting my voice through the air and hopefully telepathically. "Ambrose, wake up!"

None of my mates stir for my calls, and I brace for Franco to blow us away with his dragon fire. The world quakes, and I stumble, falling to my knees. My heart hurts as my hands splash the blood pooling around Rowan. If I didn't see his chest rising and falling, I'd freak out even more. Instead, I snatch up the athame McKenzie left behind.

Swiveling on my feet, I brace for Franco's attack. He snarls and lunges, opening his mouth wide. He doesn't scream fire at me like I expect. Instead, he jerks his head, trying to bite me. This fucker wants to swallow me whole.

Running a few feet, I launch myself into the air, shooting fire from my hands to propel myself higher. I hook my fingers to Franco's nostril and swing, hoisting myself onto his snout. He spins and gnashes his teeth, trying to knock me off. I use all the strength of my mates to hold on and shimmy my way up his nose.

His big, fiery eyes glow orange, and I do the only thing I can think of. I need an advantage over him if I'm going to survive. Raising the athame, I jerk it forward and sink it into his slit pupil. Franco screeches in pain, and I manage to stab his other eye. Thrashing, he claws at his face, cutting the side of my hip. I jump off him, my stomach flying into my throat. I summon my dragon once again, managing to catch myself on my huge feet and shoot up instead of falling the few dozen feet.

I widen my mouth, spewing magical fire at Franco, not giving him even a second to defend himself. This might be my only chance. I thrust my wings, rocketing my body forward, and I smash into his monstrous form. We slide across the floor and toward the wide balcony. I bite his neck and shake my head, ripping at his flesh. Franco jerks sideways, knocking me off of him, and he blows fire again, aiming blindly.

I claw at the floor, rushing him again. He can't fight me properly with his fucked up vision, and I take advantage of it. I swipe my claws at his sides, trying to tear him open. Breathing fire, I distract him long enough to snatch one of his wings with my teeth. At the same time, I release the magic dragon fire until his skin fries and splits, the damage ensuring he can't fly.

That's when I know what to do.

I can't leave the palace, but he can. His reign is over, and now the Litendrake Clan will fall from power with him.

"Delphia, wait. Please," Franco says, his voice ringing through my mind. "You've proved yourself to me. Let me live, and I'll give you what you want."

Sinking my teeth into his other wing, I scorch it, shredding it with my teeth, hearing him screech. I can't stop. I won't. I don't care if he begs for mercy or submits to me. I don't trust him. I'm in this position because of him. He ruined my life. He killed my mom.

"Delphia, stop." Franco fights against me, but his scratches merely sting me. They're nothing compared to the pain he's already put me through.

"No," I snap, thinking the words to him. "You deserve no mercy. You deserve nothing!"

Franco transforms into his human self and tries to flee from me in one last attempt to save himself. Green magic zaps across the stone floor, creating a magic wall. Franco hollers as he smashes into it, the force of the magic enough to send him flying back to me.

My dragon roars, the beast inside me demanding I give in to her need. I release control, and savor the power in my entire being, lit up with the most powerful dragon fire that has probably ever existed, Ambrose's magic still coursing through me.

Snapping Franco between my teeth, I yank him from the floor and chomp down, crushing his bones. He screams and pleads for his life, but my dragon is far from granting mercy. She—we need revenge. We need justice.

This is for my mom.

For my mates.

This is for me.

I jerk my head and release Franco, throwing him through the wide archway leading to the sharp cliffs below the mountain palace. Thunder and roars echo through the world around me, and I stare at hundreds of dragons soaring through the air.

They watch Franco transform into his beast, but his wings are far too damaged to fly.

In silence, I watch him fall.

Tipping my head back, I roar, shooting fire through the air.

Something shocking happens. Dragons dive toward the ground and land on the expansive world of green. As I stare at the brilliant beasts before me, I feel something strange course through my soul. I feel their collection of emotions and hear their voices whispering my name.

Queen Delphia of the Drakovich Clan.

The dragons bow.

CHAPTER 12

Magic Link

"PRINCESS, PLEASE. I NEED TO ensure there are no residual effects from the magic link." Ambrose plants his hands on my shoulders, pushing me back to cage me against the wall. "I also just need to kiss you. I wasn't sure if I'd ever get my moment."

He combs my hair behind my ear and leans in slightly, testing to see my reaction. And fuck, do I give him one. His small request sets me off, and I surprise him by crashing my lips to his and hopping up, forcing him to hold me in his arms instead of cornering me to get my attention. His worry about getting a moment with me is absolutely warranted. It took at least fifty kisses each to calm my dragons down. It took even more to assure myself that we're all okay and that Maddox could care for Rowan's wounds.

It didn't help that I couldn't stop the magical fire from bursting from me, my whole being still buzzing even now. I still can't believe what happened. I killed two people. The clans fucking bowed to me and called me their queen. It's completely batshit crazy, and my mind can't process.

So Ambrose demanded the others give him a chance to examine me alone without all of the hot emotions running wild. I need them to figure shit out without worrying about me as well. This is our kingdom. Fuck. What if I don't want it?

Spinning me around, Ambrose carries me to the sitting area and plops down on the couch, letting me straddle his lap. His lips mold against mine, and he glides his tongue across the seam of my lips until I allow him to explore my mouth. I moan at the sweetness of his kiss and how his hands seem to shock me in the best way possible as they dig into my hips.

All it takes is his one kiss to turn me completely on, and now all I can think about is wanting to be with him. He purposely waited to fuck me, despite having the chance, and after everything...I need to forget the bullshit world around us. I crave to show him my appreciation for giving me what I needed to save my mates. Without Ambrose—I can't even think about the alternative. It's too much. My soul weeps at even the thought of losing one of my guys.

"Nova, your thoughts," Ambrose murmurs, breaking away from my mouth to kiss along my jaw.

I don't think I'll ever get used to having other people be able to hear what's on my mind.

He slows down and meets my gaze. "I'm sorry. I didn't mean to listen. I just—I worry we're moving too fast. You've been through a lot today and—"

"And I really want you because of it, Ambrose. But not only that. You're my mate, even if you're not a dragon. I want to make that clear to you. You're mine." I bite my bottom lip between my teeth. "I mean if that's what you want."

"What I want? It's what I need." Ambrose's fingers spark with magic, and my shirt explodes into a million tiny pieces like confetti. "I want to be yours more than anything."

I giggle and kiss him, my body incredibly excited. Grabbing at Ambrose's shirt, I tug it up and over his head. I bow down to kiss his shoulder and work my way down, sliding off the couch and between his legs. Unlike during the times with the others, Ambrose lets me lead and plays with my hair as I unfasten his pants. The ladder of barbells lining his cock glitter in the overhead light, and I can't stop thinking about how it'll feel inside me.

Ambrose groans, his cock pulsing as I lace my fingers around it. I carefully rub my fingers over the barbells, feeling the tingle of magic vibrating through them. Peeking up, I watch him stare at me with sizzling intensity, his breath panting in anticipation. I draw it out, kissing his thigh until I reach his balls and glide my tongue over them, feeling them tighten.

"You're so beautiful, Nova," he whispers, keeping my hair out of the way. "You mean the world to me. I never expected to feel such a bond with anyone outside of my familiars, and—"

He moans his pleasure as I suck him into my mouth, feeling the texture of his cock bling. A strangely delectable taste drips onto my tongue, his pre-cum unlike anything I've ever tasted. It's fruity yet sugary and reminds me of chocolate-covered strawberries. I knew he was magical, but damn.

Ambrose whispers a spell under his breath, ripping the rest of my clothes off with magic. I laugh as the world spins. Like he can't resist pleasuring me too, he uses his magic to flip me upside down and suspends me in the air.

I grip his legs and stretch my body, doing the splits as I refuse to stop sucking him. I moan so loudly as his tongue flicks over my clit, the sensation not unlike a vibrator, getting me just right. It's almost unfair how quickly he makes me orgasm, and I close my legs, trapping his head as I scream through the intense bliss.

Humming under his breath, he pinches his fingers into my ass cheeks, enjoying my mouth for only a moment longer. I pant and gasp, my heart thrumming in excitement. Ambrose lowers me with his magic, setting me down, so I bow over the back of the couch, resting my knees on the cushion. He moves behind me and kisses my shoulder while massaging his fingers into my breasts. I wiggle my ass, feeling his hardness slide against my slippery body, just rubbing the outside, letting me feel his piercing grinding against my clit.

"You're magnificent," he whispers, aligning his body to mine. His knees rest between mine as he widens my body, and I hook my legs around him, trying to pull him into me. "So beautiful. Powerful. Mine."

With his declaration, claiming me as his, he slides into me with a moan like he savors my body. I gasp at the tingling magic blossoming between us, and Ambrose grips my hips, thrusting harder and faster, his pleasure from our passion as prominent as mine with his voice. He bumps my ass, sinking in deep, the pressure mind-blowing and his movements hitting my g-spot. I arch with another orgasm, catching sight of us in the wall mirror. Green magic lights Ambrose's eyes, and he whispers a spell once again. Sex has always been fun and incredible with my mates, and this is damn magical.

He smiles at me in the mirror, his eyes heavy with lust, and he slides his hand over my hip and to my pelvis. Heat warms my hands, my dragon fire igniting with my next orgasm, and I accidentally burn the back of the couch, screaming my bliss. It sets Ambrose off, and magic rains around us, prolonging my orgasm until I swear my hair even feels it. With a moan to match mine, he cums, the force enough to feel in my very being, leaving me experiencing the sensation of flying and never wanting to come down.

Slowing down, he rests against me, whispering another spell. Our emotions and thoughts entangle, and he opens to me completely in body, mind, and soul. The bond forming between us solidifies our decision to claim each other. Love blooms in my heart, filling me with everything I never knew I needed from Ambrose.

He slides out and shifts me to lie beside him. I snuggle close, drawing my finger along his taut chest. This moment means more than I expected. I don't know if it's because of how things happened between us or how he became my accidental mate because of his bond with the Darkonians. All I know is that I plan to spend the rest of my life with Ambrose. He's tamed my dragon and has helped me rise.

A strange noise hums through the air, growing in volume over the sound of our hearts beating. Ambrose turns and kisses me, stroking my hair, his silver gaze glowing with his magic.

"It sounds like the clans are calling for you," he murmurs, reminding me of the moments after Franco's death. "What do you want to do? We can avoid them for a little while longer."

I want to. I want to so desperately, but I also know I can't wait. I need to do this and figure out what happens next. I might be free from Franco and McKenzie.

But the High Council? Lazlo? I'm not.

Something about today feels like fate.

And it's time I face what they hold for me.

"I swear no one better pat his back or high-five him," I

say, pointing my fingers at Maddox.

He stands tall just inside the door leading to the balcony. His long hair blows in the breeze coming in, and his muscles stretch the fabric of his shirt. He looks so damn sexy, especially with the look he gives me—raised eyebrow and cute smirk. It shouts for me to just try and stop him, because he's going to do what he wants.

I stick my tongue out at him. "If you do as much, I will—"

"Spank me? Tell me to bow at your feet? Invite me to recreate the moment? Explain exactly why I torched the fucking curtain uncontrollably? Force the crazy magical asshole to apologize for making me blow a load? Because that was inconvenient." Maddox tightens his jaw, narrowing his eyes at me.

Blush burns across my chest and cheeks. "What?"

Ambrose hugs me from behind and laughs. Maddox growls, and I'm nearly certain Ambrose uses me as a shield. I can feel Maddox is only joking, but he plays his annoyance well. It's natural for him to give his brothers a hard time, and I kind of love that he starts to treat Ambrose the same. He was clear from the start that he would tolerate them because of me. But now? I think it's more than that. He respects Ambrose—Theo and Tiernan too—for remaining by their sides.

"The link we share will fade within a day. I do apologize for not warning you of the residual effects. I wasn't planning on...claiming Nova in that moment." His voice lowers with his words. His sudden shyness in his admission makes me smile and reach up, rubbing my fingers over his head.

Maddox huffs. "What do you mean you weren't planning—"

"Maddox, knock it off," I say, shooting a burst of fire at his feet.

Uh-oh. I just set off his wild side, and he stalks closer, his muscles bulging. He looks ready to throw me over his knee and spank me.

And damn it, do I want to give him a hard time. His sexual nature and constant need to ensure all of my needs are taken care of—even by others when he's not around—is ridiculously endearing. Raw and feral too.

He gives in to his nature far more than the others and uses my scent, my body language, and my thoughts to help him decide how to take care of me. I love it despite it sometimes infuriating me, and I wouldn't change the asshole for anything.

"Ambrose, shield now," I say, pushing against his back, trying to get him to move.

Maddox's eyes light with fire at my words.

"If you don't hold her still, I'll give you a damn lecture about the importance of fulfilling her needs. She doesn't always vocalize what she wants, and because you're not a dragon and in tune with what her body begs for, I won't hesitate to remind you that you should always plan to satisfy her. Feed her. Cuddle her. Fuck, you need to be prepared to punish her when she's getting to be a bit wild." Maddox cracks his neck, challenging Ambrose to summon the shield I ask him to.

I raise my palms up. "Those things are what you feel is your job to do. Have you thought that maybe I need something else from Ambrose?"

"He can make us all orgasm with the whisper of a spell. I think it's clear what his true purpose is within our clan." Maddox grins wickedly, rubbing his fiery hands together.

Ambrose tips his head back and laughs. "Is that all you think I'm useful for, dragon?"

"No, but it's the most important. It keeps her happy and her soul soaring when she cannot." Maddox gathers more fire in his palms, preparing to smolder my damn clothes right off. I can hear it in his thoughts. See it in his eyes as he devours me with his gaze. "It's time to teach her that this is how life is supposed to be now that—"

Kicking my legs up, I plant my feet to his chest, keeping space between us. "Don't even think about it. I just showered and dressed. The clans are chanting my damn name."

"They will wait." He grins with his words. "Perhaps they'll shut the fuck up if they hear—"

A fireball flies through the air, colliding into Maddox and knocking him back.

I clap my hands and tug away from Ambrose, dodging Maddox's attempt to capture me to have his way—something I won't deny no matter how many reasons I have not to floating through my mind. I never thought I was a pleaser, but damn it, I think it's because he's so adamant in wanting to do everything for me. The same goes for the rest of my guys.

"Come here, doe eyes. I'll save you from that asshole if you promise to reward me later." Rowan strolls from the open balcony, completely naked, and extends his arms out to me.

I slow down and give him a once-over. "You can't save me like that. It's too tempting."

He laughs and rushes me, not giving me a chance to run away. The heat of his body warms me up, and I can't resist kissing him. A part of me still freaks out every time I think about McKenzie choosing Rowan to sacrifice.

Turning me away and shielding me from Maddox, he

strokes his hand down my back. "Hey, it's okay. I'm okay."

The sudden change in my mood settles Maddox down, and he comes up and brushes his lips to my forehead.

He wasn't kidding about knowing exactly what I need and when. Tears burn my eyes, and Ambrose joins the two of them, whispering a spell with Kash, Theo, and Tiernan's name.

"Our mate needs our attention. She needs to confirm that we're all okay again," Maddox says, and I realize Ambrose must have called for the others.

Three bodies turn into six, and I savor the protective wall of muscle, fire, and magic around me. My heart settles after a moment, and my body chills out, and I manage to compose myself. I've been trying not to think about things, but McKenzie and Franco's actions still haunt me.

"Delphia, I know this is difficult, but as soon as you face the clans and allow them to formally show their allegiance and respect as their superior and the rightful heir to the Litendrake Kingdom, they will disperse. A female has never fought for power and won, nor has a female brought together two rival clans. The power shift was felt all through the lands." Theo touches my cheek, getting me to turn to look at him. "A number of clans already would like an alliance."

"They've come with gifts too," Tiernan says, smirking.

I groan. "This is too much. I can't handle it."

"Actually, you won't be handling it, Inmate D64901." A sharp, feminine voice cuts through the air, shaking me to the core. High Council Woman Laveau stands within a red shield that matches her glowing eyes. "It has come to our attention that your clan leader has met his demise, so I've come to return you to the Maximum Magical Penitentiary. There have been some interesting revelations recently, and the High Council would like to investigate the situation that seems to include you."

Holy fuck. No.

No. No. No.

My heart slides into my stomach, and I clutch onto Rowan.

I can't believe this is happening. My mates were supposed to take my contract and get it transferred. They should be able to because it was already created before Franco changed his mind. Ambrose was going to handle it.

"High Council Woman Laveau, I must request that you reconsider removing our mate. We have an arrangement already in order with the Litendrake Clan for Delphia's union, including the Dreki Clan."

She taps closer, her shield moving with her. "Which reminds me that they must come with me too and stand before the High Council because of their unexpected disappearance. But perhaps things can be put in order with another arrangement of their service contract."

Is she kidding me?

"Though things will change drastically because of your...illegal activity. Wearing collars will be part of the negotiations unless you choose to resist. You understand the consequences, do you not?" The witch grows in height as she uses her power in an attempt to intimidate the dragons.

"What?" I ask, my fury swelling through me. "You can't do that. It's not right."

She ignores me completely and summons a pair of magical chains. "Do not test me. You will not like the consequences, dragons. Now hand me Delphia. I will return for the Drekis."

Something inside me snaps.

Dragon fire explodes through me, surprising the High Council Woman. Her shield falters, unable to withstand my newfound power, pulled from my mates. Opening her mouth, she releases a scream. Red electricity zaps through the air, lifting my hair with its static.

High Council Woman Laveau explodes into a cloud of fire and ash with only black scorch marks burning the floor where she stood.

Oh fuck.

What have I done?

CHAPTER 13

Deadly Crimes

"STRENGTHEN THE SHIELDS. THEY'RE coming." Maddox drags me with him, not giving me a chance to think, move, or even react. "I'll take Nova. They're going to hit hard and fast."

"I'll summon the guards." Tiernan bursts into his dragon form and launches from the balcony, soaring away.

"Ambrose, shield the Drekis. The High Council can't know they're here. I doubt the witch managed to send notice of their appearance." Theo rushes beside Maddox. "Let me care for her. I'll protect her with my life and will not let them take her. Please, our mate needs you hidden and safe."

I expect Maddox to argue, but he growls and kisses me, tossing me to Theo.

My body relaxes in his arms, and I lie limply, my body in shock. I killed the councilwoman. I can't believe I did that. I just—fuck, I'm a murderer. I'm living up to the Drekis fears about me when we first met.

"You did what you thought was necessary," Theo says, adjusting me in his arms. "That's what makes you a great ruler. Do not give those who try to hurt you and rip apart our clan even an ounce of sorrow or regret. I wouldn't have you any other way."

Still, I don't respond. I can't.

The raging beast inside me still wants to burn the world down. The witch set me off, and I can't pull my dragon out of fighting mode. In a moment I should run and hide, my heart wants to stand up for myself. I want to face those who seek to destroy my world—a world that I seem to never get a chance to fully embrace.

"Fuck, they've gotten to the guards. They were already here. They're trying to sever the growing alliance." Tiernan's voice booms through my mind as he lands, shaking the room. "We're going to have to fight alone."

My whole body tenses. They can't fight the High Council. They'll be slaughtered.

Shoving my hands to Theo's chest, I push myself away and flip from his arms, landing on my feet. He growls, trying to snatch me up, but I scramble out of his way. If I leave with him, the High Council will destroy the place. They will destroy the Dragon Lands. I don't have to ask anyone to know the truth in my soul.

"Delphia, come back here!" Theo shouts, rushing behind me. "Ambrose, stop her!"

I spin and hold my hands up. "No! I won't let you hide me away and risk your lives. I won't risk them destroying the other clans. I'm a criminal. I killed people."

"Kitten, please. You can't. If you do—" Bright green light cuts off Kash's words as Ambrose casts a shield hiding the Drekis from sight.

Everything happens so fast that I freeze in my spot as brilliant blue light explodes through the room. Several figures materialize within the portal, and my dragon screams inside me to shoot my fire at them.

"Stand down, warlock," a man snaps, dressed in a familiar CO uniform that I just got used to the Drekis not wearing. "If you even open your mouth, you will be convicted of treason and stripped of your magic."

Theo growls, scooping me up to plop me behind him. "You cannot come into our kingdom and threaten our mate. Leave immediately or—"

A blast of vibrant silver power strikes Theo, knocking him into me. We land with a thud on the ground, his heavy weight smothering me. I scream, the agony rolling through him colliding into me through our soul link. Another shockwave blasts Tiernan, and the edges of my vision shadow.

"Inmate D64901, turn yourself in to us immediately and request the Darkonians to stay back. If you do not, you will leave us no choice but to deem you far too dangerous for transport. You will face immediate execution for your crimes without trial." A warlock rubs his hands together, his face elongating with his magic. He reveals sharp teeth and gathers more power in his hands.

"Nova, please. We will handle this. Don't do it." Tiernan holds his hands up, facing the High Council's team of guards. "I'm requesting a pardon on the Drakovich heir's behalf. It has come to our attention that the Liohts and Litendrakes set her up, and she was not responsible for the crimes she was convicted of. We have proof in the alliance contract, created by McKenzie Lioht before she fled."

The guard shifts his jaw, his eyes flashing red. He

stares up at the ceiling, his attention being drawn elsewhere as he communicates telepathically. He waits for a second and slowly nods his head, turning back to Tiernan. "Your warlock has thirty seconds to provide such proof."

Hope soars through my heart, my whole body buzzing in anticipation as Ambrose summons the thick contract that would turn our union official according to Magaelorum Law and establish the Darkonian Clan's right to move me from Franco's prison of a palace and to their kingdom.

Ambrose hands the contract to the guard, and it vanishes from his fingers. I tense, shifting on my feet, and peer behind me. Theo slowly pushes from the floor, coming to after being knocked out. I can't see the Drekis, but I can sense them standing close by, their anxiety as high as mine.

The guard's jaw twitches, and he stares at the ceiling once more. I hug my arms around my chest, listening to the thunderous boom of dragons flying through the air outside. The rest of the world holds its breath, and I say a silent prayer.

Red power lights up the guard's gaze, and he turns his attention to me. "Inmate D64901, your prior charges will be revisited in front of the High Court with the new charges being brought against you for the murder of High

Council Woman Laveau. If found guilty, you will be remanded to the Maximum Magical Penitentiary until sentencing. Please raise your hands. You are under arrest. If your mates intervene, they will face equal charges. Do you understand?"

"What?" I ask, my voice cracking. How did they know?

Theo growls. "You're mistaken. Delphia has been with us the entire time. I assure you that the councilwoman—"

"We have a witness testifying against Delphia Drakovich." The guard rubs his hands together. "Now stand back. This is your last warning."

A deep, guttural growl reverberates through the air, and Ambrose's magic shield explodes as Maddox blasts through it with his dragon fire.

My mouth falls agape, my whole body tensing as he charges forward.

"It was me!" Maddox shouts, his body rippling, showing off his beast trying to break free. "I killed the fucking bitch! She was trying to threaten my mate and me. She threatened to collar my clan. I'm guilty."

Oh shit.

"Maddox, no," I say, rushing to him, blocking his way. "Don't do this."

Growling, he clutches my face between his hands. "You are the Dreki and Darkonian future. Do not take that away from your mates. I was prepared to die for my brother, and I will prepare to die for you, Delphia. Do not argue. This is how it has to be. They will kill you. There is no life in Max for this crime."

I try to kiss him, my whole body begging to stop him from doing this. Hands lock to my hips and drag me back, and I watch in horror as the guards accept Maddox's admission of guilt without even questioning the truth of his words.

Bright light flashes through the air, and he and the guards disappear.

A loud boom reverberates through my bones, and I yank away from Ambrose and run toward the balcony. Red electricity zings through the air, climbing from the ground to disappear into the sky. I clutch the railing, heaving, tears burning my eyes.

"You have to stop them," I say, my voice shaking. "You should've never let him do that!"

I spin around, yanking my hair, my rage and heartache crashing through me. Kash and Rowan stand together, their eyes glassing over, their own pain resonating through me as if it's my own. Theo, Ambrose, and Tiernan remain expressionless, staring at the sky behind me.

"They're monsters! Liars! There were no fucking witnesses! We have to do something." I gather dragon fire in between my palms and thrust it at Ambrose. "Listen to me! Do something!"

His mouth tightens, his shoulders slumping. Licking his lips, he says, "I'm so sorry, princess. I can't."

"You can't? You can't!" I scream, my dragon begging for control. "You have to!"

"Nova, please come here. Let us hold you and explain," Tiernan says softly, shuffling a foot closer as if he thinks I'll attack.

"They're going to kill him." I clutch my chest, the agony coursing through me stealing my breath. "He needs me. We have to go. I'll fucking tear their world down!"

"They know it." Theo motions to the sky behind me. "Which is why none of us can go anywhere. The High Council caged our lands. They've cut us off from the rest of Magaelorum."

His words trigger my nature as a dragon, and I transform, screeching with my pain. My good senses die with Maddox's absence, and I flap my wings. I expect the world to zap me down. I expect magic to kill me for trying to leave the palace.

I launch into the air, my fire bursting free, but nothing happens to me. Magic no longer binds me.

Maddox exchanged his freedom for mine.

His life for mine.

But now, no dragon will ever truly be free.

CHAPTER 14

Death Row

I DON'T KNOW WHAT I'M doing or where I'm going. I soar high above the valley alone. No other dragons fly through the sky, and I think they've all gathered with their clans as word spreads of the magical imprisonment the Dragon Lands face.

I hate this. I hate everything about this.

How could the High Council imprison an entire species, and all because of me? My dragon's scream rips through the air in frustration, and I nosedive, following the line of magic until the ground sneaks up on me. I turn, gliding over the treetops, clawing at the branches. I want so badly to attack the barrier with my dragon fire, but every time I get close to it, something stops me.

I flap my wings, preparing to ascend to attempt it again, but a flash of blue light catches my attention from within the trees below. My whole body tenses at the sight of the portal. Fury explodes through me, and I summon my dragon fire, roaring a breath, sending orange flames over the trees.

Familiar blue electricity crackles through the air, a magical shield forming in place. I thought murder was already on my mind, but nothing compares to the heated feelings crashing through me. Lazlo Infinity steps into a clearing and shouts a spell, whipping a magical chain in my direction.

"Ti vo la coma eht!" Ambrose's spell rings through the air.

Green magic explodes from above me as he reveals himself. I've never been so relieved to have a sneaky-ass warlock as a mate. I had no idea he was riding on my damn back, but I guess I should've known that he'd be here since none of my dragon mates followed me into the sky.

Deflecting Lazlo's magical chain, Ambrose calls another spell, building a wall of power around us. His cool hand strokes the scales on my head, and his emotions flood me with his thoughts.

"Nova, will you land for me?" he asks, sending a wave of tranquility to my soul.

I roar and breathe another stream of fire in Lazlo's direction. The last thing I want to do is land and let him get anywhere close to me, but I know Ambrose has his reasons. I trust him to care for me, our bond stronger than ever, his hold on my soul more than his ability to tame my raging beast.

Expanding my wings, I catch the air, slowing down. "We should call my mates."

"They're already waiting. I'm going to extend an invitation to the warlock to stand before the princes," Ambrose says.

I nearly freefall into the trees, his comment shocking me. "Are you insane?"

"He can get us in and out if the deal is good enough." Ambrose shifts his weight, sliding forward to look into one of my eyes, his form blurring. "I swear on my life I'll protect you."

"You don't need to make me such promises. I trust you. It's just...I fucking hate him." Smoke billows from my nostrils with my thought. "I want him dead like the others, and I hate that I feel this way. I shouldn't want to murder anyone. What's wrong with me?"

"Absolutely nothing. You're a dragon. You're fierce and protective. These circumstances have been utter shit. You've done what you had to. They were not good people, and the High Council would've never served you right. We have to rise and fix our fates ourselves. It's the only way. They're too entangled with magic. You shouldn't have to sacrifice anymore for others who only see you as something to be controlled and tamed. We will use this to our advantage with Lazlo. I have a feeling he is who set us up. We can turn it all against him." Ambrose shoots magic toward the trees, opening a clearing wide enough for me to land in my dragon form.

He hops off my head and lands on his feet in front of me, raising his hands up, waiting for me to lower my head so that he can touch my snout. Bowing forward, he kisses between my nostrils and waits for me to transform. There is no way I'm facing Lazlo in my dragon form. I don't need him testing my beast.

Summoning a cotton dress, Ambrose helps me dress and summons a protective shield around us, not leaving himself open for any of Lazlo's magical attacks. We stroll hand-in-hand toward the glowing light in the trees. My heart hammers out of control the closer we get, and fire lights my hands aglow, Lazlo's presence alone enough to summon my power.

"My beautiful beast, settle down. I see I can't collar you and take you home to protect you from the High Council. I was only trying to help you." Lazlo keeps his hands at his sides, smiling at me through his own protective magical shield.

I tighten my jaw, stopping myself from screaming at him. If I open my mouth, I'll blow fire instead. I might unleash my dragon, and right now, I need to keep my good senses.

"Mr. Infinity, please do not address Delphia. She is mine, and anything you have to say can be directed at me." Ambrose pulls me in close, tucking me under his muscular arm. I slide my hand around his back, squeezing his hip. Protective on him is sexy as hell, and I love how he doesn't take bullshit from the bastard warlock. "I also realize that you set us up. We're not playing any games with you, so this is your one and only chance to join my dragon clan at the palace."

Ambrose catches Lazlo by surprise, and I savor his look of shock and confusion. He probably expected to come in here with some shitty deal to separate me from my mates. I'm so thankful to have someone who can see reason in a moment where my heart bleeds and desperation tries to make me act irrationally.

"Do we have an agreement? If not, Delphia will send you to the stars. Do not test us. She has come into her dragon power and is far wilder than any dragon I've met." Ambrose flicks his gaze to mine, his eyes lighting with magic. His pride swells through me, and it lessens the pain consuming me over allowing my nature to control me.

Lazlo rubs his hands together, sparking blue magic from his fingers. "I suppose we do."

Ambrose claps his hands, calling a transportation spell. The world ignites in bright light around us, sending my stomach twisting. I clutch onto Ambrose, burying my face into his chest, hugging him tightly as if I'll get lost in oblivion if I let go.

Growls reverberate through my bones as the world settles and my vision returns to normal. I clutch my chest, the pain and anger within my mates strong enough to leave me breathless. Kash and Rowan stand up, gathering dragon fire in their palms. Theo raises his hand to them, stopping them from attacking Lazlo on sight.

I break away from Ambrose, not giving him a chance to hold me for a moment longer, and rush the space to the Drekis. I feel terrible for abandoning them, but my heart needed to fly. My body needed to see if I could break through the magic. But mostly, I was too afraid to face them. It's my fault Maddox felt the need to take the blame for murder. He loves me too damn much, even in moments I wish he wouldn't. I've failed him and his brothers. I've ruined their clan and their lives. The fates are far from funny, cursing them with a soul bond to me, and I wish there was something I could do.

Kash lifts me up. "Don't think like that, kitten. Maddy made his own choices, and you can't carry the blame, okay?"

But I do. I always will.

Tears burn my eyes, and I hide my face, afraid that I'll start sobbing if I meet his hazel eyes. Rowan comes up behind me and sandwiches me to Kash, kissing my neck, and quietly tries to comfort me without using his words. Maybe he doesn't know what to say. Maybe he can't say anything at all because his emotions are as fucked up as mine. Regardless, I savor their closeness. I hate that I feel undeserving of them, and I wonder if they'll resent me. If they'll reject me as their mate.

"Never, Nova. Please don't take my silence as anything but support for you as my mate. I just—we should've done more. You're not alone in feeling at fault." Rowan's breath tickles the skin under my ear. He slides his arms between me and Kash, resting them on my stomach.

Lazlo clears his throat, interrupting my private moment with the Drekis. Rage explodes through me, and I jerk around, glowering at him from over Rowan's shoulder. He tightens his grip on me, keeping me back. Heat spills from me at the sight of the warlock standing like a dumbass with raised eyebrows.

"This is your fucking doing!" I shout, releasing a guttural growl with my words. "You were the witness! You were stalking me!"

Rowan and Kash stiffen with my accusation. Ambrose throws up a shield keeping us away from Lazlo. I know he's protecting us and not the warlock, but it still angers me. I want to devour him. I thought I could remain calm, but the more I think about it, the more I realize that he was never going to let me make a decision in regards to my life. He wanted me to bow to him and to help him take out the High Council. And now, because he claimed he was a witness, Maddox is gone. He's on death row.

"Oh, Delphia. I do apologize for the twist in the circumstances. Your mates were supposed to let the High Council take you away. I hadn't expected Maddox to go in your place or that the judge would let him take the blame." Lazlo frowns, his fake sorrow prodding me like a burning-hot poker.

"Shut up!" Ambrose yells, flicking his hands at Lazlo.

"I warned you not to address Delphia. She's mine."

Lazlo's features morph with his agitation. "But is she? Are you sure? I seem to know that I'm the one who holds power in this situation, and I'm only humoring you in regards to my dragon."

Theo and Tiernan both react this time, growling and morphing their features as they struggle to maintain their mortal forms. I shove harder against Rowan, wanting so badly to break free and attack.

"Lazlo!" Ambrose summons green power in his fingers.

Lazlo glowers and crosses his arms, not even intimidated by the four dragons and pissed-off warlock. He looks amused, looking at me directly.

"Listen, warlock. I need Delphia, and I won't take anything less than having her bow and serve me. You can pretend to claim her all you want, but I still have a collar on her neck, and I will break your leash." Lazlo jerks his hands out, shooting power at Ambrose. Ambrose blocks himself, but it opens the shield around me.

I push Rowan so hard that he stumbles, and I scramble over him and rush the bastard Lazlo. Gathering fire in my hands, I thrust it in his direction, setting his shield ablaze. He smiles at me, pissing me off even more. He's insane. Infuriating.

"Get it out of your system now, Delphia. And hurry. If I know the High Council like I think I do, your mate's execution will be fast." Lazlo twists his lips with his words. "Unless you feel you have enough mates and losing one isn't a problem. You obviously won't be without—"

I scream and pound my fiery hands against the shield, shattering it. Lazlo's eyes widen for a split second, and he chants a spell, lashing a magical chain at me. Green power rains through the air, but Ambrose isn't fast enough. My dragons can't reach me either.

My body trembles and shifts. Scales bloom on my arms, and I fight against Lazlo trying to chain me.

"Delphia, bow to me, and I'll save your mate. Help me take down the High Council, and I'll allow you to live your lives in contracted freedom. You will only serve me when called. It is more beneficial to me to have you reign over the Dragon Lands and influence the beasts that can stand up to magic." Lazlo grinds his teeth, his focus torn between me and deflecting Ambrose's magic.

"What about Quillon? You know he controls Kash." I heave a breath, my mind settling down as I start to consider his reasoning. "I need all my mates free from control."

"Bow to me," Lazlo repeats. "Do it, and as long as you keep your end of our bargain, I will give you what you want. I'll bring Quillon for you to break. It must be you who gets him to return power, but I will help ensure he wants to."

"Nova, no." Ambrose's voice cuts through the static buzzing through the air. "We will find another way."

"Your warlock has far too much faith in the fates. The only way out of the Dragon Lands is by someone able to access a portal or with dark magic. Do you plan to make a sacrifice, Ambrose?" Lazlo steps closer to me.

I swivel and meet Ambrose's glower. I could never ask him to practice such magic. I know that what he casts now already takes a toll on his life. Looking at the others, I say, "I will not let anyone else sacrifice anything for our clan. This is my burden and deal to make. It is my job to protect you all. Trust me and my decision. You can't ask me to put myself above Maddox. I would do the same for all of you."

"Nova," Tiernan says.

I shake my head, tears streaming down my cheeks. "Don't argue with me. This is better than the alternative."

"I want to look over the contract." Ambrose clenches and unclenches his fingers. "I will not let you take advantage of my mate in her desperation. It affects all of us, and if you're that in need of help for the High Council, allow me to assist. We can bind magic if it ensures I get control too."

Lazlo flares his nostrils, his eyes darting from Ambrose to me. "You understand the risk?"

"I do." Ambrose rolls his shoulders. "She's worth it to me. My familiars' happiness is worth it."

"Then you have a deal. I'll prepare the contract and ceremony." Lazlo steps closer to me. "Now bow, my beast."

I straighten my back. "Once you prove to me you can do as you say. Take me to Maddox. I need to see him."

Twitching his fingers, he summons magic and snatches my wrist. "As you desire."

The world turns white.

CHAPTER 15

Visitation

MY HAIR DANCES AROUND IN the magic breeze whipping through the hallway of the Visitation Center. I try to tug my hand free from Lazlo in case I need to summon my dragon fire. A part of me feared he'd just kidnap me and hold me hostage. I knew of the chance, but I was counting on Ambrose's binding of magic to be more appealing to him.

And now I stand outside a familiar door to a room I

wish I never saw again. Lazlo tightens his fingers around my wrist and peers around. He zaps the door with his magic, flinging it open, and I frown at the empty room before us.

"Wait here. Do not leave. If you so much as make a noise, I will not be able to summon your mate." Lazlo pushes his palm to my back, shoving me forward.

I spin, my body wanting to flee, the memory of being attacked by Lazlo in this room as fresh in my mind as my stay here. In a burst of blue magic, Lazlo vanishes, and the door slams shut. I rush to the corner of the room and duck, trying to hide from the two-way mirror and the window cutout in the door.

Fucking fuck. I was not expecting to be left alone. Panic seizes my lungs, and I gulp in deep breaths, hoping to settle my nerves.

"What is this? Take me back! I said no visitors!" Maddox's bellowing voice rings through the air, and I stand upright but resist flying at the door.

"Take your small mercies, Dreki. You're lucky I have a debt with the Infinity Coven, or you wouldn't see outside of the fucking pit until you lose your damn head." The CO's sharp voice stabs into me. I gather fire in my palms, preparing to hurt the fucker for surely manhandling my mate.

"She has fifteen minutes, Infinity," the CO says, shoving the door to the visiting room open.

"Make it thirty, and come join me for a bit. I have a few things I'd like to discuss." Lazlo's voice remains even despite the threat lacing the CO's voice.

My eyes widen at the sight of a familiar guard with wings, and I automatically turn my gaze away. It takes everything in me not to flip him off.

"Go in, fucker. Thirty minutes." The guard shoves Maddox forward, tripping him as he forces him into the room.

Falling on his chained hands, Maddox growls deep in his throat but doesn't try to retaliate as the door slams closed. I release a whimper, my whole body craving his closeness. Maddox whips his head up, his eyes no longer glowing with his dragon fire. Brands glow on the backs of his hands, and he hoists himself to his feet despite being chained with magic.

He bares his teeth. "Delphia, you shouldn't have come. What were you thinking? How could my brothers—"

I launch at him, shutting him up with my mouth. I can't stand the thought of any space between us and trap his hands between us, ignoring the crackling shock of magic the best I can. Maddox spins and slams my back into the wall, his desire to give in to my affection running hotter than ever. I hook my arms around his neck and kiss him with every desperate fiber of my being like I'll die if I don't.

"You can't distract me. I need an answer," he mutters, using his knee to hold me up, making me straddle it since he can't grab my hands well with the chains.

"I need you to just shut up for a second. What you've done—I'm so angry with you." I smash my mouth to his and nip his lip.

"I should piss you off more often, cookie." His voice lightens with his comment. "And then punish you. You can be spitting-fire mad all you want, but I made the right decision. They'd have executed you."

I yank his hair and force his head back. "They are going to execute you. It's why I'm here. I'm not letting it happen."

He cocks his head to the side, flaring his nostrils. "Damn it, Delphia! Don't tell me you did what I think you did."

"I did what I had to." I narrow my eyes, refusing to back down.

"You keep doing that. Why can't you let me do what I feel I need to for fucking once? It's my job to protect you as the leader of the Dreki Clan and your mate. It's my job to ensure that you don't go through any more bullshit than you have to. Having you do this—whatever the fucking deal you made with Lazlo—it's not fucking worth it. My brothers will be there for you. The Darkonians will help you through. I cannot live, knowing that you chose me over everything else. It's selfish. It's wrong."

I swing my hand and slap him across the face, my anger getting the best of me. Tears escape my eyes, and a sob clenches my chest. I bawl my eyes out, just straddling his knee under his silent scrutiny. How dare he think he has the right to just die. To be executed on my behalf for a crime I committed and he didn't. He has no right to assume that I can live without him, even with his brothers and the Darkonians. And I'm furious that he doesn't see himself as important as I do. I will not let him just fucking sacrifice himself. I won't.

"You are in so much trouble, you fucking ass!" I scream, my voice high-pitched through my tears. "I should push you to the floor and spank you until you turn into the same damn color as my dragon is. You are crazy if you think I'm going to just turn into some compliant little mate and accept anything less than having my whole damn clan by my side."

"Delphia, you don't understand—"

I clutch his cheeks. "No, you don't fucking understand. I'm not letting you go. I'm not standing by and losing you. I will destroy the entire High Council, all of Magaelorum, and even the damn Mortal World for you, Maddox. You are important—as important as your brothers and the Darkonians. And me. I know it pisses you off that the fates cursed you with my complicated life and my psycho-murdering ass, but you're going to have to deal with it. I will fight for you. I will lose my humanity and give in to the wild beast inside me, tainted by my mom's criminal past and her same attitude for doing the shit she did. Do you understand, Maddox?" Fire flickers from my palms, setting the dimly lit room aglow.

Maddox growls deep in his throat, his chest bumping into mine as my words sink in.

And then he kisses me again. Our bodies turn aglow with my dragon fire as I heat up his entire being, filling him with what the witches stole. I savor his mouth on mine, his tongue gliding between my lips as he deepens our kiss. I don't even care that he's dirty from the pits. All I want is to give him what he wants and needs. I want so badly to prove to him that I will save him. I will do whatever it takes to bring our clan together. Fuck the High Council. Fuck everyone against us.

"Fuck me," Maddox says, his grumbling voice vibrating against my mouth. I know he can't read my mind, but he still feels my soul. "Sit on my face. Let me taste you. I can't hold you like I want, and it drives me crazy."

I laugh breathlessly and slide off his knee. "I'm doing whatever the hell I please, inmate," I say, sliding around him. Stretching my arms around him, I pop the buttons on his jumpsuit open, taking my time to explore his pecs and abs as I tug it off him.

Maddox twists his body, spinning around so fast that I can't move, and he encircles me with his arms, using his chains to lock my hip. Bowing, he tears at the front of my dress with his teeth, managing to drag it over my head. Using his knee again, he lifts me up, sucking each of my nipples into his mouth. I moan and rock my body, grinding myself against the hard bone of his knee. I'll get off on him any way I can. I don't care. I just want to be with him.

Managing to get his hands on my ass, he lifts me up completely, setting me on his shoulders to bury his face between my thighs. "You taste so good," he murmurs, blindly strolling toward the wall to balance me better as I squirm. This damn talented dragon. He could probably be bound and blindfolded and still manage to get me off.

He flicks his tongue over my clit, his desperation and desire bringing me to my peak in only minutes. I yank his hair, rocking on his shoulders, wanting to ride his face while I soar through the hurricane of ecstasy crashing through me.

He swings me around, plopping me down on the metal table, chilling my ass. I grab for him and lace my fingers around his massive hard-on. It's been a while since Maddox and I have been intimate alone, and he looks ready to devour me inch by inch.

He licks his lips and watches me stroke him for only another minute. Standing at the end of the table, he stretches my legs, not even caring if anyone sees us. I don't give a fuck either. My dragon wants this too badly to think of modesty. I'll take what I can, when I can, the world around us be damned.

"My beautiful mate," he says, aligning our bodies. "You piss me off to no end."

"Punish me then." I pant and squirm before him, barely able to control myself from flying at him. "Show me how mad I make you. Let me feel your wrath."

I gasp as Maddox pinches my hip as he flips me over and thrusts into me from behind. He spanks my ass hard enough to make me jump, and I moan as his fingers lock into my hair and yank my head back to kiss me. I moan at his deep thrusts, his hard body smacking mine like he's trying to fuck my dragon free so he can punish her too. I stand on my tiptoes, the pressure and pleasure aroused in me, turning me submissive and docile. I scratch my nails into the metal, my dragon claws splitting free of my fingers to etch into the metal top. Heat pours from me, my dragon fire blazing and burning. The metal glows red, but Maddox remains unfazed, fucking me like the beast he is, smacking me and gathering my hair. His cock hits me hard and deep, feeling as if it rearranges my insides in the best way possible, and even his fucking balls slap me, hitting my clit just right that I make my lip bleed from biting it.

"You're a fucking bad girl, cookie. So fucking naughty," Maddox says, growling and biting the back of my shoulder.

"You like it," I say, squeezing my thighs together. "You can't wait to punish me all the time."

"Damn straight. I want your ass aching. I want you to remember what I'm capable of." Maddox whacks me with the glowing chain just hard enough to set my body off again. The electric magic shocks me in such a way that I orgasm again.

I scream out in pleasure, my whole body lighting with the fire and magic awakened inside me. Maddox grunts, his cock pulsing as he cums. The chains smack the table above my head as he sinks on top of me, pressing my hot body into the cool metal. Resting on his elbows, he gives me enough space to turn over and teases me by sliding back inside me like he plans to go at it again.

"I can't get enough, Delphia," he murmurs, kissing me softly, his use of my birth name getting to me in the best way possible.

I caress my fingers to his cheek, savoring the sensation of our bodies entangled. "You won't have to. I swear I will get you out of here."

He sighs. "I still wish you wouldn't. I can't stand the thought—"

I cut him off again, afraid that my heart can't handle his argument. "I can't stand the thought of not having the hundreds of babies you plan to curse me with, you asshole. So stop it. Just hang on and trust me, okay? I am your mate, and you've made enough sacrifices."

Maddox smiles, his whole face lighting up. "You want a huge clan, don't you?"

"I just want to fill the world with dragons as brave and strong as you are—as kind and loving and fierce as your brothers and as persistent and tough as the Darkonians. As magical as Ambrose. I'll do anything for that life and future."

He kisses me once more. "I love you, Delphia. I love you with everything in me and everything I have to give. You were wrong about the fates cursing me with you. I've been blessed. You've saved me time and time again, and I know you'll save us all now. My perfect dragon mate. My queen."

"Five minutes, Delphia." A knock taps with the words, stealing all of the good left within me. "I proved to you what I have to offer. Now it's your turn."

I snuggle Maddox close once more. "I love you, Maddox. I swear we're going to be okay."

I just hope I can keep my promise.

I just hope I can survive bowing down to Lazlo.

It might be the only way I rise—perhaps trapped with a leash—but my dragon will soar.

CHAPTER 16

Bow to Magic

I SCREAM AS LAZLO'S MAGIC sears across my chest, branding an infinity symbol over my heart. Heat and fire haven't bothered me much since awakening my dragon, but holy fucking shit. The agony that sizzles across my skin with his mark steals my consciousness. I don't know how long I blackout for, but it's long enough to snap my eyes open with my cheek planted to the stone floor.

"Give her space. She will adjust momentarily." Lazlo's

voice booms through the room.

"She doesn't need space. She needs me." Theo snarls with his comment. Footsteps slap on the floor, and a warm hand caresses my back. "She needs space from you to adjust, you asshole. That fucking hurt her. I don't understand why you had to mark her. The contract should've been enough."

"Theo, it's—"

"I don't want a reason, Ambrose. I want that shit off her," Theo argues, gently helping me to turn over.

He and Ambrose were the only ones allowed in the room, because having the rest of our clan together in one place obviously makes Lazlo nervous. And he should be. Kash, Rowan, and Tiernan don't linger far from us, maybe even outside the door, and they feel like destroying the warlock for hurting me.

"It's for her safety. With my mark, she is off-limits. It will not only protect her from magical attacks, but it will also ensure no one can control her beast...except for me." Lazlo circles us, rubbing his palms together. "Shall we test it out now?"

"No!" Theo and Ambrose shout in unison. Ambrose steps between Lazlo and me, gathering magic. "It works, and you know it. You will not put her through any more anguish. She bowed and kept her end of the bargain. Now it's your turn. Retrieve her mate immediately."

Lazlo sighs and rubs the back of his neck. Annoyance rushes through me. He's not going to do it. He lied to me. I should've fucking known.

The room door crashes open with a blast of dragon fire, and the rest of my mates rush in, preparing to take Lazlo out. He shields himself from all of us, knowing exactly what crosses our minds.

"It will take me some time to accomplish, but don't worry. I assure you that I will get him. But first, I'm going to need a few things." Lazlo vanishes with his words, only to return with two figures.

I nearly lose my shit and transform into a dragon.

"Quillon will need an escort into the Mortal World to retrieve something for me. I'd like you to go with him." Lazlo whacks Quillon on the back, sending him shuffling forward.

"No fucking way," Kash snaps, his dragon fire lighting his eyes. "Nova can't stand him. There is no way you can make her help that asshole."

"Like fucking hell do I trust that bitch." Quillon folds his arms over his chest. "She'll fucking burn me alive. She's tried before."

"Because you made my mate bow!" Damn it. Quillon brings on a dozen aggravating memories to the front of my mind. He tried to make my life miserable. He forced me to dance for him. He wouldn't let Kash turn into his human form. Of course I'm going to burn him alive the second I have the chance. The only reason he's still alive is because of Kash.

"Delphia is who I need to go, but if you're that afraid of my little beast, perhaps you can take your own. I'm sure you have some catching up to do." Lazlo smirks, his eyes glittering with his blue magic. "It's imperative that we learn to work together. Plus, it'll give you time to negotiate your terms."

Hair sprouts on Quillon's cheeks as he unleashes his lycan form. "Our terms? Fuck our terms. I'm never letting go of Kash—"

I launch at Quillon and knock him off his feet. Lazlo doesn't intervene and allows me to get in four slaps across the bastard lycan's face before even clearing his throat. Growling, Quillon thrashes, unable to grab my hot wrists. Seeing him so frightened beneath me makes this so much better. He should be afraid of me. He's a damn snack and not the good kind.

"Rose! Rose, get her the fuck off me!" Quillon shouts, snapping his teeth, trying to bite me.

"Oh, no you fucking don't you murderess fairy." Green magic zaps through the air. Ambrose blocks Rose, who silently stalks forward.

"All right, firecracker. That's enough. I'll kill that bastard if he hurts you, and I want to protect Kash for you." Theo drags me off Quillon, restraining me in his muscular arms.

I try to blast fire at Quillon, but he rolls a few times, scrambling to get behind Rose as if the tiny, pink-haired fairy could truly protect him.

Ambrose claps his hands, sending magic through the air. Everyone apart from Lazlo freezes, including me, and Ambrose rubs his hand on the back of his neck. I scrunch my face, glowering. How could he spell us like this?

"Princess, please. I want to kill the asshole as much as you do, but right now, you're not thinking clearly. Allow me to help you ground your soul. Maddox's absence is affecting all of you." Cupping my cheeks with his hands, he bows in and kisses me, keeping his voice low. "I know the last thing you want to do is go with a monster who hurt you and your mates, but I don't think there is any way around it."

I puff a breath of air through my lips. "Why do you have to be so reasonable?"

Brushing his lips to my ear, he whispers, "Not always, but I can use this. I gathered the residual magic left behind in McKenzie's wake. I'd like to find your aunt. She could help us. She's obviously powerful enough to vanish without a trace. We can do that too. Lazlo can't use you if he can't find you. There is powerful magic that will break all ties, so he'd be unable to call you."

I blink a few times as his words sink in. I hadn't thought much about McKayla since she left us reeling with her unexpected revelation. "What do I need to do?"

"What Lazlo says. Quillon will take you to the Mortal World, and I can follow." Meeting my eyes, he stares at me as if he can see my soul. "Please have faith in the fates. I know it seems as if they're against you, but they're not. The fates allowed for you to claim two clans and punish those who've messed greatly with life's plan. Things will work out as they should. I know it."

If only I had the hope and faith he carries. But I don't. I can't leave my life or mates in the hands of some invisible force and hope it works out. The only ones I can put my faith and trust in are my guys. I can trust me.

"Okay," I finally whisper. "But it's not the fates I'll put our lives in the hands of. It's you, Ambrose. You and the rest of our clan."

He smiles and kisses me. "That's even better, my beautiful mate. Do you know why?"

I purse my lips in silence.

"Because you're unstoppable." He releases me from

his magical hold. "No power will ever truly contain you."

"I swear if you try anything stupid, I'll leave you stranded here and won't tell anyone where you are until it's too late for Maddox." Quillon keeps space between us, clenching his fingers into fists. His threat only makes me angrier. He's a stupid piece of shit for thinking these kinds of threats will keep me in line.

"If anything happens to my mate before we get back, I'll rip your limbs off and feed them to Kash. Ambrose will keep you alive, though I'll make sure you wish you weren't. Don't test me, lycan." I huff a breath of smoke, hoping to scare Quillon. "Now stop trying to be a tough-ass and keep moving. I want to get the fucking amulet and return to Magaelorum."

I still can't believe what Lazlo wants. Apparently, he and a couple other witch covens portal back and forth between Magaelorum and the Mortal World. It's how they bring lycans over, despite them being an abomination to the High Council because they were human born. And now, we're supposed to find some amulet that was in the hands of a couple of lycans before they disappeared—or died. I honestly don't care.

"The cabin should be around here somewhere." Quillon glowers at the world in front of us. "It wasn't too far from the unauthorized gateway. There was a coven of witches that lived nearby."

I want to ask him what happened to these witches and how the hell they managed to live in the Mortal World, but a strange energy hums through the air, drawing my attention. Kash snakes his arm around my waist and pulls me into his side. He's been silent since leaving Magaelorum, and I know it's because he's on guard. He feels responsible for not only my safety but also for accomplishing this task. Maddox depends on us to help Lazlo prepare.

"Don't touch anything. This whole area is spelled." Quillon glances at me and Kash over his shoulder. "What we're looking for is...shit. Damn it."

My eyes widen at the array of bones—which I'm nearly certain belong to humans—lining the walkway leading up to a boarded-up cabin. There are so many skulls, at least two dozen or more. Whatever happened at this murder cabin wasn't good. It probably lived up to every horror movie expectation of finding lycans living in a cabin in the woods.

"Careful, asshole," Kash says, speaking up for the first time. "I don't want to have to save your ass. Are you sure this place is even abandoned?"

"Do I look like I've fucking been here before?" Quillon bares his fangs with his comment.

I hold my hands up, stopping the two of them from arguing for once, and shift to look into Kash's eyes. "We can handle anything. It's why we're here. He knew Quillon was incapable of doing this alone."

"I can't fucking do it at all. You are the only one that can find the talisman and pick it up properly. It'll hurt me. It was created to help pass along the curse. If I handle it, I'll go on a biting spree. As much as you probably don't care, I do. I don't want to create a bunch more assholes for the High Council or anyone else to use." Quillon stops a few feet ahead of us and inhales a deep breath. "It's close. Why don't you look around?"

"You sound like you actually care," I mutter, tugging Kash along with me to walk up the stairs leading to the porch. The last place I want to go is inside this rundown cabin, but it's the most sensible place to look.

"I only fucking care about remaining useful." Quillon rubs his fingers on the back of his neck. "If more lycans come into existence, Lazlo could decide to break one to bend to his will like he has with you. I'm not cool with becoming useless."

And for a second, I thought he might've cared a little bit about someone who isn't the asshole he sees in the mirror daily.

"Unless you take a cure and turn mortal again...or have you forgotten our deal?" I shove past him, purposefully knocking him out of my way. "Then you can live out your life like you wanted to. I don't get why you suddenly changed."

"Changed? No. The only fucking reason I wanted a cure was to avoid Max. But now that Lazlo—" Quillon snaps his mouth shut, peering around. "Fuck. Do you hear that?"

A blast of green light rains through the air, startling me. Quillon turns to say something, but Ambrose shoots power at him, freezing him in his tracks. Kash strides to Quillon and flicks his cheek. I can't help the laugh bubbling from my throat. I wish I could shut up that ass so easily. Ambrose never fails to surprise me with what he does with his magic.

"I found your aunt's location. We have to hurry. The magic shielding her is strange. I've lost her twice just when I'd get a connection." Ambrose grabs my hand and turns to Kash. "I can only transport Nova. Will you be okay here?"

Kash doesn't look like he wants to stay behind, but he nods. "I'll find what Lazlo needs. Just keep Quillon frozen. If I have to hear him speak another word, I'll bury him or something."

He doesn't mean what he says, because it's impossible for him to act against Quillon, but I know he needs to feel in control. Throwing my arms around him, I kiss him, showering him with my affection.

"We won't be long. I don't even know if she'll want anything to do with me, but I have to try anyway." I squeeze him again. "Stay out of trouble."

He chuckles. "I should be telling you as much."

I peel myself away from Kash, knowing he will never be the first to let me go. Ambrose offers his hand to me, and I let him spin me to him and lift me up. He prefers carrying me during teleportation, and I don't mind it either. I'm certain that none of my mates would willingly let me walk if I allowed it.

The world brightens, blinding me. I grind my teeth through the feeling of falling, my stomach twisting with the blanket of magic around us. Something weird tickles my skin, the sensation blooming goosebumps over my body. I try to ignore it, but it's uncomfortable. I squirm in Ambrose's arms, rubbing my hands over my face and arms.

"I feel like ants crawl all over me," I say, scratching my fingers into my hair.

"It's the deterrence spell to keep people away." Ambrose chants a spell under his breath, setting a shield aglow around us. The sensation stops, and I puff a breath through my mouth.

Ambrose sets me on my feet as we stand in the middle of a forest with nothing around us. This can't be right. There aren't any signs of life. I link my fingers through Ambrose's and peer around. I can't see much but tree after tree.

"It's hidden, but I sense it." Ambrose strolls forward, taking me with him. "I don't think I can break through without proper preparation."

I sigh. "So it's here?"

He nods.

"Can they sense someone trying to find them?" I ask, squinting as if it'll help me see through the magic.

"I think so. It's why their shields have enhanced." Ambrose waves his hand in front of him and sends magic sparkling through the air. "I can take you back to Kash, and we'll try again later."

Annoyance burns within me, and I tug my hand from his and strut through his shield. Gathering dragon fire in my palms, I suppress the icky sensation coursing through me and shoot a stream of orange flames through the air.

"McKayla! I know you're here!" I shout, feeling my dragon awaken. Scales bloom on my arms as she tries to break free, but I keep her contained by releasing another burst of fire. "Come and face me! I've come a long way!"

A deep rumble of a growl echoes through the forest, and I freeze in my place at the sight of a huge lion stalking in my direction. Ambrose grabs the back of my shirt, yanking me away, but the lion launches and crashes into the both of us.

It roars in my face, blowing my hair back.

"Get off me, or I'll light your ass up. Don't test me." My words lace with a guttural noise, and smoke billows from my mouth. "I'm here for McKayla."

"The High Priestess is under the protection of the Fire Mountain Clan. You will have to face our army if you think you can take her from us, guard. The High Council will regret—"

Guard? He thinks I'm a dragon guard? "I'm not a guard or whatever. My name is Delphia Drakovich." It's hard for me to refer to myself by that name, but it would be the one anyone would know me as. "She raised me."

The lion tilts his head, his growl silencing as the lion gets off me and shifts into a man. He stands butt-ass na-ked, crossing his arms over his chest, and shifts his gaze from me and to Ambrose, standing in a weird haze behind me. Shit. It's like I managed to get through the shield, but he didn't.

"You're Delilah's girl," the man says, tightening his

mouth.

I nod my head. "Now, please. Let my mate in and take me to McKayla. It's important."

Blue portal light flashes through the air, and I jerk my attention to the female figure emerging. My aunt's face lines with her frown, and what I thought would be a happy reunion leaves me feeling like a cold wave put out the flames inside me. She studies me in silence, cautiously shuffling closer with red magic in her palms.

"Aunt McKayla," I say, my voice coming out hoarse as my tongue tries to stick to the roof of my mouth. "Please let my mate in. We don't have much time. What you did—fuck. Everything is messed up. Please."

McKayla shifts her gaze away from mine and to Ambrose. "Your mate? That is the warlock guard of the Darkonian Clan. You were fated for the Dreki Clan. I can't allow him in. He is in alliance with Franco Litendrake."

"Franco is dead," I snap, balling my hands into fists. "So is McKenzie and one of the High Council members. I killed them. Now fucking let Ambrose in. He's not going to hurt you. He helped me find you."

McKayla looks to the naked man in consideration. How can she remain so guarded? She raised me. She knows me. Why is she doing this? It's her fault that I had to deal with all of this mess. It was bad enough without having her start a damn war or whatever.

Stomping closer, I snatch McKayla by the shoulders, not backing down even with the lion-shifter's warning growl. "Please, Aunt McKayla. I'm in trouble. One of my mates is in trouble. The High Council sealed off the Dragon Lands from the rest of Magaelorum." It's so weird talking to her about all of this. I believed she was human my whole life. It should be her catching me up and not the other way around. "I had to bow to a warlock named Lazlo—"

"What?" McKayla sucks in a sharp breath, my words triggering a look of despair on her face. Her eyebrows knit together, her face frowning. Tears glass her eyes, and she rubs her hands over her cheeks. "You bowed to the Infinity Coven? Fuck, Delphia. Why would you do such a thing?"

"I just told you. One of my mates is in trouble. He took the blame for me killing High Council Woman Laveau when it was me. This whole situation is fucked up. I'm here because I need help."

McKayla waves her hand, sending red power bursting through the air. The shield shifts and brings Ambrose through, leaving him standing in shock, staring at the three of us.

"Where are the rest of your mates? You were never intended to come here after the fates guided you away from me, but it seems that it was important for us to cross paths again like I had with your mother and her mates. She entrusted me with your care for as long as you needed."

"Is that why you never looked for me after I ran away?" So many emotions crash through me. I haven't thought much about the months leading up to my decision, and I can't truly explain why I left when I did, but for one of the first times, I might actually believe in the fates, knowing that it wasn't a witch who led me away.

"Nova, I know you want to catch up, but we need to hurry. We can only stay away from the lycan for so long before the magic wears off. Lazlo will sense your absence." Ambrose takes my hand and looks at McKayla. "I'm sorry for our intrusion, but the magic here is unlike anything I've ever known. I need to know if there is a way to end a contract and hide my mate from a powerful warlock."

"She can stay here. The magic we use isn't easy, nor is it something you can handle on your own. The Fire Mountain Clan is bound together, and the only way to accomplish what you need is to join us. I'm afraid of what is in store if she leaves. Lazlo Infinity is a powerful warlock with a taste in collecting magical beings. He will destroy Delphia's humanity." McKayla holds out her arm to me. "I trust that you can find her mate and locate me again?"

My mouth falls agape. "I can't stay. Maddox is in Max."

McKayla tightens her lips. "You need to do this for yourself. It is a mate's duty—"

Fire burns in my palms. "Don't you fucking say that I should leave Maddox to the fates. They will execute him. Lazlo is helping me get him out in exchange to fight with him against the High Council."

Her lip trembles. "You'll die. You can't possibly face them. They've been ruling Magaelorum forever. Lazlo might think he can overthrow them, but it's not that simple. Please, Delphia. Stay."

I shake my head. "No. I can't. I'm getting my mate. I'm not letting him die on my behalf. My other mates are still trapped in the Dragon Lands too. It took Lazlo and the damn lycan who controls another one of my mates to even get here. I did not come all this way to go into hiding. I came to tell you that I took care of your fucking problem with your coven and the Litendrakes. I've come for Ambrose to get what he needs to help us all."

"I'm sorry, Delphia. It will take longer than a single visit to help your warlock learn the magic. It's taken centuries to perfect and comes at the highest price imaginable." Aunt McKayla grimaces with her words. "I wish there was more I could do. I can't risk the community of

Fire Mountain and leave. I help stabilize the magic. The High Council is already on alert, and I must protect those here. Let me protect you. We have over a thousand creatures here, and we live in unity. It's—"

"I already said no, McKayla," I snap, my anger getting the best of me. I don't know why I allowed Ambrose to even bother. "I'm needed elsewhere. I'll just—I'll handle it myself. I don't need you." I haven't needed her in years.

"I'm truly sorry, Delphia. I wish in my heart that things could've been different. I do. I wish I could've stopped you from leaving in the first place, but the fates ha—"

"Fuck the fates. They've been ruined. Everything has been ruined. This is why I've agreed to work with the fucker warlock. At least he isn't afraid to try to change things. If he helps me get my mate back, then my life will be what he makes it. It was already over anyway. I never had a chance." Tears burn my eyes, but I don't let them fall. I won't let her see me cry. Turning to Ambrose, I hold out my hand. "I'm sorry this was a waste of magic and time. Let's go get Kash and the dickhole. I think Lazlo might summon us soon."

"Delphia, wait." Aunt McKayla grabs my shoulder. Rubbing her fingers together, she creates a strange vial on her palm with a glowing lavender elixir. "Give this to the lycan. It's a cure for his curse. If he's not a lycan, Lazlo can't use him."

I don't know how to react, staring at the vial. A part of me wants to throw it at a tree and watch it shatter. Quillon is the last damn person who needs mercy and miracles from my aunt. It feels like a slap in the face that she offers help to the fucker in the first place. But another part of me is relieved and in shock. A cure? She fucking has a cure for lycanism? That means that Quillon will have to free Kash. He will finally have his freedom instead of being enslaved to that bastard.

"Thank you, High Priestess," Ambrose says, taking the vial from me to tuck it away. "I will not consider this a rejection of help. I understand the purpose you feel you must follow as I follow the fates with mine. But do know, I have faith in Delphia, and we will be back. I do hope you will help us when we do."

Aunt McKayla slowly nods her head. Bringing her hand to Ambrose's head, she whispers a spell. "I've given you what you need to return. Blessed be the fates, dragon guard."

Ambrose picks me up. "Blessed be."

CHAPTER 17

The Cure

"JUST STAY NEARBY. IF YOU all are too close, he'll be even more of a dick." I wring my hands together, rolling the vile between my palms. "He thinks you'll kill him the moment he takes it, so you need to only intervene if necessary. I'm going to shove it down his throat if I have to."

"Come on, kitten. I'll restrain him and Row can pry his mouth open. We'll just choke him with it. He's already said he changed his mind. Playing nice won't get us anywhere." Kash bounces on the balls of his feet.

"He's right, Delphia. You'll just be wasting your time. We don't know when Ambrose and Lazlo will return, so the faster we proceed, the better it'll be. I'm sure Lazlo doesn't want to lose his easy access to the Mortal World. The High Council is up in arms everywhere." Theo massages his fingers into my shoulders. "You don't even have to face him. Why don't you come with me to my suite?"

"Now isn't the time to fuck, Theo," I say, tipping my head back to smack it against his chest. "It's too hard to control myself around all of you, and I need to keep a clear head. Keep those cocks away from me for the next day until we get Maddox."

"Damn," Tiernan says, raising an eyebrow. "Do you think having us distract you is better? Ambrose has opened communication with Max. We will know if anything changes with Maddox."

"He'd be furious if he knew we weren't taking care of your needs," Rowan adds, sneaking between Tiernan and me to hug me. "You know how he gets."

Damn them and their attempts to reason with me.

"We can survive a day or two. I'm starting to think that it's all you ever want to do with me." I nudge Rowan with my hands, getting him to walk backward until I can dodge around him.

"Because it is for me, Delphia." Theo's eyes flash with his dragon fire.

I sigh and keep the four of them back. "Well, we need to find some new hobbies we can do when all of this is behind us. Go on dates. Get to know each other outside of our bodies and souls. I don't even know your favorite color."

Theo play-growls. "That's not important—"

Tiernan whacks him in the stomach. "The same emerald as your eyes, Nova. For both of us. If you let the Drekis handle the lycan, I'll tell you anything you want. Just...let us take care of you."

His eagerness nearly makes me give in, but I hear Quillon yell for Rose to get out of his room. Pink magic sparkles through the crack, and I press my lips together, listening and waiting for a moment. I think he just got out of the shower, and I don't exactly want to knock on the door only to have him answer naked.

"It's okay to change your mind, kitten," Kash says, speaking over the quiet settling between us. "You don't have to always do everything, you know."

I twist and kiss him, getting him to stop trying to persuade me out of this. It has to be me. Quillon will fight like a dirty bastard and use his claws against my mates if they storm the room. As awful as Quillon is, I know he has a vulnerable side. He also has a thing for me—or did—before he realized that there is no way in hell I'd ever be with him. I just hope that I can fool him long enough. Kash needs his freewill.

"Give me five minutes and wait here. If any of you make a sound—" I snap my mouth shut and sigh. "I'm handling it. No more arguing. Now back your sexy asses up and stay out of view."

Reluctantly, my mates shuffle back and out of the way of the door, ensuring that Quillon won't see any of them and automatically send me away. I peek at them one more time and hold my index finger to my lips. I listen to Quillon in his room, shuffling around and doing something I can't decipher. Soft music hums, and I use the sultry beat to put on my performance smile. I'll fake it until I shove the cure in his throat.

"Quillon?" I say, calling his name as I knock on the door. "Can we talk?"

"The door's unlocked, Red. It better just be you. I've dealt with enough dicks today. I don't want to see any more." Quillon's voice rumbles through the door.

I turn the knob and crack open the door. Sucking in a breath, I gather my nerve and stroll in, searching the spacious suite until...this mother-fucking bastard.

I tip my head back and stare at the ceiling. "A little

warning would've been nice, asshole."

Quillon chuckles, getting a kick out of my reaction as he lies naked on his bed with his damn cock in his hand. He fucking did this on purpose, wanting to get a rise out of me. I smother the fire burning in my palms and force my feet to move forward. I don't want him getting any satisfaction from messing with me. It seems like he's turned it into his sole purpose in life.

"And miss seeing the look on your face? Come on, Red. Your pussy has to be fucking tired of getting stretched and pounded the hell out of. Haven't you ever thought that it might be nice to remember what a little normalcy is like?" Quillon wags his eyebrows, trying to get me to watch him stroke his little nub. He's so small look-ing, especially with his nest of pubes that make him look like a bird abandoned his worm in search of a snake else-where.

"Nothing about that thing is normal." I close my thumb and index finger together, showing only an inch of space.

"It can be if you give it a little tug. Maybe you'll put me in a good enough mood that I won't think of all the ways I could torture you and your mate when Lazlo finally finishes this bullshit with the High Council." He arches his hips like it'll help him look bigger, but it really is a lost cause.

"You know what? Fine. I'll see if I can stretch it out." I stride forward, struggling to maintain my composure as he realizes the huge fucking mistake he made with his pervy suggestion. "I can't promise it'll put you in a good mood. It might take a lot of strength to get it to stick."

Flopping over, Quillon rolls himself in his blanket, finally covering up. Laughter bursts from my mouth, and I sit on the edge of his bed. He hops up and puts space between us. I've never wanted to be close to Quillon, but now? I want to do so just to teach him what it's like to live in fear and be uncomfortable. He needs to learn that I'm no longer playing his games, nor will I just keep my mouth shut. If he wants to threaten me to receive sexual acts, I'll make it so he thinks twice about ever trying to do so again.

"What's wrong, dickhead? I thought you wanted me to jerk your cock. And you think I'm the fucking tease." I raise my eyebrow and clench my fist, pumping my hand in front of me in short bursts just to show him how I'd just have to shake my hand a little.

"You're a psycho, Red. I don't trust my dick anywhere near you." Quillon clutches his blankets around him, peering past me like he considers rushing to the door.

"You act as if it doesn't just fall off or get sucked in or

whatever when you turn into my future lycan rug." I give him a long once-over, watching him squirm. "But you know what? It doesn't have to be that way."

Quillon narrows his eyes, meeting my stare with a glower. He doesn't respond right away and shuffles back toward his closet and blindly grabs a pair of pants from the small shelf. Instead of looking away, I train my eyes on him as he drops his towel, clearly trying to get me to break. But I've seen him enough that despite being repulsed, I'm not threatened. All I feel is annoyance and pity.

"What do you mean?" he asks, his nerves clear because of his shaking hands as he pulls his pants up. "Be what way?"

"I came across a way for you to keep that bird food." I twirl my finger, motioning to what looks like a lump under his pants. Either I've gotten so used to gigantic cocks, or I swear he's gotten smaller. I recall thinking he was average, but maybe it was all in my head.

His jaw tightens as he studies me. It doesn't dawn on him that I'm talking about a cure, so I don't push it as much. Maybe I need to convince him otherwise. Trick him. If I'm not against murder to save my mates, I'm damn well not against lying.

"It'll also help you grow. Consider it a gift." I slide off

his bed and tug the vial out of my pocket. "Who knows, maybe I'll want to test it out if it works." I hate myself a little for saying the words...because ugh, hell no.

But Quillon loves the thought, his body hardening at my suggestion.

Strolling closer, I circle him, drawing my finger across his hairy chest. He tenses, but not because he's scared. He's confused and curious. A part of him wants to know what my plan is regardless of how much he knows I hate him.

"I'm not against hate sex. I found it fun with Theo. I just...I have desires that require a little more to work with." I shake the vial in front of him. "What do you say? Want to find out? I'll even wait."

Swaying my hips, I dip low until my knees touch the floor. He groans under his breath as I act as if I'm ready to give him a blow job. He clenches and unclenches his fingers, the sinewy veins winding up his muscles pulsing. It takes everything in me to keep my eyes on him as his head takes him into fantasy land, but I know I can't back down. If I do, my plan won't work. He'll get his good senses back, and if he does, I know he won't take the cure. He's already said as much.

"Nova," he murmurs, licking his bottom lip before sucking it into his mouth. "What kind of game are you playing? I don't fucking mind, but I need to know. You want something from me. I can tell."

I break my gaze from his and reach out, pinching my fingers into his hip. "I've told you already."

"Prove it." He wags his eyebrows. A cocky bastard smile creeps on his face, sending my chest tightening. Fuck.

I can't do this. I've already taken it too far.

The stubborn part of me wants to push just a little more. I can't have him think that he beat me at my game. So I guess I'm going to touch his cock...in the only way I'll ever want to.

Surprising the hell out of Quillon, I hook my fingers to the waistband of his athletic pants and yank them down. My skin crawls, my hand begging me to change my mind. It looks like it'll feel like an uncooked mini-hot dog or maybe a limp mozzarella stick that was left out of the fridge. Ugh.

He intakes a breath and has the nerve to touch my hair. "Fuck, I've thought about this over and over again."

I bat my eyelashes. "Me too."

Swinging my arm, I punch him in his junk hard enough to knock him back. Quillon growls with his yell as he bows forward to clutch himself. I knock my hand to the back of his knee, buckling his leg, and he falls forward.

His bare ass hangs out of his pants, and he's too stunned to react. I tackle him, using the strength of my thighs to pin his arms at his sides. He freezes in confusion like he's unsure what's going on.

I smile and bite my lip, far too satisfied to be in this position with Quillon. "Come on, baby. I like it rough. Don't let me down." My sickly-sweet voice turns his gaze heavy with lust. The fucker actually believes this is part of some sort of fantasy. "Now open up. I need you to hurry the fuck up."

Quillon purrs like a damn cat and drops his gaze down my body like he expects me to burn my own clothes off and sit on his jerk face. He lies placidly beneath me, his chest rising and falling with his panting.

"Hurry? No, Red. I'm going to take my damn time with you." He flicks his tongue out as if his sloppy gesture will get me excited. "I'll transform a bit and really make you scream my name." His facial features shift as hair sprouts from his cheeks, and his nose elongates into a snout. A long, flat tongue curls from his mouth like a dog's, and he licks my pants in an attempt to show off his freaky skill. I might be impressed if I didn't ride my mates' faces all the time. Dragon tongues, even in mortal form, have a lot to offer.

I hum under my breath and hold up the vial, shaking

its contents. "After you take this, so we can have fun together."

Quillon's eyes narrow on the potion, and I tighten my legs, preparing to shove it down his throat. "Each other? No. I want those fucking dragons to know what it's like to have a lowly lycan make their girl—"

I slap him across the face and shove my hand to his forehead. "You're taking this even if I have to force it down your throat."

Snarling, he clenches his teeth together and shakes his head. "Get off!" he yells through his teeth.

My hair hangs down, sweeping with my movements. "Not until you take this!"

His eyes reflect in the light, his body growling as he shifts completely. "You're fucking insane, Nova! What the hell is that? I'm not taking shit from you."

"Like hell, you aren't. I wanted this to be easy, but I know you. If I told you what this was, you'd refuse." I pop the little cork off and pinch the top of his snout, sneaking my fingers under his slimy lips. I'll pry his mouth open if I have to. "It won't kill you, so just open up."

His eyes widen, and he thrashes, breaking out of my grip. "Get that shit away from me! I told you I changed my mind about the cure. I'm not taking it."

"Then you're going to fucking let Kash go! I'm not

doing this shit anymore with your bitch-ass." I punch him in the side of his snout as my anger gets the best of me.

"You'll kill me! I'm not losing my protection." He snarls, catapulting upright to land on his feet.

I hold on tight and sink my nails into the top of his snout. "I'll take you to the damn brink of death now if you don't. Be a good fucking boy and take the damn cure. I'm not allowing you to have control over Kash anymore. We had a deal, so just fucking take it or I'll—"

Blue light sparkles through the air with Lazlo's portal magic. I cling onto Quillon in his beast form as he spins me around. It's now that I realize his bedroom door hangs ajar, and my mates stand in the hall, watching me. They don't intervene, but I can feel how much they want to. I think Lazlo's arrival is the only thing stopping them. I don't give a fuck, though. He said I could make Quillon take it, so I am.

"My beast, release the lycan," Lazlo says, his voice calm.

I whip my head in his direction, my whole body zinging. My hands automatically release Quillon, and I fly back with a screech. Two muscular arms catch me. Ambrose sends green magic sparkling around us, stopping Quillon from attacking me. He snarls with his silent threat. Lazlo puts his hand on his hairy shoulder and gets his attention. Quillon shakes his body like a wet dog and transforms back into his human self.

"She has a cure!" he shouts, pointing at me. "Take it from her. I don't want it."

Lazlo's eyebrows shoot up on his forehead. Giving me a once-over, he studies me like he can figure out exactly where the hell I got a cure for lycanism. I half-expect him to demand me to share the information, but all he does is hold out his hand.

"Be a good beast and give it to me. I'll hold onto it until Quillon is ready to take it. Now isn't a good time for him to return to the Mortal World." Lazlo wiggles his fingers. "We have too much to do."

I glower. "But you said—"

"Give me the cure." Blue electricity crackles in his eyes. "Now."

My body reacts to his command. Rapping against my ribcage, my heart threatens to escape me. I wiggle in Ambrose's arms, trying to escape, but he refuses to let me go. Kash growls from behind me, his anger growing enough to entangle with mine.

"I don't think so. I put in a great amount of effort and a sacrifice to create such an elixir. I'll not be entrusting it in your care." Ambrose snatches the vial from my fingers, and it vanishes in a flash of his green magic.

Lazlo narrows his eyes, pursing his lips. The hairs on my arms stand on end, and I brace for them to start a magical fight with me in the middle. If a strange ringing noise didn't echo through the room, I might've had to transform into my dragon to just put space between the two warlocks. McKayla was right about Lazlo. Even with my mates by my side, he is dangerous. His control over me scares me.

I'm afraid I've made a far greater mistake than I realized.

Lazlo jerks his head back and stares at the ceiling. "It seems things have changed, and the High Council is proceeding with Maddox's execution sooner than later. I just got word from my source."

My blood cools as the warmth of my anger leaves me.

Lazlo holds out his hand. "Come on, my beast. Let's prepare. We have a lot of work to do."

CHAPTER 18

Submit to the Monster

"YOU CAN'T JUST TAKE HER alone." Ambrose crosses his arms over his chest. "She needs her mates to stand by her. This is dangerous. You could get her killed."

"It'll be far more dangerous to try to conceal a whole dragon clan, even with you. Where we're going, the magic is far more powerful than you realize. The High Council is gathering to confirm Maddox's charges and discuss how to proceed with his execution. With the way the Dragon

Lands are currently facing unrest, they will make sure their power is clear. Without Laveau, they've asked three others, including myself, to join them." Lazlo flashes his elongated fangs at Ambrose, trying to threaten him to stay back. "You need to wait for us at Max. That is where it will occur. Can you handle that?"

Ambrose flares his nostrils. "Of course, I can. I just h—"

Locking his fingers to my shoulders, Lazlo sinks his sharp nails into my skin, pulling me to him. My stomach flops as he casts a teleportation spell, not giving Ambrose a chance to argue. My ears ring with the hum of my mates' growls, but they fade just as quickly as the rest of the world. I stiffen at the icky sensation of magic crawling over my skin. It feels like it had when I found McKayla, and it repulses me in a way that makes me rip away from Lazlo.

"Vi tien ala tu go te," Lazlo chants, his voice humming around me. Heat encircles my neck, and I gasp as the invisible collar burns and tightens around my throat.

I try to tug at it, but pain smolders my fingers. I can't force words out to even scream, and Lazlo swings his hand, sending me crashing into a stone wall. Agony swells through my back, and tears sting my eyes. What the fuck is he doing?

Lazlo yanks his invisible chain and drags me a foot closer, only to throw me back and pin me to the wall in his magic. Fear tightens my chest. Stomping forward, he grows in height, trying to intimidate me.

It works.

"Listen, Delphia. I want you to know your place. You have a tendency to disobey, and it could get us both killed. I will not have everything fall apart because of your hot temper." He shocks me with a burst of magic. "Do I make myself clear? You will be concealed with a spell during an important discussion. The sensitive magic can detect almost anything, so no talking or moving. You will stand where I leave you. If we're caught, you'll be the one who ends up dead, not me."

My mind whirls with his words. Fear seizes me tighter, and I say a prayer to the universe. Aunt McKayla might've been right. I might die because of him. Because of this, I know I have to prepare for anything. I will not lose Maddox, nor will I lose my own life. If it means I remain obedient and follow Lazlo's command, then I guess I'll be his good beast...until I no longer need him. Then I can devour him.

"Now stay close. The High Council is waiting." Lazlo releases my collar and drops me to the floor.

I gasp and clutch my neck, scrambling from the

ground to follow behind him into a dark tunnel. I have no idea where we are, but magic lingers everywhere. Whatever spell Lazlo used on me makes the tunnel glow with power in a blend of every color. The rainbow light buzzes and hums against me but doesn't touch me. The blue shield keeps a centimeter of space around me.

Lazlo stops when the tunnel dead-ends, and he raises his hands and presses them to the rock wall. Chanting a spell, he prods it with his magic until it cracks and fissures and crumbles into a doorway. I hesitate, staring at the cloaked figures standing around an altar. Golden thread glitters in strange symbols within the dark fabric. The four figures turn their attention in our direction, and I freeze in my spot. Lazlo claps his hands, gathering magic around us until he stands before me in a cloak similar to what the High Council wears. With a twitch of his fingers, he drags me behind him and leaves me freaked the hell out against the wall behind his empty seat.

Two more figures appear in the magical room and greet the High Council members with bows. They adorn their bodies in dark robes and join the circle around the altar. I slow my breathing, afraid if I gasp or something, I'll get noticed. It's strange to watch the group of witches gather in silence without even looking at me.

"Blessed be the fates, we welcome you into our chambers. The times have been unfortunate, but it is in your stars to guide us on the path to fruition among the creature lands of Magaelorum." The female voice rings through the air, and the woman at the head of the altar flicks her fingers and lights dozens of candles through the room. "Blessed fates, we have heeded to your warning and have protected our home from the beasts of fire and rage until we have the strength of completing our circle of power once more."

"Tonight, we gather the three most powerful coven leaders to join our ranks in guiding the High Council in the direction to bring peace and power, stabilizing the magic we've spent millennia after millennia ensuring remains strong." Pulling his hood back, an old warlock peers at the other members of their circle. Deep wrinkles cut across his aged face, and I'm nearly certain the guy is beyond ancient. He's probably seen the millennia he claims to have filled with magic.

"High Priest Infinity, High Priestess Shadows, and High Priestess Gildedrod, please join us for the ceremonial prayer to begin our meeting." Another woman tugs her hood down, revealing her ageless face and dark complexion with bright red eyes. She must spell her features unlike the old man, because even though she looks young, her presence screams old as hell.

The witches hold their hands up and gather magic in their palms—blue, green, red, silver, gold, purple, and strangely black. Their chants fill the air, the words indecipherable yet melodic like a song. Magic swirls from their palms, blending and moving like a rainbow show of electricity dancing to the rhythm of their prayer. I've never seen anything like it before, the sight terrifying yet fascinating, helping me remain utterly still. It baffles me how this small group of witches has such great control over all of Magaelorum.

From what I've gathered just from being in Max, there are territories for every creature imaginable—beyond the Dragon Lands, there is a place for vampires, mermaids, fae, shifters, witches, and who the fuck knows what else. So where are they? Why don't any of them get a say? I know the dragon clans have their leaders. Why doesn't everyone get a voice?

I never really thought much about that question until this moment. And now? Fuck. I need to chill. I'm afraid my inner beast will rouse and awaken, set off by my anger.

"Blessed be the fates, always in our favor," the witch at the head of the altar says, lowering her hood finally.

I nearly slam my back into the wall. I thought the old man looked old, but this woman could very well have been around for thousands of years, her skin tight against her bony face with black eyes sunken into her skull.

"Blessed be," the rest of the witches say in unison, following the old woman's lead in summoning chairs to sit around the altar table, facing one another.

"First thing on our agenda tonight is to discuss the unrest in the Dragon Lands and how to proceed with the Drakovich queen. As you all know, she was never intended to rise to such power, nor was she supposed to entangle her soul with the Dreki and Darkonian Clans. They were never intended to have an alliance," the old warlock says, leaning his elbows on the table.

"The answer is simple, High Priest Helio. We bring her back to Max in her mate's place. We all know she was responsible for the death of Laveau, and if the word were to get out that we allowed her mate to take her place, the Laveau Coven might retaliate for not giving them the opportunity to decide the Drakovich female's fate." This comes from the beautiful dark-skinned witch with red eyes. She slowly turns her attention to each of the witches to see their reaction. "Maddox Dreki and his dragon clan have served us well until someone tampered with the arrangements and let the fates free."

"You want to execute a female dragon before she has reared offspring? What a preposterous thought. Their species numbers have already dwindled significantly after the

Fire Battles, and they never could get them up again. That's why we allowed Maddox to take her place." The fourth witch, one who hasn't spoken except to chant, stands up from her seat. "The unrest is bad enough."

"Do not forget what happened with the wolves of Lulupoterra. We lost a significant amount of power because of the extinction of their species. Relying on lycans is bad enough. I refuse to stand by and lose the power that comes with dragon fire," High Priest Helio says.

Wolves of Lulupoterra? Shit. Whatever happened to them sounds bad.

"I have to agree." Lazlo straightens his shoulders, meeting the gazes of the High Council members. "Which is why I also must request that you don't execute Maddox Dreki. It would be a waste of significant power."

My heartbeat picks up speed as Lazlo mentions my mate.

"I think it'll better suit our needs to collar and contain him. As you know, I have a—"

The creepy old woman waves her hand, cutting Lazlo off. "No. If we don't serve justice for High Priestess Laveau, it'll put the rest of us at risk. A point must be made, and executing him for the crimes will make an example that even those loyal to our cause aren't safe from consequences."

"Collaring him is a better example to make. You're letting the old ways influence you, and those times are long gone." Lazlo grows taller in his seat, showing off his monstrous façade. Even with fangs and an elongated nose, he doesn't compare to the skeleton witch.

She remains unfazed. Actually, they all do. It freaks me out a bit, because if the High Council isn't afraid of Lazlo, why should I believe we can even accomplish what he wants? Fuck.

The longer I stand here, the more anxious I become. It feels as if ants crawl up my legs, trying to force me into moving and breaking the spell keeping me hidden.

"Do not speak as if you are a permanent member of the High Council yet, High Priest Infinity." High Priest Helio gathers magic between his hands, the black color managing to glow despite its darkness. He threatens Lazlo by matching him in height, but where fangs should be in a monstrous façade remains a gaping mouth with only gums. I'm starting to believe these witches should've died long ago, and the only reason they remain is because of their magic—and not good magic. I can feel the darkness in the air. "Your invitation can be revoked."

"Then revoke it. Prove that you don't need me and find out what happens when your strength wavers. To assume we'd all get in line and do as you suggest is far beyond the scope of reason. You've paved a path far too treacherous to navigate alone, and your poor decisions are why we're in this situation in the first place. Had you listened to me to begin with, you'd have never had such difficulties with the dragons. They are a simple species and easily manageable when content." Lazlo turns and peers at me from over his shoulder. "Keep loose collars, open skies, and don't break up clans. Instead, learn how to use them, and we'd have a great asset on our side." Is that what he's doing with me? He went from threatening to giving in to my wants and desires but only after cornering me. Is this why Lazlo claimed to be a witness of Laveau's death?

Whatever his reasons are, all I know is that I don't like them. I hate that he's talking about keeping control of my entire species, which extends long past the leash he hooks on the collar around my throat. He's not only looking to overthrow the High Council. He wants to steal the remaining power he craves.

"It works rather well for lycans as well, but I find the mortal beasts better alone unlike the dragons, who work best as a clan." Lazlo eyes me from his spot again, stretching his arms over his head to make it look as if he grows bored. "I can prove it."

I stiffen, holding my breath. I expect him to reveal that I'm in their chambers, but he doesn't. All he does is send a pulse of power through me, sending my skin buzzing. Why he does it? I think he's trying to make sure the collar remains in place.

"Give me Maddox, and I'll have the Dragon Lands tamed and ready to serve." Lazlo peers around at the silent High Council and the other two guest witches.

No one responds to him, and I think the main four council members communicate telepathically as magic zaps back and forth between them. I slow my breathing, hoping it helps control my racing heart. Lazlo claims he'll collar Maddox if they release him. All I can hope is that he's not serious. I never discussed how he'd get my mate, only that he would. And damn it. If that's the case, and Lazlo does what he says he will...he's dead. They all are. I will not be used like this. I won't.

"You make a fair point, High Priest Infinity," the skeleton witch says, remaining expressionless.

One of the guest witches stands up and fists her hands. "What? You can't be serious. He's not even on the council, and you're suggesting he can claim an entire territory with some of the strongest beasts? Do you how dangerous that is? Lazlo is known to—"

"Silence, High Priestess Shadow!" the old man snaps, summoning power and blasting it at her.

"Wait, High Priest. I'd love to hear what she has to

say about High Priest Infinity," the skeleton witch says. She flicks her fingers, undoing the spell that froze High Priestess Shadow.

Lazlo growls and slams his hands on the altar, shaking the table. Candles flicker, and magic ripples across his skin. His back straightens with his obvious anger, and I dig my nails into my palms, bracing for the shitshow unfolding to turn into a fight.

This could be it.

Lazlo might call upon me to stand up with him and without even returning Maddox to me.

"This is ridiculous! I will not stand here and wait for Cassandra to try and sully my good standing when she should question her own worth." Lazlo growls and leans forward, threatening the council with a glower.

High Priestess Shadow—Cassandra—throws her hands out and shocks him with an orb of magic. "Try and sully? Lazlo, you've gone—"

"Enough!" Flinging out his hands, High Priest Helio blasts magic through the room, knocking everyone out of their seats.

Pain shocks me, stealing my breath, and I slam into the wall. Sparks shoot from my skin as the magic breaks Lazlo's spell on me. I drop to the floor, my legs giving out. The witches summon magic, preparing to fight each other.

The skeleton witch jerks her head and glowers at me.

"The Drakovich female!" she yells, summoning glittering power in her palms. "Who brought her in here?"

Shit. Shit. Shit.

My dragon awakens, triggered by my fear and need to survive. With the way the High Council looks at me, I feel as if they'll kill me at any minute.

"Tell me!" the witch hollers. "Who brought the beast?"

No one responds.

Lazlo warned me that if it came down to him or me, I would be the one not making it out of here alive.

Fire bursts in my palms.

The skeleton witch shouts a spell. She attacks.

CHAPTER 19

High Council

"STOP, HIGH PRIESTESS ZELKI! DON'T hurt her!" The woman with red eyes summons a wall of magic and blocks the skeleton witch from me.

I shield myself with fire, my mind and body on edge, and my dragon begging to be unleashed.

"Back down now, Lana. I will not ask again." High Priestess Zelki bares her jagged teeth and calls more magic to her palms.

Thrusting it around the room, she blasts everyone back and clears a path for herself. She strides in my direction, her eyes glowing with silver energy. I try to back up even more, but the wall blocks me. I can't do anything but stand tall and not back down.

"Stay back! I don't want to hurt you," I say, calling upon my dragon fire, growing the orbs in my hands until the world glows with firelight instead of magic. "I just want my mate."

The witch ignores me and shouts, "Vi te lon attatita!"

My body stretches out as I float and stick to the wall. Fire shoots out at my sides from my hands, scorching across the floor. I try to fight and move, but I can't do anything. High Priestess Zelki chants her spell again, and agony tightens my muscles. It feels as if she's going to rip me apart with her magic.

"Stop!" Lana, the dark-skinned witch, shouts. "We need her!"

"We need peace and submission. She's untamable and out of control like her parents. She puts all of Magaelorum at risk." High Priestess Zelki leers at me, a strange look on her face. Is she satisfied with her power over me? Fuck yeah. Will it last? I'll eat her alive to stop it.

"That's why we'll cage her," High Priest Helio mutters.

She scowls. "No. This ends here. Her mate will be next."

My eyes widen, and I open and close my mouth, trying to speak. Fear clenches my chest. Flicking my gaze to Lazlo, I try to beg him for help with my eyes, but he turns his face away. None of the other witches do anything to stop High Priestess Zelki, choosing not to argue with her any longer.

The skeleton witch closes the space completely and grows in height, meeting my gaze. A wicked smile curls her lips, and she reaches out and caresses her fingers along my jaw and works her way down my neck and to my clavicle.

"Prepare a heart cage. We will not let her go to complete waste." An athame materializes in the skeleton witch's hand, and she aims it at my heart.

Fire smolders through my body. Energy zings over my skin, and static lifts my hair away. I can't believe this is happening all over again. What is it about a dragon's heart that draws witches to wanting it? What kind of power does it bring?

The second High Priestess Zelki sinks the tip of her athame into my skin, my dragon roars inside me. Fire explodes from my body, lighting the woman aglow. Flashes of green magic zap through the room. A spell whirls through my mind, and I realize that Ambrose remains linked to me. He's using magic to counteract whatever the High Council plans. I scream in anger, blowing out a breath of fire across the room. High Priestess Zelki manages to use a shield to protect herself, but Lana blasts her in the side, taking advantage of her distraction.

"Bi lu tono vienita!" Lazlo's voice rings through the air, and the collar on my neck illuminates with his magic. I almost don't believe it. He uses his power and proves that it was him who brought me. "Delphia, settle down. Do not harm the High Council, my pet."

"Your pet?" High Priestess Zelki whips around and gathers magic in her hands, turning her anger on Lazlo. "This was your doing?"

"Your ways are far too outdated. Of course it was my doing." Lazlo deflects her magic with a sweep of his fingers. "I knew what it would take to bring peace to the dragons, and I've put things in order."

"You traitor! You've turned against us," High Priest Helio snaps, his face morphing with his anger. Sharp lines deepen across his wrinkly face, and he strides toward Lazlo, gathering magic. "You had no right to enter the Dragon Lands before things were discussed. I should—"

"Cu vi fio no la vientita!" Lazlo shouts, yanking the leash of my collar and dragging me to him. "Delphia, og eht erif raor!"

My body hums with energy, and fire shoots from my hands, flooding the room in glowing flames. The witches scatter and draw their shields, caught off guard at the intense magic-laced dragon fire coursing through me.

"I'm going to teleport you to the prison yard. Get to Maddox." Lazlo shouts another spell, growing the wall of flames between us and the council. "Get ready. They will follow. I'll keep them back."

I tense, my whole body yearning to transform into my most powerful form. If the room wasn't so small, I'm sure Lazlo would make me do it now.

"Ta vi lota for wit ri!" Lazlo shouts his spell, and bright blue light erupts before me. Shoving his hand into my back, he knocks me forward and into the portal.

I flail my arms as the world spins and he releases me. He's purposely separating us. My stomach flips, and my head pounds with my heartbeat. The bright light dissipates, leaving my vision shadowy. The hard floor turns soft, and the scent of dirt fills my nostrils. I rub my eyes and spin around, spotting dozens of figures loitering in the unfortunately familiar prison yard. The dark sky overhead reminds me that this isn't the time for shifters. The prison yard will have the vampires and witches running about. If they spot me, they will attack. I know it.

I don't get a chance to think about anything, because rainbow light flashes through the air. Lazlo shoots power at the High Council, and people scream. I kick my ass into gear, jogging forward, afraid that the witches will abandon Lazlo and go after me.

Fire billows from my hands, clearing a path before me. Inmates rush to get out of my way, and I thank the fates that I still have my power here. It gives me the strength to keep moving and to not look behind me. The only thing I need to do is get to Maddox. If I can get to him, I can protect him. I can keep him safe from the High Council and the rest of the prison until the rest of our clan comes.

My shoes sink into the damp dirt of the prison yard, and I head in the direction of the pits. I would transform into my dragon if I wasn't worried about the witches, because damn it. My legs don't seem like they can carry me fast enough. My soul screams, my whole body sensing Maddox nearby. One minute. That's all it's going to take me to reach him. One minute, and he can help me control my dragon and remind me of everything he taught me about keeping each other safe. I never thought I'd look forward to him threatening me with immense pleasure as a reward or getting smacked in the ass with his baton if I do something dangerous.

"Maddox! Maddox! Which pit are you in?" I shout, afraid of drawing attention but not terrified enough not to find him as quickly as I can. I know the guards have been keeping him in the pits because of how dirty he was when I saw him in the Visitation Center. "Maddox!"

"The traitor was taken from his pit a moment ago," a soft, feminine voice says, drawing my attention to my right. My heart stalls at her words, threatening to slip to my feet. "He's been called for execution."

I don't have time for this bullshit, but I also don't have time to look either. I groan and spin on my feet, glancing into three empty pits before finding a woman with dark hair staring at me through her grate.

"Where would they take him?" I ask, glowering down at her, my dragon fire swelling in my palms.

"The courtroom is usually where, but I heard Council Woman Zelki demand a private execution." Blue magic flickers in the witch's eyes, but it's only the residual effect of it lingering.

I swear under my breath. "How do I find them?"

"Use your beast. She'll lead your way." The witch waves her fingers. "Hurry. I feel the High Council preparing to lockdown."

"What is your name? I'd like to thank you later," I say, searching the yard.

"Heather."

Using my dragon strength, I flip her grate covering from the pit, sending it flying. The soft-spoken witch backs up, watching me from below as I unleash my dragon. My vision changes as I grow in height and expand my wings. Using my tail, I help her out of the pit, and she runs in the other direction, searching for shelter.

Magic zaps through the air, and I catch sight of High Priestess Shadow as she tries to hook a magic chain to the collar Lazlo controls. Opening my mouth, I breathe a breath of fire, sending her tumbling away as it hits her shield.

"Maddox!" I scream, my dragon roaring with my mental call to my mate. "Maddox, where are you?"

"Delphia." His soft voice trickles into my mind, igniting my whole body in fiery relief. "They're taking me to the outlands. Do you remember where my living quarters were before? Hurry."

Expanding my wings, I launch into the air, blowing another breath of fire at the prison yard, hoping it distracts the remaining High Council members long enough for Lazlo to attack. I soar low, avoiding the building until I get a clear view of the mountain with the cave Maddox lived in, choosing to stay in his dragon form when he was a CO during his time off.

Magic sparkles through the air below, drawing my attention away from the mountain. My dragon screeches at the sight of two COs shoving Maddox into the dirt. Swinging their batons, they beat him down and knock him onto his stomach. I scream again, sending a wave of dragon fire through the air so brightly it turns the world light as if I've brought the sun with me.

A huge wall of magic shoots up around the guards with Maddox, shielding them from my fire. Fury rushes through me. I spot the skeleton witch materialize a few feet away from them, her power as hot and vicious as mine as she thrusts her arms up, trying to attack me.

"Nogard it vu!" she shouts.

I freefall out of the way of her blast, nosediving and blowing another breath of fire. Her light collides with my fire, and a boom echoes through the world. A crack splits the ground, breaking the earth apart until it strikes the high wall surrounding the prison. Magic showers through the air, humming with static. It distracts the witch enough that she's too slow to maintain a shield, and I swoop down, stretching my legs out.

"Nogard it vu!" High Priestess Zelki screams, throwing magic at me.

I fail to dodge out of the way, and it smashes against my wing. Spiraling out of control, I screech, trying to grab onto anything within reach. I hit the ground, shooting up dirt and debris, shaking the ground all over again. Pain steals my breath, shadowing my vision. The witch rushes me, gathering more magic, and once again, she thrusts it at my big beast form, keeping me down.

"Get up, Delphia!" Maddox shouts, his voice ringing through my mind and through the air. "Delphia, damn it! Get your ass up!"

I lift my long neck, but my body refuses to cooperate. Everything hurts, and my scales still crackle with the witch's magic. Blowing another breath of fire, I manage to keep her away from me long enough to transform into my human self. I push up on my shaking hands and peer at the electric world around me.

My chest tightens.

"Delphia Drakovich, you've made a grave mistake. The High Council will not tolerate such uprisings. Under the Magaelorum Law, I hereby declare you guilty of treason, attempted murder, and murder. You will perish by beheading alongside your mate. The dragon clans will see what a disgrace you are to your species. May the fates bring you misery in the afterlife." High Priestess Zelkie swirls her hands, calling upon her magic. My naked body lifts into the air as she draws me closer.

"No! No!" Maddox roars, thrashing against the

guard's hold. Fire lights his gaze, and his dragon screams to break free.

And then he spits fire, his beast breaking through the magic containing his dragon. The skeleton witch throws out her hands, shielding herself. It breaks her spell on me, sending me to the ground. My body buzzes, the magic in the air crackling.

"The barrier has been broken!" one of the guards shouts, unfurling his wings. He rubs his hands together, sparking his hands aglow with neon orange magic like I've seen Rose do. "You fucking bitch! You knew that force of magic would make it unsta—"

Maddox unleashes his dragon fire, roaring as he shakes the world around us. It engulfs the fae man, swallowing him whole. Glittering dust drifts through the air and fades on the gust of wind from Maddox's dragon wings. The guard was right. The spell keeping everyone's power contained has faltered. Magic and fire of all kinds light the night.

"Nogard it vu!" The high priestess summons magic, protecting herself as Maddox destroys the other guard before he can fight. A bolt of magic shoots at Maddox, striking him in the chest. The earth rumbles, his massive body crashing into it.

Rage consumes me, and I transform back into my

dragon form. I push away the pain in my wing and launch forward, kicking off the ground instead of taking flight. Heat builds in my chest to warm the rest of me, and I attack High Priestess Zelkie, clawing and breathing fire at her shield.

I don't stop, summoning the strength of Maddox and the rest of my mates. Thunder booms through the air, filling up my entire being with relief. With power. Green sparks dance across my hulking body, lighting my glittering red scales with a new light. I tear at the shield, refusing to stop.

High Priestess Zelkie's magic falters, and I crash through, scratching my claws into the ground at her sides. She screams and tips her head back, staring up at me. I whip my head forward, snapping my teeth around her, feeling her body collapse and magic tickle across my tongue. Flinging the witch into the air, I unleash a wave of dragon fire, smoldering her within her magic.

Another stream of fire joins mine, and then another and another. They stand with me as we face one of the witches who thinks we're beneath them and deserve to be killed or caged. The world quakes as my mates stand by my side to destroy the witch determined to see us fall.

It's her biggest mistake.

Dragons don't fall. We fly. We soar.

Summoning another wave of fire, I break through the skeleton witch's shield completely, and she explodes within the fire, sending magic rippling through the air.

I screech in excitement, my heart feeling as if it comes together as my mates land by my side. Ambrose jumps off of Theo's back and rushes to me.

"My beast!" Lazlo's voice shouts, echoing through my mind. "My beast, come to me."

My whole body shakes and ice fills my soul.

There's nothing I can do as magic drags me away from my mates.

I should've known this wasn't over. My imprisonment as Lazlo's pet has just begun.

CHAPTER 20

Unleashed

"AMBROSE, DO SOMETHING!" ROWAN RUNS after me in his dragon form, using his wings to propel him forward without flying.

I scratch my claws into the ground, trying desperately to find something to cling on to. A roar of desperation rings from me, and I whip my head, looking between Rowan and the world ahead. Pain cuts through me as my body scrapes across the wild terrain of the outskirts of the prison yard. I don't know how Lazlo has such power over me, but it terrifies me. How can he summon me like this? I feel as if I'll break at any second.

Creatures of all shapes and sizes fly through the air above us. Some fight each other and others look to be fleeing. Without the magic caging the prison in, a riot adds to the battle between Lazlo and the High Council with prisoners in between.

A bolt of glowing black magic shoots through the air, setting what looks like one of the fae aglow. The man falls from the sky in front of me, and there is nothing I can do to stop from crashing into him. His body hangs lifelessly, slung across my front leg. I can't believe this is happening. I don't know if I should try to get him off and risk crushing him if he's still alive, but I don't want his body on me either if he's dead. It's now that I realize the remaining members of the High Council attack the prisoners, killing everyone they can. Lazlo must've done something to incite the inmates into joining him and attacking. Maybe he offered them freedom. Whatever it is, I'm not sure whether to be thankful or not.

"Ambrose, hurry!" Tiernan calls, swooping above me. He lands in front of me and braces himself for my impact.

I relent to my need to fling the fae man off me and claw as hard as I can into the ground, leave huge crevices in my wake. But the magic is too strong. I can't stop, and Tiernan won't move. I huff a breath and shoot fire into the air, my whole body aching with the force of hitting Tiernan's solid form. His claws sink into my sides as he anchors us together the only way he knows how. I cry out in my mind, my dragon raging in fear and pain. Still, he doesn't release me. The primal side of him will do anything to save me. He tries flapping his wings to slow me down and snaps at trees and whatever he can as we pass them by. Theo joins him, but nothing works. My mates can't overpower the magic dragging me by a leash right into the middle of a power struggle with magic.

"Vi tota le got yu dititia!" Lazlo's spell booms through the air, sending a shockwave of blue magic exploding in the sky like a firecracker. It stops Ambrose in his tracks, and he shields himself. "Delphia, I command you to protect me! Your mates can either stand with us or risk losing you!"

I growl and spit fire in front of me, creating a wall of flames that cuts off the High Council members from Lazlo. My body acts on his command as if I'm now trapped in my beast form, unable to do anything but allow my dragon control. Magic zaps through my fire barrier at Lazlo, and I throw my huge body forward, physically protecting the warlock.

The High Council's chants hum through the air, and a shock of rainbow light electrocutes me. I shudder through the pain and anguish, trying to force my body to cooperate with my mind. I'll die here in this spot, protecting a vicious man if the High Council keeps attacking me.

"If you want your mate to survive, protect her!" Lazlo shouts, parting his magic and allowing my mates closer.

Theo and Tiernan reach us first in their dragon forms, and their presence distracts the High Council long enough for Lazlo to summon a shield. Growls and snarls, spells and blasts of magic mingle with the screams of creatures getting trapped in the crossfire. He's not protecting himself or anyone else. He's trapping the council.

"Tota de la can yo ito!" Lazlo holds his palms toward the sky, a flurry of magic dancing around him. My body hums with an energy so intense that I roar a breath of fire, trying to dispel it. If any more fills me up, I might explode.

"Lazlo, stop! You'll kill her!" Ambrose shouts, but I can't see him.

Lazlo ignores him, and it's now that I realize that he's not filling me with energy. He links us and pulls from mine, the sensation of his magic burning through me. "Blessed be the fates, take my offering and bind my power to those who serve me."

No. No. No. Bowing is one thing, but binding me? Holy shit.

His blue magic strikes through the cage he creates, hitting High Priestess Gildedrod in her chest, knocking her off her feet. Twirling his hand, he uses a spell to drag her through the cage and in our direction. Her screams ring through the air as she tries to call on her magic, but nothing happens. The witch's eyes widen as she skids to a stop a few feet away. The world quakes around us. Maddox, Rowan, and Kash all land to join me beside Lazlo. I expect them to fight, to do anything to stop him, but they remain stoic in their dragon forms. They're not here to stop Lazlo. They're here to help me by protecting me.

Fire fills the air as they surround the High Council, keeping them caged within Lazlo's shield. My mind, body, and soul go to war. I should pity the High Council's position. I shouldn't care about what happens to them. And really, I don't, but I don't want my mates involved. I want so badly to fly away and not be at the front of their destruction. I've killed too many already. I will never be known as anyone but a killer for the rest of my life. I'm no longer a victim of the fates or bad circumstances. I'm a villain right alongside the worst warlock I know.

How will my mates look at me the same?

Will I look at them any differently?

I don't want to find out.

"Ambrose, what's happening? What do we do? I'm a puppet. I can't fight his magic." I send the thought telepathically, hoping that Ambrose or one of my other mates hears me. I whimper in my dragon form, my insides weak while my body remains strong and compliant to Lazlo.

"Just stay strong, princess," Ambrose says, his voice swirling through my mind. "I need something more powerful to tap into. This is dark magic, and only dark magic can twist the fates back into our favor."

I call out in my dragon form as agony courses through me at his words. My attention whips to Lazlo as he stands over the witch. Magic sparks from me to him. My body gives out on me, and I thump against the floor, lying flat.

All my mates roar at once, feeling the same pain I do. Stretching out his arms, Lazlo stills the air, seemingly slowing down the world outside our circle, bringing silence around us and cutting off the calls of my mates.

"It is a great honor for you to bow beneath me," Lazlo says, rubbing his hands together. "Your sacrifice will save Magaelorum. It is far past the High Council's time ruling. May you rest among the stars and be blessed by the fates."

The witch's eyes widen, and she shakes her head. "Please, High Priest. Choose someone else. I don't deserve a blessing of this sort. I'm not on the High Council and can be of better use serving you in this lifetime. You know I agree with you and what you wanted." High Priestess Gildedrod clutches her hands together as if she silently prays to her fates to save her. She can't do anything with the weird magic pulsing through the air. "Please, don't do this. You know my coven has power—"

Lazlo flicks his fingers, shocking her with magic. An athame materializes in his hand, and he stalks closer to the witch, purposefully growing in height. I continue to release smoke and flames into the air, my body buzzing and ready to bow to his command even if my heart and soul want nothing to do with it.

"That's exactly what I want, Betty," Lazlo says, calling the witch by her first name instead of using her title. "Dolea cov tetiata von mika! I call upon the Infinity ancestors to bind our magic."

"No! Please, no!" the witch screams as her magic glows around her, crackling across her skin. It travels through her body, lighting her veins up. Lazlo's spell gathers her magic from her being and draws it to her heart.

Lazlo stomps forward, chanting his spell again. The witch falls onto her back, her body convulsing as her heart lights aglow. Wind whips through the air, the scent of fire and dirt and something sickly sweet like cough syrup bats at my senses. My claws dig into the ground as I wait in silence for another command. As Lazlo's magic controls the witch, it loosens its grip on me. I find the strength to push up from my belly and tower behind Lazlo, meeting the witch's gaze from over him.

"Stop him, please!" she screams, her skin rippling with the force of her magic. Pain laces her words, making it nearly palpable.

I roar in response, shooting fire through the air. I couldn't help her even if I wanted to. She stood by and did nothing as the High Council targeted me. Vengeance burns through me, but I'm fireproof. I savor it like the fucked up monster I've become.

"Dolea cov tetiata von mika!" Lazlo positions himself above the witch, aiming his athame at her glowing heart. "The fates bless me with your magic. They will give me the power to see this through and put Magaelorum on the right path once more. No longer will power be wasted. The fates bless me to tame even the wildest beasts."

I screech with his words. His power yanks at my collar, forcing my head to the floor, showing the truth of his words.

The witch stills, her eyes wide and her mouth open in a silent scream. Lazlo slices the dagger across his palm, stretching his fingers out only to curl them around the hilt of his athame. Jerking his hand down, Lazlo stabs the blade into the woman with a yell. "Vet que folio datack beemis fritia tu!"

The world shakes, and gold magic pours from the witch and into Lazlo, entering the blade and into the cut on his palm. His blue light mixes and twines with her gold magic, turning an intense shade of green similar to Ambrose's.

With the thought of my mate, I listen to his muffled words swirling through my mind. Something strange prods at me, and the collar around my neck loosens, allowing me to rise to my feet. Lazlo's attention focuses on the witch as he steals her magic and life.

"Blessed be the fates, please cut the bonds that should've never been formed. I ask you to accept this life and bring my mate to me. Ala vit ja otto! Ze hilo fi eht eta! One heart to bind seven. Ze hilo fi eht eta! Bind my clan as one. Ze hilo fi eht eta! Give us the strength to overcome the power breaking us. Ze hilo fi eht eta! We will be whole again!"

Ambrose's green light ricochets through the air, bouncing from Theo and Tiernan and to Kash, Maddox, and Rowan. They roar and shoot fire toward me, setting me ablaze in their dragon fire. My skin heats, and my heart soars with the relief my mate's power brings. A sharp pain whips through my body, knocking me off my feet.

"Bi lota ki vientita! She's mine!" Lazlo shoots a blast of power at Ambrose, sending him flying back. Skidding across the dirt, his tether to me snaps, and I watch in horror as all of my mates collapse around me. "Everyone will bow to my power!"

Screams rip through the air, and I turn my attention to the High Council, bowing on their knees in shock and agony, their bodies breaking to Lazlo's will. I never thought the most powerful witches in all of Magaelorum would be afraid of one man. They don't fight back. They do nothing but bow, screaming for mercy.

Here they are, acting as if Lazlo is the be-all, end-all of warlocks. And maybe he is.

He has a beast as his pet, after all.

He has my mates.

"Inmates of the Maximum Magical Penitentiary!" Lazlo bellows, his voice echoing through the night. Silence falls through the prison yard as the inmates stop fighting and begin to gather, Lazlo's presence alone enough to command their attention. "I've come here tonight to call upon some of the most powerful creatures in all of the lands to rise and stand beside me as we show the High Council that their power and control is long overdue. Their authority has done nothing but put our lands and your species in jeopardy. They've taken things that should've never belonged to them. They've guaranteed that you were caged like undeserving and weak beings, but in actuality, you're here because they fear your power. But as I stand here, I say no more!"

Holy shit. His speech is convincing enough that if my throat didn't tighten, I might actually believe he was here to help us. But like the High Council, he's only here to control everything he can.

The inmates can't see what I do. All they see is the High Council imprisoning them. Some unfairly, some not. It doesn't really matter to them in the end as long as they escape the punishment forced on them by the ruling witches—witches that don't care who lives or dies here as long as they remain in control.

"Join me! I have freed you from the magical chains that bind you. I have opened the cells and stopped those who seek to control you," Lazlo continues, twisting his hands, whirling magic through the world. He's such a liar. I'm certain it was me and the skeleton witch who broke the magical barrier. If I could speak, I might call him out—no, I would call him out. Because witches and vampires begin to cheer. Some bow. They just swap one source of power to another. They'll never truly be free.

A buzzer rings through the air, and guards rush from

the buildings. I spot fae, shifters, and strange creatures flooding the prison yard, looking confused yet excited. Growls and shouts, catcalls and whistles ring through the air, the cacophonous sound of the inmates growing louder and louder.

"You see! We can stand together and finally take what belongs to us. First Magaelorum from the High Council and then perhaps the Mortal World. We will all be free!" Lazlo claps his hands together, dropping the magical cage from the High Council. "Delphia, my pet. It's time. Show the High Council their mistakes. Show them what power we have. Execute them by dragon fire. Show Magaelorum what you're capable of."

My whole being ignites in anguish, but I can't resist.

I can't do anything.

Opening my mouth, I screech out.

Fire engulfs the world.

CHAPTER 21

Freedom

MADDOX'S HUGE FORM CRASHES INTO my side, knocking me off course. Fire blazes across his face but doesn't burn him. My body fights against his control, and I kick and snap my teeth, trying to break free.

"Maddox, please! Please, I can't stop. I don't want to hurt you," I say, my voice pleading with him through our mind link.

"I will not let this fucker put you in this posit—"

Maddox roars in fury, whipping his tail around. He knocks a man with wings away as several faes use their magic against my mate to get him away.

The second my body feels his weight lift, I flap my wings and throw him off me. My heart and soul scream in anguish, but the power controlling me doesn't relent.

"Split up!" Ambrose shouts, yelling through our mind link as he speaks to the others. "I need Nova pinned long enough for me to snap her chain. The rest of you keep everyone back. Don't let the High Council go either."

I blow another breath of fire and use my wings to launch into the air several dozen feet. I screech and circle, diving out of Theo's reach as he tries to capture me. The High Council shoots magic blindly, trying to take me out first as Lazlo watches everything from below like we're putting on a damn performance. Another dragon—an unfamiliar asshole inmate—sinks his teeth into Theo's throat and flips him midair, using his weight to shove him toward the ground.

My dragon soars around again, and my attention returns to the High Council below. Heat smolders through my entire being. I stretch my wings, tucking them close to nosedive faster than I've ever done. Smoke billows from my nostrils a moment before flames expel from my mouth, searing across the ground and over High Priest

Helio. He screams, trying to chant a spell, but Lazlo calls his own magic to shut the warlock up, realizing that my mates aren't going to stand by and watch me destroy everything. They want to protect me from Lazlo, turning me into Magaelorum's most vile, heartless dragon princess who will turn the world into fire and brimstone.

"Blessed be the fates, give me the strength of this sacrifice to withstand dragon fire," one of the other witches says, summoning an athame. "Ji lono ka fi abo we te vata!" she shouts, throwing it at High Priest Helio, sinking it into his chest.

He crumples as his magic blasts from him, knocking not only me back but also Lazlo and a dozen other onlookers. I can't even soar to my feet before the witch summons an orb of red and black magic. She shouts another spell and casts it at me, setting my body ablaze.

I screech and hit my back on the ground as agony seizes my muscles. Lazlo ignores me, calling upon the inmates to stand with him. He focuses on the witch, giving Ambrose a chance to close the space.

Rowan flies and lands on top of me, using his heavy body to pin me to the ground. My dragon fights and thrashes despite my mind's pleas to resist.

"Nova, hey. Look at me. Feel our bond. Lazlo can't control you completely. You're mine, and I will not let him have you like this." Rowan's voice swirls through my mind. "Please, you have to look at me." Using his clawed foot, he pins my head in place and bows in, forcing me to meet his familiar hazel eyes.

My heart thuds erratically, trying to escape me to be near him as my body refuses to comply with my mind.

A figure draws my attention to Rowan's head, and I spot Ambrose climbing up and standing. Green magic dances in his palms, sending static through the air.

"Nova, listen to me. I've weakened the chain on your neck, but you have to break it. You have to fight." Ambrose rubs his hands together. "There is only one way to do it."

He doesn't have to say the words to know the truth in my heart. If only my body would listen to me. If only the pull of Lazlo's magic didn't convulse through me, knocking Rowan and Ambrose away.

"My beast, finish this!" Lazlo shouts, zapping me from the ground. "Finish this, or I'll destroy your mates. I'll destroy you!"

I scream with his words, watching as he shoots power at Kash, lassoing him with a magical chain. Staring in horror, I watch as he uses whatever link Quillon has over my mate and takes it as his own.

Red tints my vision, my shock and fury pushing me

forward. The ground rumbles with each of my powerful footsteps. Launching up, I fly over Lazlo and Kash, my dragon's focus hooked to the remaining council members.

"Fight, kitten. Don't let him control you. Fight," Kash says, his dragon snarling, the sound reverberating through my being.

But I can't. I can't stop my dragon until the High Council disintegrates within my fire.

Heat builds within me, and magic pulses over my skin. Blue and green colors blend with the fire glowing in my veins as Ambrose's magic tries to steal Lazlo's control. The energy grows more intense, and I lose focus of the world.

As if my soul splits from my body, I watch my beast from the outside as it gives in to Lazlo's command, a part of me wanting nothing more than to see the High Council perish. And not only them. Lazlo too.

Screams pierce the air, and my soul and body crash back together, sending my ears ringing. I whip my head toward Lazlo, the disconnection in me merging as one. His control vanishes with the death of the remaining council members as my fire sets the prison yard aflame.

"Het ca lula vet!" Lazlo shouts, zapping me in the chest.

Ice steals my warmth away, and my body zings as I

transform from a dragon and into my mortal self. I drop to my knees, my body weak and aching, unable to do anything without the power Lazlo forced into me. Tears burn my eyes, and I curl in on myself, tucking my knees to my chest.

"My beast, how dare you try and turn against me," Lazlo says, his chest heaving as his features morph. "I felt you break your chain, and I can't have an untamable beast ruining everything I've fought hard for. I thought you were better than this. I thought you knew your place."

Lazlo flicks his fingers at me, sending me rolling. Pain burns my skin as my body scrapes the hard ground. A few inmates close in on me, tightening my chest with fear. I'm naked, vulnerable, and barely have enough energy to get to my feet, let alone fight.

Fire burns across a circle around me. Maddox and Theo shield me with their flames, stopping the inmates from grabbing me. They'll destroy them if the fuckers so much as touch me. If only the inmates were hindered and powerless. The fire doesn't stop a man, whose hand lights up with yellow power—another warlock. He sets his sight on me, chanting a spell, winding a chain of light in his hands. He's going to try to leash my collar now that I've freed myself from Lazlo.

The warlock swings his hands. "Hata be veta—" His

spell cuts off with his screams.

Bright flames engulf him as Rowan attacks him with his dragon fire. Landing by my side, he picks up the warlock and flings him through the air. Lazlo blasts magic at Rowan, the energy strong enough to knock him on his back. It gives Lazlo the opening he needs to cast a shield around us, blocking me from my mates once more.

"I thought we had an agreement, Delphia. You bowed to me." Lazlo saunters closer, shocking me with magic again.

"Please, I know. I don't know what happened. Don't hurt me." My teeth chatter, and I remain on the ground, trying not to lose myself to the pain and exhaustion consuming me. I hope my weak voice is enough to get Lazlo to stop. I hope he believes the lie coming from my mouth. "I didn't mean to break the leash. We still have an agreement."

Towering over me in his monstrous form, Lazlo studies me. Magic glows in his eyes, and he tips his head, assessing me. I pant, my painful breaths making it harder to stay focused. If I can distract him long enough, maybe Ambrose can do something. My soul feels Ambrose's power prodding at me, trying to help, but Lazlo is too powerful.

"The terms have changed, Delphia. I don't trust you

any longer. You will bow and remain caged to be used at my will when I need you. Your clan is too wild. Controlling you with them around takes too much of my energy." Lazlo tips his head back, peering at my mates blasting fire at the barrier. "As for the warlock...say goodbye to him."

"What? No," I say, managing to push up on my hands. "You can't change the terms. We had a deal."

"I can change the fucking fates, you wild beast! I can do whatever the hell I want, and right now, I want to put you down. You broke our deal. You resist too much. The only reason you're even breathing is because I don't like to be wasteful. This is your one warning. Accept the new agreement or perish. I have no use for you otherwise." Lazlo shocks me again, sending me to my stomach. I convulse under his power, my body and mind wanting nothing more than to unleash my dragon, but she remains trapped in my exhaustion and Lazlo's magic.

"Lazlo, stop!" Ambrose yells, calling on a spell that shakes the world around me. "This is your last chance. Nova is ours!"

Flinging his hand out, Lazlo drags an inmate forward and through his barrier. Horror widens my eyes, cooling me even more at the sight unfolding before me. Summoning an athame, Lazlo stabs the strange warlock in the chest, sending magic shooting through the world. He offers the fates another sacrifice, stealing the man's magic.

"Accept the deal, Delphia!" Lazlo hollers, his chest heaving with his anger. "Do it now, or I'll destroy your mates. Don't test me! Il be ti votatito calla me ti og!"

Blinding light steals my vision, and a wave of magic shoots from Lazlo like a shockwave, blasting everyone within a few dozen feet of us away. Pain ricochets through my soul, feeling all six of my mates collapse. Lazlo's dark magic unleashes a flurry of dread as he proved himself to be no better than the High Council.

The ground cracks open with the force of his magic, splitting the prison yard in two. People scream and scramble away, trying to stay out of Lazlo's path. The power he possesses gets to his head. Before, he had to worry about the High Council. But now? No one can stop him.

Except me.

Even if doing so ends my life, it's a risk I must take. This monster of a man deserves the same fate as those he has destroyed. He deserves to know what it's like to have his power and freedom ripped from him.

"Fight, princess. Fight. We give you our strength and power. Don't let him win." Ambrose's voice whispers through my mind. "Co let ti vi atta go lu. I call upon the fates to bind my body, mind, and soul to my familiars and their mate. Co let ti vi atta go lu. Blessed be the fates to give Delphia the strength of three plus three. Co let ti vi atta go lu. Unite us as one entity and set her free."

The earth quakes and my mates fall silent, their constant growls and threats vanishing. A jolt of magic strikes me in the chest, arching my back. My dragon rouses at the newfound strength and power buzzing through me. Six magical tethers glow through the air, solidifying the connection I have to the men I love. It's enough to gather their strength, love, and hope for our future inside me. It's enough to help me rise and face the monstrous warlock who ruined my life, yet who also helped me become whole. My stars aligned with the most powerful, incredible beings in all of the universe, and I will not let Lazlo steal them from me.

"Bow, Delphia!" Lazlo shouts, thrusting his magic at me.

I blow fire with my screech, and Lazlo's power gets lost in the heat of my dragon's anger. His face wrinkles with his annoyance. His confidence wavers. Shouts call through the air, but I don't turn my gaze away from Lazlo. I narrow my focus on him, my beast wanting nothing more than to consume him.

Lazlo gathers more power, his whole body aglow with its light. "Vi at oto fi—"

Jerking my head forward, I snap at his protective

shield, surprising him enough to make his words falter. He snarls, his sharp fangs trying to intimidate me. If he threatened me like this even a few weeks ago, I'd have been terrified. But now?

I roar, shooting fire and Ambrose's magic in a long stream that lights the night. It's like the sun comes to the ground, heating everything within Lazlo's magical shield. I push against it, refusing to stop. All I can think about is what life will be like once he's no longer in it.

How freeing it will be.

Magaelorum will no longer be at the mercy of witches or magic. It will take a lot for them to try and rise again. Lazlo was right about their time coming to an end. I feel it deep in the heat of my core. I feel it through the souls of my mates and even through the power of the onlookers around us.

Things will change.

I will ensure it.

My mother started it with her mates. With McKayla. And now, I plan to finish it. I plan to be wild and free and unstoppable to prove to all of Magaelorum that no one is above each other. Our power is intended to blend and grow. It's the only way for every territory and species to thrive.

Lazlo's chants turn into a holler and then a scream.

My fire breaks through his shield completely.

With one final breath of fire, I torch the warlock, sending magic exploding through the air. Something weird shifts inside me as magic rains over me. The tightness around my throat vanishes as my collar snaps and disappears. Flames eat away at the ground before me, and I stare in awe as they devour every last drop of Lazlo Infinity's magic.

Silence settles through the prison yard, and I bow down, my body giving out on me. I rest my head to the ground, watching as creatures of every kind follow my lead and bow beside me. I should be weirded out, but something about the gesture comforts me. Shifters, vampires, fae, witches, and others all join together as one, surrounding me. No one fights. No one does anything. They all look to me.

But I don't look back. I look to my mates.

Ambrose dusts himself off as Maddox, Kash, Rowan, Tiernan, and Theo all transform into their human forms, striding through the crowd butt-ass naked to me. I gather my will, my mind, body, and soul wanting to take the form they do as they surround me. Ambrose summons a big shirt, tugging it over my head. My knees tremble, but I manage to remain standing tall.

"My beautiful mate," Ambrose says, spinning me

around. "What have you gotten us into?"

Theo play-punches him in the shoulder. "The chance for a better future."

"Finally fucking freedom," Maddox adds.

I lick my dry lips and smile. "But what now? What happens now?"

"We call upon the leaders of every territory to come together as one." Kash scoops me up, unable to control his need to hold me for a minute longer.

"I think we might also know of a witch who can help." Ambrose offers me a smile. "A big change is going to occur, and we can use all the help we can get."

I slowly nod my head as his words sink in. That's exactly what we need. Everyone to help. This is how life will grow and change and become better than ever. A select few witches shouldn't have the power to control entire species, nor should they be able to rewrite the fates.

"As long as everyone agrees to leave things to fate. No one can mess with our lives again." I hold out my arms to my mates.

With the fates comes freedom. It also comes with the ability to choose which paths to take and to discover where we are fated to go. It gives us the chance to build a world together.

And together with my chosen mates, all who feel as if

they've been fated to be mine, I know our lives will be everything I never knew I'd dream about.

Together, we will thrive.

CHAPTER 22

Payback

"DO IT OR END UP in the new Max." Kash twists the back of Quillon's shirt in his hand. "We've agreed not to pardon your dumbass. If you don't open a portal, we will find someone more willing."

"You'll get out of Magaelorum and the cure. It'll be your only mercy." Ambrose rubs his palms together.

"Agree with them. It's far better than what Nova came up with." Rowan punches Quillon in the stomach, winding him.

Kash remains strong, taking any of the pain Quillon experiences like the badass, sexy mate he is. Theo and Tiernan call to us from overhead, and I watch them descend and land with a thud in the middle of the clearing.

"The murderess fae princess has been returned to the Fae Lands and left to the Courts. She put up one helluva fight and is now safely the being of her namesake—thorns and all," Tiernan thinks to me, transforming into his handsome, muscular human self.

"Rose is a rose?" I ask, my eyebrows shooting up.

"Well...not for long. She pricked someone, and he picked her." Theo comes up beside his brother and waves a pink rose around. "Hey, lycan. I got you a gift. Enjoy." Grabbing Quillon's hand, he slaps the rose into his palm.

Quillon growls under his breath. I expect him to throw the flower back, but he surprises me and tucks it into his jacket pocket. "Fucking fine. I'll do what you ask."

I smile and hop onto Kash's back, peppering his neck with kisses. All of my mates choose to stay together, and Ambrose stands beside Quillon, ensuring he opens a gateway to the Mortal World properly.

A blue portal lights the world in front of me. I snuggle Kash more tightly, my mind and body spinning with nerves and excitement. I can't believe we're going back to the world I grew up in. It seems so long ago and strange. But we have one more thing to do.

Shoving Quillon forward, Maddox forces the lycan to lead the way. Rowan holds onto my waist from behind like he wants to ensure we all stay together, and Theo and Tiernan finish off our group, blanketed in the protection of Ambrose's magic.

Cool, salty air mingles with the scent of pine trees, and I stare around the forest. A stream trickles nearby, flowing lazily and almost out of place, the water glowing with a strange blue light. But we don't stand here for long.

Flipping me over his shoulder, Kash pulls me into his arms and gets me to wrap my legs around him. We all walk in silence as Ambrose navigates the way until the sound of a car horn blares in the distance. My heartbeat thrums in quick beats, and I wiggle in Kash's arms until he sets me down, and I can glimpse the quaint downtown area of a town named Evergreen Beach.

"That's the place," Ambrose says, motioning toward a small apartment complex a block away. "Welcome to your new life."

Quillon spins to look at us, and Kash rushes forward, tackling him. Rowan and Maddox cheer him on, and Ambrose summons a metal rod.

"But before you go, we gotta tag your ass. It's what we've all agreed on to keep tabs on you. We can't have you trying anything stupid. Someone hold him still." Kash smacks Quillon on the back of the head. "Brace yourself fucker. This is going to hurt."

Rowan and Maddox pin Quillon to the ground, and I bounce on my feet. Kash holds up the metal rod to my mouth, and I gladly blow on it, turning it red with my dragon fire. Ambrose twirls his fingers, twisting the red-hot rod. Quillon thrashes and tries to break free, his fear so obvious that it's nearly palpable.

"Take a breath, douchebag." Kash rips up Quillon's shirt, exposing his back to him. "Be thankful I'm not branding your forehead or ass."

"Wait! You don't have to—" Quillon's plea cuts off with his holler, and he stills beneath Maddox and Rowan, blacking out.

The seven of us surround the annoying, infuriating lycan and watch the dragon fire branding fade into a puckered dragon design with the words "Property of the Drakovich Kingdom" swirling around it.

"Time to give him the cure. Who wants the honors?" Ambrose asks, waving the vial between Kash and me.

I snatch it from Ambrose. "Hold his head still, Kash." Kicking Quillon in the ass, I flip him onto his back.

"Someone wake him up."

Ambrose flicks his fingers, shocking Quillon with magic until his eyes snap open. Growling, he tries to fight, swinging his arm. Kash releases him with a laugh, letting Quillon get to his feet. I shake my head and roll my eyes as he bolts away like he can escape us.

"Hustle, lycan! I'm coming for you!" Kash yells, his voice light with laughter. Inhaling a deep breath, he shoots dragon fire in Quillon's direction, singeing the clothes off him.

Quillon screams and pats down his reddening skin. Twisting, he glowers in our direction. I fold my arms over my chest and smile sweetly at him, giving him a long look.

"At least your beastliness won't scare anyone." I point and laugh at his cock. "And hey, look. You can see the angry inch!"

My guys holler, striding past me to capture Quillon once more. They're fucking with him, giving him hope and taking it away. It's a far sweeter revenge than locking him up could ever be. He'll now live out a human life, cursed with mediocrity and a pathetic existence.

"Looks like two, maybe," Theo says, his voice remaining even. "But don't worry. Ambrose can fix that."

Chanting a spell, Ambrose engulfs Quillon with magic, freezing him in place. Coarse hair sprouts from his body so long and thick that he won't even be stopped for indecent exposure. I laugh and clap, jogging the rest of the way to Quillon.

"Hold still, fuckface." Kash grabs the top of Quillon's head and forces his mouth open by shoving his fingers into his cheeks.

I shake the vial with the lycan cure in Quillon's face and pop the stopper on it. "Have a miserable life. We'll be monitoring you." Pouring the elixir into his mouth, I wait for Kash to force him to swallow it before patting his cheek. "That's a good boy."

Locking his fingers to Quillon's shoulders, he vanishes with Quillon for a split second before returning. Ambrose pulls me into his arms and hugs me close. "He won't remember anything, so we don't have to worry about him again. The Fire Mountain Clan keeps an eye on this town as well."

I bob my head and motion for my mates to surround me. "I can't believe it's finally over."

"Thank the fates," Kash says, kissing me. "Ready for our last stop?"

Nuzzling my nose to his, I respond, "More than ever."

McKayla hugs her arms around herself, burying her face

into my hair. "I was so scared for you, Delphia. I've been praying to the fates ever since you left."

"And they came through." Rowan holds my hand, swinging my arm back and forth.

Opening her arms more, she pulls Rowan to us, embracing the two of us the best she can. "I can't thank you enough for standing by Delphia. All of you. I should've known that like her mother, the Drakovich heart was big enough for more than one clan."

I swipe my hand over my cheek, brushing away my stray tear. Now that I have time to enjoy catching up with my aunt, I finally get to fill in the missing pieces of my life.

My mom might've found her fated mates in the Drogony Clan, guards that worked at Max long before I was born, but she also did claim a Litendrake prince, who turned his back on the old ways.

I almost don't believe that the fates set my life to repeat hers, so it could—we could—finish what was started with my birth.

"Oh, fuck. Delphia? Where the hell did you come from?" A blond woman strides from the forest outside of the hidden community of Fire Mountain. Her familiar blue eyes rove over me, assessing my mates as we surround McKayla.

"Careful, Lyric." A man with vivid lavender eyes pulls her in close.

A playful bark sounds from behind the two of them, and I watch as a shiny, silver wolf bounds around the two of them and blocks their way. I blink a few times in curiosity, wondering if—

The silver wolf stretches, turning into a grown-ass, completely naked guy with blond hair. I automatically glance away, listening to something that sounds like flesh smacking flesh.

"Sterling, damn it. Delphia grew up in the same town as me. You can't just transform and show her your schlong." Lyric bares her bottom teeth and turns to me. "Please excuse my mate. He's unashamedly comfortable letting his pendulum swing free."

I laugh and peek over my shoulder at my mates. "Sounds like my dragons. I met two of them butt-ass naked."

Widening her eyes, Lyric glances from me to my guys. "Dragons?"

"Dragons are nothing, princess." Ambrose points to Sterling. "They're—they're wolves. I had no idea they still existed. I have so many questions."

"And we have answers. I thought I'd invite the Lunar Crest pack here to welcome you all. What happened with the Wolf Lands was a tragedy but beauty came from it. The packs learned to adapt and grow together, and now they're stronger. The dragon clans can be too." McKayla touches her hand to mine and Lyric's shoulders. "You're proof of it, Delphia. This is why I'm asking you to stay. At least for a while. Learn what you can to help your lands adjust to the changing fates. We'll protect you. The falling out could be—"

"No." My mouth says the word before my brain has time to process it. "I can't leave the home I just got back."

"She's right, High Priestess. The Dragon Lands are looking to the Drakovich Kingdom for guidance." Ambrose drapes his arm around my shoulder. "Magaelorum needs us more than ever."

"But without a lycan...it'll be difficult for you to come back." Worry lines McKayla's eyes, and she sucks her bottom lip between her teeth.

"What about a familiar?" Lyric smiles and bumps her shoulder to the man with lavender eyes. "I think Flynn might be able to help create a gateway from the Dragon Lands to the Mortal World with my help. We've done it for Lunar Crest."

"It'll be difficult without the power source in Magaelorum to anchor the gateway." Power flickers in Flynn's gaze.

"What about two power sources? A whole clan?" Tiernan steps forward and glances between Ambrose and Flynn. "My brother and I have soul-bonded to our guard. We're as one."

"When we solidify our bonds to Delphia, we'll all share our souls. It's the way of the dragon." Maddox smacks Ambrose on the back. "And our warlock."

I smile. I can't help it. Maddox was the last one I ever expected to claim Ambrose as part of our clan. I never knew I could be happier.

Flynn, Ambrose, and McKayla turn to each other with their magic crackling through the air. Nodding slowly, Flynn says, "I think it'll work."

"Is everyone sure about this?" McKayla asks, twisting her lips to the side. "You can always return here if you change your mind. Fire Mountain is open for every creature."

I bob my head. "And I hope Magaelorum will be too, someday. We've called upon the leaders of all the lands to gather. We're going to make sure things change."

Throwing her arms around me, McKayla hugs me. "May the fates bless you always, Delphia."

I smile. "Thanks, Aunt McKayla. I should tell you I go by Nova now. Delphia was the stolen Drakovich heir. But me? I'm the mate of the Dreki and Darkonian Clans."

"You're still Delphia to me, cookie," Maddox teases, swatting me.

Theo pats his back. "Our infuriating, beautiful, stubborn queen."

CHAPTER 23

Stars Aligned

"THE LEADERS HAVE GATHERED," AMBROSE says, popping his head in to look at me standing in front of a full-length mirror.

I adjust the bodice of my dress, showing off more of my cleavage. "Are you sure I have to be present? Theo—"

Tiernan hugs me from behind. "Throwing my brother to the fray already? I like it. Being an alpha-asshole on a power trip was always his thing."

Rowan laughs, lighting his fingers with flames. "Maddox will keep him in line...maybe. Probably not. They've probably already put every leader in their place and—"

I groan and shake my head, whipping my red hair around. "Damn it, you two. You better be wrong. The last thing we need is for others to start comparing us to the ruthless High Council. We're just going for being a council, remember?"

Kash chuckles from the hallway behind Ambrose. "They're just teasing you, kitten. Those bastards haven't stopped complaining about wrapping things up and sending everyone on their way so we can return here and get to work preparing for all the babies we plan to knock you up with."

I sigh a breath through my nose. "So not helping."

Ambrose twirls his fingers, spinning me around. Using magic, he pulls me away from Rowan and Tiernan and into his arms. He brushes his lips to mine and smiles, loving how freely he can give me affection. "Don't worry, Nova. I denied both of them when they asked me about a spell to keep you fertile year-round or to increase your odds of multiples."

"Which are already high," Tiernan teases, sneaking a kiss to my cheek.

I bat his shoulder and wiggle out of Ambrose's embrace before the four of them start something I'll want to finish—mostly them—but with their mindset, it'll be me first, times a million. And then I'll never want to leave.

"No more talking about babies or sex or anything that will leave this gown burned and torn to shreds until this gathering is over." I wag my fingers and duck under Kash's arm, dashing away before he can grab me next.

I don't make it far as my body freezes, and I float a foot in the air, suspended in Ambrose's magic. He spins me around and smiles. Rowan dodges past everyone and snatches me from the air, pulling me into his arms.

"Ambrose, not fair," I say, fake-glaring over Rowan's shoulder.

He chuckles and winks. "My magic only evens my odds against your power. Plus, I can't have you flying away now. Your dragons like chasing you far too much."

"I can't always be easy to get," I tease, swinging my legs up and around, hooking my knee over Rowan's shoulder.

Laughing, Rowan lets me straddle his shoulder as I prepare to swing off him and into the air. Kash catches me before I land, and I kiss him and grab his cock through his pants. He play-growls and throws me onto his shoulder, picking up his pace until he breaks into a sprint. I shriek and cling onto him as he launches with me in the air, throwing me out as he transforms. Swooping beneath me, Tiernan catches me on his back, and Ambrose slides up behind me. I never knew how much I'd love riding my mates in all their forms, either playfully like this or in the way they enjoy most.

The Dragon Lands shine silver under the full moon, and Kash and Rowan soar around us as we fly toward the Freeland, the area previously dominated by the High Council, which now belongs to everyone. I clutch onto Tiernan's neck and press my cheek to his dark, glittering scales. Feeling the power of his body awakens my dragon, and my core warms at just being close.

"Look, Nova. I don't think I've ever seen anything like this. And it's all because of you." Ambrose points to an open area where creatures remain in their true forms, mingling in the vast space. A huge bonfire glows in the center, bringing warmth and light to the area, blending with dragon fire and magic.

"Will I ever get used to this? There are so many species here that I never knew existed." I narrow my eyes like squinting will help me prepare for our descent. I'm a leader of the dragon clans. I can't be all wide-eyed and in awe.

"Hell yeah, you can, doe eyes. I love that expression. It's my favorite, and I'll ensure no one says a damn thing."

Rowan's voice hums in my mind as he listens in on my thoughts.

I smile and stretch my arm, waiting for him to fly flush against Tiernan, allowing me to touch him. "No fighting, okay?"

"Only broody glowers, promise." Rowan puffs out a cloud of smoke through his nostrils.

Tiernan dives down, his descent stealing away my ability to respond as my heart jumps into my throat. Ambrose swears behind me, adjusting his arms tighter around my waist. Spreading his giant wings, he slows and lands, running a few feet. He lowers his head, and Ambrose uses his magic to help me slide to the ground. Tiernan bumps his big snout to my ass as I step away. I spin to whack him only to have Maddox catch my wrist and pull me to him.

"Are you being naughty, cookie?" Maddox asks, his deep voice serious. "Don't think there isn't time for me to—"

With my free hand, I smack him on the ass, startling him. Maddox growls and tries to catch me in his arms, but I dodge past him and bolt away. I regret running immediately, because Ambrose was right. My guys love a game of chase.

"You all better put some damn clothes on before you make everyone else feel inferior," I call, cackling like a maniac.

Maddox shoots an orb of fire at my feet. "You're demanding the wrong thing. I'm already dressed."

He knows I'm talking to Kash, Tiernan, and Rowan, but he can't help teasing me anyway. Inhaling a deep breath, I summon power in my palms and chuck it behind me. I hit Maddox in the gut, setting his shirt ablaze, showing off his abs.

"That's more like it." Maddox picks up his pace, reminding me of all the times we've worked out together and trained. His reward and punishment system is the same, and I can't stop thinking about him catching me and how I almost want him to. "Now it's your turn."

Ah hell.

He's utterly and completely serious.

"Don't you even think about it," I call, pushing my legs to move faster. "We have things to do."

"Only each other. This is all just a formality." Maddox shoots a fireball at me, missing me by an inch.

I clench my jaw and blindly throw my power behind me. "I swear to the fates, Maddox. If you burn this dress before—"

A wave of fire engulfs me, singeing my clothes and leaving me standing butt-ass naked in the middle of the clearing. We're still quite a ways from the bonfire, but the last thing I want is to have the leaders of the other territories see me like this.

"Nice aim, you bastard," Maddox says, charging at me and scooping me up.

Theo laughs and high-fives Maddox, and the two cocky bastards each swat my ass. Green magic sparkles through the air, and Ambrose dresses me all over again. All of my mates groan, not as thankful as I am.

"You guys need to take a breath and control yourselves," Ambrose says, freezing Maddox and Theo with magic long enough to help me to my feet. "Don't make me help you."

I tilt my head and look at Ambrose curiously. "Do it. Help them. I want to know what that entails."

Theo growls, gathering fire in his palms. "If you so much as—"

My eyes widen, and I cover my mouth, spinning to look at everyone as they moan and grunt in unison, sounding as if...

Tipping my head back, I release a loud-ass laugh and cup Ambrose's cheeks between my hands. "I can't believe you did that. You know you're going to be in so much trouble, right?"

Ambrose inhales a long breath. "I already am. My bond ensured it."

I flick my gaze down to his pants and back up. Laughter bubbles in my throat again, and I cover my heated face. I knew Ambrose was magical, but damn. I can't believe he went so far as to use magic to make all of them cum—himself included because of his cock bling.

"Yeah, you fucking are. You forgot our mate. What were you thinking?" Maddox adjusts his pants, looking ready to lunge at Ambrose.

"Maddox, it's oka—" My whole body tenses with my shocking orgasm, and if Ambrose wasn't holding on to me, I'd collapse to my knees. I gasp and moan, my body refusing to release me from the wave of pleasure until I melt into my warlock's arms. It's my turn to glower. "You fucker. I—"

Dazzling magic lights up the sky, cutting off my words and drawing my attention away from Ambrose. Excitement rushes through me. People cheer, and I spot as figures dance around the bonfire. A beautiful melody trickles through the air.

"Looks like the celebrations are starting. Come on, Nova. It's time to join the leaders." Ambrose rushes me, scooping me up.

The rest of my mates surround us in a solid wall of sexy muscle and power, and I climb high on Ambrose to sit on his shoulder, wanting a better view of the gathering.

Shifters part away from each other and open a path for my clan. I smile, drinking in the view. Huge lions, bears, and tigers mingle with men and women in all attire. Some naked, some not, but everyone looking comfortable and natural together.

I peer ahead and spot those chosen to represent their territories. Inhaling a deep breath, I suppress my nerves. This is the first time I'm standing among those not intent on destroying us, nor am I standing among those deemed criminals. I thought it would be weird or a bit leery, but it feels so normal.

"Queen Delphia, it is a pleasure to meet you," a woman with brilliant ice-blue wings says. Cool air drifts around her with her movements. "You have the support of the Fae Lands' Winter Court."

"As well as Summer, Spring, and Autumn," a male fairy says, his red wings glittering with millions of sparkles.

I nod my head and slide off Ambrose's shoulder. Maddox and Theo take their places at my side, representing the leaders of the Dreki and Darkonian Clans with me as the Drakovich heir, showing the union of several clans possible with one woman.

"The Witchlands also offers you their support and would like to ensure the rest of Magaelorum that we have no intentions to fall onto the path of the former High

Council. Our covens were just as bound by magic, and it feels amazing to finally follow the fates as we were intended." Silver magic dances around a beautiful woman with dark hair. "Blessed be the fates, Queen Delphia. I offer you this token of our loyalty."

Ambrose steps forward and takes the amulet from the witch. "This is very kind of you, High Priestess." Turning to me, he motions for me to turn around to fasten the necklace around my throat. "It's a good luck charm for a fertile, prosperous, and peaceful future."

My mates love the hell out of the sound of that, their excitement and appreciation flooding through me. Witches before never gave anything without a price, so the truth of the High Priestess's loyalty is clear.

One by one, the leaders of different clans, covens, pods, prides, and more greet my mates and me showing their acceptance and appreciation for the change in Magaelorum. As I look around at the gathering, I can't help thinking about my mom. I wonder what she was like. I wonder what her mates—my dads—were like. I wish she were here to see this. I hope she knows that I am proud to be her daughter, and without what she did, I wouldn't be here like this with my mates today.

"We will ensure all of the clans remember your mother's legacy, cookie," Maddox says, tugging me away from the crowd. He cups my face and smiles. "She will not be known as a criminal. She will be remembered as the powerful dragon who chose to fight for the fates and freedom."

"I love that," I say, snuggling close. "And you."

My mates engulf me in their arms, breaking us away from the gathering. We rush toward the clearing with a new lightness in our hearts and souls. Charging ahead of them, I incite a game of chase, laughing and dodging out of their reach. Fire and magic dance through the air, and I let it consume me as I change into a form I love.

I roar, unleashing fire into the night sky. My mates join along with me, and I snatch Ambrose up by the shirt, setting him on my back. His laughter fills my senses, and I flap my wings, leading our way into the sky.

I never expected to be captured, freed, and saved by my mates. I never expected a life full of love and magic and everything I could ever want and need.

Taking flight, I soar through the air high above Magaelorum. Above the place I'm meant to be. I'm so happy to finally have a future with my mates. And best of all, the perfect home.

The Dragon Lands will be better than ever.

We'll guarantee it.

CHAPTER 24

Together Forever

"I DON'T SEE THE POINT in putting this on. We're just going to get naked." Rowan cracks his neck, pulling at the collar of his suit. "Wouldn't you prefer to enjoy the view of us all standing how you like for the ceremony?"

"He's right, kitten." Kash summons dragon fire in his palms. "Here, let me help you with that dress. You look hot as fuck in it, but that only makes me want to scorch the thing keeping us apart."

I tip my head back and laugh. "We tried that twice already, and none of you could stay in control long enough to finish."

"I think you remember that wrong. We finished...several times." Rowan winks at me, trying to pull me from his brother.

I blast dragon fire at his feet. "Go get in place, or I'll make you put on a tie like Maddox."

"I'll just use it to tie you—"

Bright green light flashes through the air. Rowan doesn't get the chance to finish his sentence as Ambrose intervenes and steals him away. He should've joined the others a couple minutes ago but purposely took his time getting dressed, which is a lot further than we got for our last attempt to bind all of our souls as a clan under the presence of only the fates. No party and gathering. No strangers. Just the seven of us together in an intimate ceremony, which is exactly what I want—if we can make it through.

"Third time is a charm," Kash says, spinning me around to drink me in.

"It better be. Ambrose will freeze us in our spots otherwise," I tease, grabbing his jacket lapels and pulling him closer. Brushing my lips to his, I kiss him sweetly. "Or at least you five. Maybe I'll have him do it anyway, so I can grab you all by the—"

Kash play-growls and snatches me up, striding toward the archway of our suite. He adjusts me to his shoulder, carrying me like a damn caveman or some shit. Breaking into a run, he bolts down the grand hallways. When there would usually be other dragons around—guards, family, allies, and who knows who else—the Darkonian palace remains empty. We have all agreed to keep it this way until the end of mating season that could start next week. I'm excited yet scared, but no matter what, I'm the happiest I've ever been in my life. I'm so ready for this. For my future.

Groaning, Kash sets me on my feet and spins to pin me to the wall outside Ambrose's altar room. "Keep up those thoughts, kitten, and we're not making it inside."

I press my hand to his chest, keeping a couple inches of space between us. "I can't help it."

He leans forward and kisses me, sliding his tongue in my mouth, humming deep in his throat. "I love it. I love you."

I smile. "I love you too."

Green light sparkles through the air, wrapping around the two of us. Ambrose chants a spell, dragging us into the doorway of the altar room. I giggle, clinging onto Kash until I hear the deep intakes of breaths from my other mates. Their desire for me can't be contained, and even if only seconds pass where we've been apart, they act as if they're seeing me for the first time and like I'm the most beautiful woman they've ever seen.

"Because you are, kitten," Kash says, responding to my silent thought. Setting me on my feet, he guides me forward and slowly spins me in the aisle, sending my short dress sweeping out. "Isn't that right?"

"So sexy," Rowan says.

Theo pretends to spank the air. "Naughty."

"Everything I ever imagined and more, cookie. Now get that hot ass over here so I can kiss it." Maddox snaps his teeth playfully together. "I've been waiting my whole life for you, and I'm done waiting another second until we're all bonded as one."

My heart flutters at his words. "Look at you, sounding all romantic."

He narrows his eyes. "Just wait until I get that dress off you and claim you how you like."

I giggle and shake my head. "I love you, you wild beast."

"Just wait until you let me have you as a dragon." Maddox blows out a breath of smoke, his eyes lighting with fire.

"Veta viana go te hel ita," Ambrose says, dimming the

room before setting it aglow with magic and candlelight.

Everyone's attention pulls to him as he stands in a ceremonial robe with metallic threads embroidered within the fabric, creating strange symbols. I didn't think my heart could pound any harder, but Ambrose sets my dragon wild with emotion, love, and a deep-seated need to draw closer to my mates—our clan.

I can barely contain myself. Kash has to tighten his hold on me, stopping me from flying down the aisle. The looks of awe and adoration crossing my mates' faces light heat in my core, shooting it through the rest of me. The short stroll down the aisle, lit with magic, feels like a journey in itself, and the overwhelming need to finally stand before my mates and turn our union official sends tears of happiness clouding my eyes.

"It is a great honor to be gathered with the fates as our witness as we bind our souls as one under the name of the Drakovich Clan," Ambrose begins, summoning magic in his palms. "Dnib eht luos semit neves. Ekam ruo nalc sa eno." Twirling his fingers, he scatters his magic through the room, setting all of us aglow. "Kash Dreki, as the last born, it is your duty to present our gorgeous mate to our clan. Do you accept the position as the soul who tethers her, so she may remain grounded yet be set free?"

"I do," Kash says, turning me toward him. Tucking

my hair behind my ear, he bows in and kisses me once more. "Forever and always, Nova. I love you."

I steal another kiss from him, letting him take both of my hands in his. He shifts out of the way and offers me to Maddox and Theo to take. I smile, holding both their hands as they guide me to stand in front of Ambrose.

"Maddox Dreki and Theo Darkonian. Your duty as the leaders of your clans will be the guiding light of our mate's soul. Do you accept the positions of teacher and caretaker, ensuring her every need on a mental, physical, and spiritual level? With you both, her soul will remain strong, binding us as one." Ambrose touches his hands to each of their chests. "Yam eht setaf wohs ycrem nehw ehs seog dliw."

"I do," Maddox and Theo say in unison, bowing to each other first and then turning to me.

I take a moment to kiss each of them, smiling with so much joy filling my entire being. I never thought about anything like this. I've known since I've met my mates that they all follow a role, and I love hearing them accept the things they've always wanted in our relationships.

"Don't forget that sometimes you're going to need some punishment," Maddox teases, licking his lips.

"And rewards," Theo adds, grinning.

I kiss each of them once more and turn to Rowan and

Tiernan. Maddox and Theo hand me over to their brothers and step back to join Kash, creating a circle around us. Rowan winks and kisses me, unable to wait to shower me with his affection. Tiernan joins him without waiting for his turn, and I laugh and groan as the three of us share a kiss.

"Tiernan and Rowan, as the middle ground of our clan, it is your duty to teach balance and be the security our mate needs. With your souls, you will stand strong by her side, being who she needs under any circumstances. Do you accept your roles as guardians, warriors, and protectors to our mate, promising to always ensure she can overcome everything in her way?"

"Hell yeah," Rowan says, pulling me into him.

"Absolutely. I do." Tiernan joins our hug, and I laugh as they each kiss my neck, so ready to finish the ceremony as much as I am.

"Vita be con le xi su." Ambrose gathers a green orb of power in his palm. "Nova, as the warlock of our clan, I promise to fulfill my duty as your power source, guard, and the keeper of your soulmates. With me, I bind our souls long past life and into the stars, our fates together forever."

Ambrose uses magic to bring me into his arms, hugging and kissing me, whispering how blessed and worthy he feels to be claimed as my mate. The others close in around us, encircling me with their towering muscular bodies just the way I like. I can't move much without touching any of them and feel like the sun in their universe, lit by everything they are to me.

"Lastly, Nova Delphia Drakovich, as the center of our clan, do you accept your duty as our mate, being the foundation in which we thrive in mind, body, and soul. Bi lo wit ca norna. Your love and life will bind us as one, and through you, our future will grow with power and prosperity." Ambrose takes my hand and chants a spell, lighting my palm aglow with power. "Do you accept to carry the end of our tethers forever as our one true mate?"

"Yes, yes, yes," I say, letting the energy sink into my skin. "I do."

"Tel ti og da sie nalc reve!" Ambrose shouts, motioning for my mates to link their hands together.

Blinding light erupts from my heart, spilling out in six magical tethers that connect to each of my mates, binding us together. A wave of different emotions crashes into me, stealing my breath away in the best way possible as their minds and emotions mingle with mine, making it feel as if we are one.

Seven bodies and one amazing soul.

My perfect life.

"Blessed be the fates," Ambrose says, his eyes shining with joyous tears. "Under the stars and the fates, I announce our union as the Drakovich Clan. Now you all may kiss our mate."

"Fucking finally," Maddox says, scooping me up into his arms. "Let's celebrate."

Nothing has sounded better.

"I can't get enough of you," Theo murmurs, gliding his tongue over my shoulder and to my spine. "I need more. I'm insatiable."

I arch my back at the sensation of his mouth working its way down as he takes his time to explore every inch of me. "Whatever you want."

"Give her a good ass-kissing, brother. She deserves it from you most. It's how she forgets you're a dick." Tiernan leans closer, sucking my bottom lip between his teeth.

I gasp as Theo digs his fingers into my ass cheeks, spreading me wider from behind. Chuckling, Kash props up on his elbow, smiling at me. Tiernan strokes his fingers between my legs, and I moan in pure ecstasy at the different sensations awakening my body.

"She likes that," Kash says, his eyelids heavy with his lust. "She wants our lips all over her body."

Just the thought of my six mates kissing me everywhere blooms tingles between my legs. Rowan squeezes into the space between mine and Tiernan's body, stretching my leg up as he positions himself to kiss my clit. I squirm, my body buzzing as my two mates kiss and lick and suck me at the same time, teaming up to set off my wild side.

"Damn, she wants more of us. Can you feel her desire?" Maddox sits up on the bed, his place on the outside this time as my mates trade spots without complaint, never fighting over me as they share.

"I'm soaking in it," Rowan murmurs, flicking his tongue and moving his head, his rhythm pushing me to my peak.

"We're all about to be." Ambrose rubs his fingers together, sending a shockwave through me.

I'll never get used to his ability to make me cum at the snap of his fingers, his magic igniting a wave of lust through the room.

"There she goes," Rowan says, shifting up. He wipes his face with his fingers and pops them into his mouth. "Nice and slick."

Blush warms my face. I don't think I'll ever get over how the six of them communicate and practically cheer each other on when it comes to my pleasure. I should be used to it, but I'm not sure I ever want to be. The thrill of them working together excites me on a level I never knew I had. Taking care of all of them at once is also an adventure I crave to experience, testing my body's limits and discovering new ones. It's as if I'm performing aerial acrobatics again with adrenaline coursing through me, pumping pleasure with every kiss, spank, hair pull, stretch, and more.

"Let me feel," Maddox says, climbing over Tiernan and Rowan until he kneels at the edge of the bed and pulls me closer. Grabbing my knees, he spreads my body wider and aligns his cock to sink inside me. He groans and tips his head back. "So incredible. Feel what you've done, Ambrose."

"Me too," Theo says, beating Ambrose to me. Instead of climbing on top, he adjusts me onto his chest and cups my boobs.

Ambrose hums under his breath, Maddox's invitation turning him on even more. I can feel all of their desires mingling with mine. He summons a bottle of lube and tingles burst through me before Ambrose even squirts it onto me. While my body was made to handle many mates, Ambrose's magical lube makes things crazy intense in the best way possible.

Theo moans as Ambrose helps him glide into my ass,

the way my body stretches, burning my muscles yet setting my heart ablaze.

"Make some room, warlock. I can't get enough. She wants us all." Maddox squeezes beside Ambrose in what feels like an impossible tangle of our bodies.

Pressure builds between my legs as Ambrose shifts one of my legs up and over my head, half-kneeling and half squatting to be able to share my body with Maddox. I moan at the sensation, wondering how it feels for them, triple penetrating me in a way that leaves me lost in their lust.

Kash kisses my lips, stroking himself beside me. I reach out my hand and join his, his body slippery with lube. Tiernan guides my other hand over his thick girth, letting me feel the weight of his cock bling as I blindly rub his tip, letting him fuck my closed fingers how he wants.

"You too, Rowan," I gasp, licking my lips. "I want to taste you."

Rowan gathers my hair, straddling me just enough to guide his cock into my mouth. Pleasure courses through the room, our moans and sounds of passion filling the air. I ride the high of bliss, created by my mates, and Ambrose whispers a spell to make me orgasm over and over until my mind turns to mush, and all I can think about is that these six sexy men are mine. Forever.

Their lust and ecstasy blends with mine until all of us reach our peaks, and our bodies and souls hum in contentment. No one bothers moving as we lie together, hugging and loving each other as a clan. As a family. As mates chosen and fated but destined to be together. With our bond and strength, we will never fall again. We will never face a world against us because we've helped create one as perfect and remarkable as we are together.

With the magic of our soul bonds, we will always embrace the best parts of us—our devotion, love, and our untamed dragon hearts.

"What do you say, kitten? A soak in the mud bath, some food, and all the cuddles?"

I smile and nod. "I can't think of anything that sounds better."

EPILOGUE

The Dragon Heirs

"ANOTHER GIRL!" MADDOX SHOUTS, HIS voice rising over the pounding of my heart. "That's seven to one. I almost don't believe it. Good job, brother!"

"Hell yeah! I'm an uncle again!" Kash sways back and forth, bouncing with our daughter on his hip. "Look, Delilah! Isn't she beautiful like Mommy?"

"Purty-purty," Delilah chants, clapping her chubby hands.

"I'm so proud of you, doe eyes. You did great." A warm hand touches my forehead, and Rowan combs my damp hair from my face. "She's ours and so beautiful."

Another contraction hits me hard, stealing my breath. Maddox shouts for me to push until the pain and pressure eases with the sound of another whimpering cry.

"Oh, shit! Eight to one. Another girl!" Maddox says, his voice bellowing with excitement. "Tiernan, you're up! Looks like you and Rowan were both right."

Shaking Tiernan's shoulders, Theo stands behind him and watches Maddox and Ambrose clean up another precious daughter of mine with hair as dark as her dad's. I stretch my arms out, my body weak with exhaustion but my heart and soul fuller than ever.

Maddox and Ambrose bring me the babies and help me hold the two of them in my arms. Tears prickle in my eyes as I hold my newest daughters, turning our clan from fourteen to sixteen from just our second mating season. I never thought life could get any better, but as I stare at all of my mates as they hug and cheer and love up on our children surrounding us, I know this is only the beginning of the best moments of our lives.

"They're perfect, aren't they?" Tiernan says, draping his arm over my shoulder.

Rowan cuddles on my other side, the two of them

smiling and drinking in the sight of our daughters. "Just like our mate."

With our love and strength, and our power as the fiercest dragon clan in Magaelorum, I know our future is as bright as our dragon fire and the magic we've built as one. And now, with the freedom we fought for, our children will never have to worry about contracts or witches or anything keeping them down. They will fly wild and free as the fates intended. And like us and our clan, our children will never be tamed. Our wild hearts will never again be caged.

~The End~

Thank you so much for reading Saved by Her Dragons! I hope you enjoyed the series! For fun, giveaways, games, and more, join my Facebook Group at the Paranormal Center for Matches and Mates.

Other Reverse Harem Novels by Ginna Moran

THE VAMPIRE HEIRS WORLD

La Vega Vampire Showstoppers
Vampire Nights

The Divine Vampire Heirs
Blood Match
Blood Rebel
Blood Debt
Blood Feud
Blood Loss
Blood Vows

The Royale Vampire Heirs Series:
Rebel Vampires
Rebel Dhampir
Rebel Match
Rebel Heir
Rebel Fight

Academy of Vampire Heirs Series:
Dhampirs 101
Blood Sources 102
Coven Bonds 103
Personal Donors 104
Blood Wars 105

THE MATES OF MAGAELORUM WORLD

The Pack Mates of Lunar Crest:
The She-Wolf Games
The Wolf-Mate Trials
The Omega Hunt
The Witch Chase
Winter Wolf Games

Fated Mate of the Dragon Clans
Caged by Her Dragons
Freed by Her Dragons
Saved by Her Dragons

SEVEN SINNERS WORLD

The Seven Sinners of Hell's Kingdom
Her Personal Demons
Her Deadly Angels
Her Darkest Devils
Her Sinful Saints

ABOUT GINNA MORAN

GINNA MORAN IS the author of over seventy novels including the popular La Vega Vampire Showstoppers, The Pack Mates of Lunar Crest, The Seven Sinners of Hell's Kingdom Academy of Vampire Heirs, The Divine Vampire Heirs, and The Royale Vampire Heirs Why-Choose novels.

She always carried a fascination for all things paranormal and wrote her first unpublished manuscript at age eighteen. Her love of the supernatural grew stronger through her adult life, and she now spends her days with different creatures of the night. Whether it's vampires, werewolves, dragons, fae, angels, demons, or mermaids, Ginna loves creating and living in worlds from her dreams.

Aside from Ginna's professional life, she enjoys binge watching TV, crafting and design, playing pretend with her daughter, and cuddling with her dogs. Some of her favorite things include chocolate, mermaids, anything that glitters, learning new things, cheesy jokes, and organizing her bookshelf.

Ginna is currently hard at work on her next novel and the one after, and the one after that.